Kiss & Sell

BY BRITTANY GERAGOTELIS

ISBN: 1493633805
ISBN 13: 9781493633807

First Edition: November 2013

To my husband, Matt, my favorite kissing partner.

Chapter One

THE FIRST DAY of my freshman year of high school started out the same as every other year.

New clothes. Check.

Different faces. Yep.

And once again—*completely kiss-free.*

"I'm serious, Arielle, it took me practically an hour this morning just to pick out the perfect outfit," said McCartney. "I mean, what you wear on your first day pretty much sets the standard for the rest of the year, you know?"

My friends, McCartney Janning, Phineas Haywood and I walked toward the front doors of Ronald Henry High School trying hard not to act like it was our first time doing so. As McCartney went on about her new threads, I glanced down at my own outfit. It'd taken me all of five minutes to decide on a pair of dark denim jeans, and a black tank top underneath a cropped-top featuring the words "Who is A?" on it. Not exactly double-take-worthy, but it would guarantee that I'd blend in with the crowd. And blending in meant not being singled out as a lame, newbie freshman.

Along with the non-flashy outfit, I'd smoothed my long, red hair back into a low ponytail and dusted my eyelids with a soft green shadow that perfectly complimented my eyes. And even though I was wearing two-inch heels, I still barely hit 5'3". Taking some clear lipgloss out of my pocket, I reapplied the shiny stuff to my lips just like *Teen Vogue* had suggested in the issue I'd read the night before.

"So, after about twenty different outfits, I ended up going with the first one I tried on," McCartney finished, taking her first breath since she'd began talking.

"And *that's* what you decided on?" Phin asked, snorting loudly. He examined McCartney's mini skirt, white top, black tie and bright pink satin jacket with mock horror.

"Hey, now. Don't knock the outfit," McCartney said, stopping briefly to glare at Phin. "Don't even get me started on *your* fashion choices."

"What's wrong with my outfit?" Phin asked, gesturing to his choice of skinny jeans and a plain black tee.

I knew they were mostly joking with each other, but being that I had no desire to start the year off with an argument, I decided it was time to break it up.

"Okay, okay. Back to your corners," I said, laughing at them. "You both look great. Like you *belong* here."

"Yeah we do!" Phin said, putting his hand up for a high five. When neither of us reciprocated, he let his arm fall to his side weakly.

I shook my head and smiled. *Boys could be so incredibly clueless sometimes.*

Once we reached the front door, the three of us stopped in our tracks, ignoring the fact that others would have to swerve around us to get by. One by one we reluctantly looked up at the words chiseled onto the building above the doorframe. "Education prepares you for real life."

What's more real than high school? Seriously.

"We ready to do this?" I asked.

Phin and McCartney didn't respond, but both took a step through the doors and into the hallway. With a silent prayer, I joined them and we began to move as a group past the lockers that lined the walls, and further into school.

As we walked, I tried to survey the scene without appearing too much like a nerdy tourist. But as I glanced around, my mouth dropped open slightly from what I saw.

Everywhere I looked, there were couples. Some were holding hands, others were leaning up against each other, seemingly attached at the hip. But more than that, there was *kissing*. A couple at my right was practically all over each other. As they made out, the girl tangled her fingers up in the guy's hair and he stuck his hands deep into her back pockets.

Must be some pretty tasty lipgloss.

I made a face and then turned back to McCartney and Phin.

"Are you guys seeing what I'm seeing?" I asked hissed at them.

Phin pulled his messenger bag off his shoulder as he read off the numbers on the lockers for his own. When he found it, he punched in the code to the electronic lock and placed his stuff inside.

"What? New school, same boring classes?" he asked, staring into the metal container like it was a Rubik's Cube.

"Yes, but no," I answered. "Look around! Everyone's making out. I feel like I'm in the basement of some suck-fest!"

"And how would you know?" McCartney asked, raising her eyebrows at my comment.

"Ha, ha," I said.

"She's got a point, Arielle," Phin said, slamming his locker door shut and leaning against it. He surveyed the couples around us. "I hate to say it, but maybe the reason all of this is bothering you is simply because *you've never kissed anyone before.*"

"Uh—*nooo*!"

Okay, so I was a little quick to deny this fact, but it didn't mean Phin was right. Right?

"I just think that all this PDA is a little *gross,*" I continued. "I mean, seriously! Get a room, people." I turned on my heels, only to run right into another couple who'd been swapping spit behind me.

I looked back at my friends and pointed at the couple. "See what I mean?"

I stalked off, taking my time so that Phin and McCartney could catch up with me.

"You know, Arielle," McCartney said seriously. "You may be the only person left in our class to be a lip virgin."

"That's not true," I said dismissively.

Right?

I looked around. "What about Arnold Becker?"

We all examined Arnold thoughtfully. He was currently standing at his locker, talking to himself and pressing his hair down into place with his own spit. No way this guy was getting *anyone* to kiss him.

"Arnold's been hooking up with this girl at chess camp for the past few summers," Phin said, still staring at the guy.

"How do you even *know* that?" McCartney asked.

Phin just shrugged.

Finding out that Arnold had somehow managed to snag smooches from some chess chick, and I was still—as McCartney so bluntly put it—a "lip virgin," made me want to throw up. My eyes widened as realization hit. "I'm the last one in our class to kiss someone," I said slowly as I let the words escape my lips.

"Please don't freak out," McCartney said, looking at me concerned. "Phin and I will come up with a plan."

"We will?" Phin asked.

"We *will,*" McCartney answered and then added, "Arielle, girlfriend, this is going to be *your* year. The year you get your first kiss."

"Better start puckering," Phin said with a smile.

"Oh, goody," I said under my breath as I walked into my first class.

"I can't believe we already have homework!" I whined as we stumbled through my front door after school.

McCartney and I collapsed onto the oversized living room couch. We lay across the cushions, our heads meeting side-by-side in the middle and allowing our legs to drape over the sides. Phin fell back into the corner of the room and onto a big pile of pillows.

"I know! I've got math, science and a three-page paper on what I did this summer," McCartney complained. "And somehow I don't think that telling Mr. Simmons about my summer fling is going to fly."

"Speaking of work and flings," Phin said, resting his arms comfortably behind his head. "We still need to come up with a plan for project GAAK."

"Gaak?" I asked, confused.

"You know, G-A-A-K," Phin said. I continued to stare at him blankly, until he rolled his eyes. "Project Get Arielle A Kiss. Hello?!"

"Good call," McCartney said, nodding.

I sat up and looked from McCartney to Phin. "I didn't think you guys were actually serious about that."

"Are you kidding?" McCartney asked. "Girl, it's about time someone ventured to where no other man has been before—your lips."

"There just hasn't been a good opportunity yet," I said, lying back down on the couch. "Or anyone worth kissing."

"That's *so* not true!" McCartney said. "You've had crushes on plenty of guys at school and you were asked out, like, ten times last year."

Darn McCartney and her freakishly good memory.

"Yeah, but not by anyone I actually *wanted* to hang out with," I answered. "It's bad enough I get so nervous around guys that I want to hurl, but why go through that for someone I don't even like?"

"For free food and a movie?" McCartney asked.

"To get some cuddle time?" Phin chimed in.

"I don't know," I said skeptically and shook my head. Even with the prospect of free food or the potential for some good, clean, PG-13 fun, I wasn't exactly sure dating just anyone that asked me out was worth it.

"What don't you know?" my mom asked as she entered the room.

"Nothing," I said quickly.

McCartney sat up on the couch and settled back into the cushions. "We're starting a special project to help Arielle get her first kiss, Mrs. Sawyer," McCartney piped up.

"Arielle!" Mom exclaimed. "You haven't had your first kiss yet?!"

I glared at McCartney, who shrugged her shoulders. I'd been hoping the parental unit wouldn't find out about this particular Arielle fun fact until *after* it was a story that we could all "laugh about later..."

"Arielle, you know that kissing and dating is all a part of growing up," Mom said, in her best counselor's voice. She sat down on the ottoman in front of me, placed her hands together and rested her chin on her fingertips. Great. Looks like the doctor is officially in. "It's healthy to be curious at your age, honey. It's nothing to be ashamed of."

Ugh. Please. Stop. Talking.

"Mom!" I finally exclaimed, exasperated and embarrassed. "I've asked you not to treat me like one of your patients—*especially in front of my friends.*" I said the last part practically through my teeth.

See, my mom is a pretty famous marriage counselor and sometimes she has a problem turning off her role of "professional" and just playing the role of "parent" when she's at home.

"Sorry, sweetie, but I just want you to feel comfortable with your sexuality," she continued.

"Ew, ew, ew, ew," I said, placing my hands over my ears, and squeezing my eyes shut, in an attempt to drown out what she was saying.

Weren't there laws against kids and using cruel and unusual punishment?

My mom stopped talking and stared at me. Standing up, she threw her arms in the air, giving up. "Fine, Arielle," she said as she walked over to the computer that was set up in the corner of the room. "But you know you can always talk to me about stuff like this."

"I know, Mom," I said, relieved she was leaving the topic alone. "I just don't really want to, you know?"

Mom took one last look at me and then began to type away on her keyboard. I turned my attention back to my friends.

"Thanks a lot," I whispered to McCartney.

"We still need to come up with a plan," Phin said.

"Hmmm...we could always just start setting her up with people," McCartney offered. "She's bound to find *someone* to kiss."

"She could join the school play. They're doing a kissing scene this year," Phin said thoughtfully.

"Oooh, we could organize a kissing booth to raise money for the band or something," McCartney said. "Then, you'd get more than just one kiss."

These were my choices? I stared at my friends with a nauseated look on my face.

"It would be good practice. You know, to have to kiss people over and over and over again," Phin agreed.

So not impressed, guys.

"Uh, no. But thanks for trying," I said, shaking my head and covering my face with my hands.

"Yes!" Mom shouted out all of a sudden. "An autographed copy of my book just sold on eBay for forty dollars!"

"You're selling your books on eBay now?" I asked, thankful for the distraction.

"They go for a lot more if I sign them first," she explained, still looking at the computer screen.

That's when I noticed that the room had gone quiet around me.

I glanced over at McCartney and Phin slowly, and saw they were both staring at each other with their eyes open wide.

"Are you thinking...," McCartney started.

"...what I'm thinking?" Phin finished.

I knew it wasn't a good sign when they started finishing each others' sentences. It was like having an angel on one shoulder and the devil on the other, and both were whispering into my ear. Except that they were both more like devils.

"What? What just happened?" I asked and looked from one to the other.

McCartney and Phin scrambled to get up and then grabbed my arms and pulled me toward the stairs and up to my bedroom. When we were in the safety of my room, they plopped me down on my bed and stood there smiling at me.

"What?" I asked, completely confused.

"We have the perfect G.A.A.K. plan," McCartney said.

"We'll have you kissing someone in no time," Phin added.

"Do I even want to know?" I asked carefully. Neither of them answered, but both wore matching smiles on their faces.

That's a negative, ghostwriter.

Chapter Two

ALL I COULD think after McCartney and Phin told me their genius plan, was that they'd either smoked something or that they'd gone completely insane. And not the cute Britney-Spears-letting-her-infant-son-drive-her-car crazy, but the Michael-Jackson-dangling-his-baby-out-a-window or Tom-Cruise-jumping-all-over-Oprah's-couch-like-a-maniac crazy.

"You guys are *seriously* considering this?" I asked as they turned on my computer and sat side by side in front of it.

"It's perfect!" McCartney said, turning around to look at me. "We are going to sell your first kiss on eBay."

EBay, Schmebay. This was my so-called love life we were talking about here. And their answer was to hand it off to the highest bidder? As if there was enough money in the world for that. And besides, there's no way that I'd sunk that low yet.

Had I?

"EBay exists so people can sell *items,* not *people,*" I said, crossing my arms over my chest. "Or their kisses."

"I heard that one guy tried to sell his mother-in-law on eBay, just because she bugged the hell outta him," Phin offered, tapping away at the keyboard.

Now they were lumping me in the same category as annoying in-laws. I tried to burn the backs of their heads with my best death ray stare, but neither of them even flinched. I sighed, giving up on punishing them for the time being.

On the bright side, I could always sell McCartney and Phin on eBay and buy a new set of friends if this whole G.A.A.K. thing went terribly wrong. I quickly snapped out of my brief daydream and realized I was still in the land of loony.

"You guys, no one's going to want to bid on my first kiss," I said. "If I can't get anyone to do it for free, why would anyone *pay* to kiss me?"

"It's the intrigue of the whole thing," McCartney answered. "Now, are you in or out?"

I took a minute to think about how potentially embarrassing their plan could be. If people at school found out, it would be like social suicide. And I sort of had the desire to get out of high school alive.

"Don't you have to be at least 18 to post something?" I asked, looking for a way out.

"She's right," Phin said, looking at the screen.

"So, we'll get an adult to sign off on it," McCartney said. She stood up and walked out of the room. Phin and I looked at each other, as McCartney disappeared. This was not good.

A few minutes later, McCartney was back and my mom was standing in the middle of my room alongside her.

"Mrs. Sawyer, we would like permission to sell Arielle's first kiss on eBay," McCartney said. "But we need someone over 18 to say it's okay."

"You want to sell her kiss on eBay?" my mom asked slowly.

"Well, you know, it's about time she kissed someone already—you said that yourself," McCartney said. "We're just trying to help her along. Give her a wider selection to choose from."

"Plus, it'd be an experience she'd never forget," Phin added.

"And you want to do this?" Mom asked, turning to look at me.

Did I want to? I mean, obviously I had to do *something*, because there was no way I was going to end my freshman year still having never kissed anyone. That would be the ultimate humiliation. And by having guys bid on the opportunity to kiss me, it *would* take the pressure off of me wondering whether they did or didn't want to kiss me. Because, duh?! They already obviously would by that point. And it *could* be kind of fun to see who bid. Might even give me a clue about who was crushing on me...

Oh, God, did I just manage to talk myself into this?

"I guess it would be okay," I mumbled. "I mean, do *you* think it's a good idea, Mom?"

"Well, I think it's healthy to want to experience your first kiss," she answered, crossing her arms. "But I think we would need to lay down a few ground rules, to ensure that you're not prostituting yourself."

Here it was—your everyday mother/daughter prostitution talk. Can't exactly say I'd been expecting it so soon, but really, when *was* a good time to talk to your child about turning tricks?

"Mom!" I exclaimed, embarrassed. "It wouldn't be like that."

"Just think of how it sounds to 'sell a kiss' though, Arielle. Prostitutes are people who sell their bodies for money," my mom answered. "So, we'd need to have some rules, so that this isn't at all like one of those experiences."

Mom had always been a big believer in rules. Oddly, my friends liked this about her, because Mom also believed that rules were better when we came up with them together. You know, so they fit individual situations. I knew better, though. In the end, whatever rules Mom wanted me to follow were the rules I was going to have.

"Like what kind of rules?" I asked, suspiciously.

"Well, I think that any money you raise should go to either a charity of your choice, or be donated to your school, that way you're not getting paid for it," Mom said.

"Sort of like the kissing booths they do to raise money for school sports or clubs," Phin said, nodding his head.

"Okay, that sounds fine," I said. "What else?"

"He has to be around your own age. No one two years older or two years younger than you," Mom said.

"That's actually smart. You wouldn't want your first kiss to be from some old skeeve," McCartney said miming throwing up. "Or from a 10 year old. Talk about robbing the cradle."

"And lastly," Mom continued. "If, in the end, you don't like the guy who wins the kiss and don't feel comfortable about things, you don't accept the money and you don't kiss him."

Suddenly having my mom in on the plan, felt more like a blessing than a curse. With a list of rules drawn, I actually felt better about the whole idea. I never would've thought that having *more* rules would be a good thing (and certainly would never admit it to anyone currently in my room), but now I was glad she'd laid down the law. And, I had no real reason to say no to the plan.

"Okay," I said, finally. "Sell my kiss on eBay."

"Yeah! You rock, Arielle!" Phin said trying again for a high five. I didn't move. Phin frowned. "Why do you guys always leave me hanging?"

"Just let me see what you're going to post before you send it," my Mom said as she walked out the door.

"Sure, no problem," McCartney yelled after her. Then with a smile, she added, "Let the bidding begin!"

"I can't believe that I'm agreeing to this," I said, groaning from my place on the bed.

"You know you don't have to, Arielle," McCartney said, sympathetically. "You can always say no and we just won't post it."

"Hey, I worked hard on this profile!" Phin exclaimed. "I mean, this is a work of *art*. You don't just delete a thing of beauty."

"He's right. Really, I'm okay with this," I said, mostly to convince myself once again that I was indeed, okay with it. I sighed. "Let me read it again."

I got up and took a seat in front of the computer.

MY FIRST KISS COULD BE YOURS

14-year-old Arielle Sawyer is looking to get rid of her first kiss. That's right, no other lips have touched hers—here's your chance to be the first one there. All bidders must be between the ages of 14 and 16 and have good personal hygiene. Jerks need not apply. Arielle is a good-looking, talented and bright gal, who we're sure, once she's had a little practice, will be a fine kisser. Help make her dreams come true and kiss the girl!

"You think I'll just be a 'fine' kisser?" I asked, putting my hands on my hips. "Not a 'great' kisser, or an 'awesome' kisser, but a 'fine' kisser?"

"I just don't want to put too much pressure on you by saying you're going to be the 'best kisser ever,' before you've actually ever done it," Phin said.

"Oh," I said. "Well, maybe I could just kiss *you* and get it over with and then we'll see who's a 'fine' kisser." I faked like I was leaning in for a sloppy smooch, pushing out my lips and batting my eyes at Phin enticingly.

"No way, Red," Phin said, covering his mouth with his hand. "It would be like kissing my sister or something. I'm *so* not going there with you. No offense, of course."

"I was just teasing you. Jeez, tell me how you really feel," I said and plopped back onto my bed. "And for the last time, stop calling me Red!"

Ever since I'd met Phin back in third grade, he'd insisted on calling me Red every once in a while just to annoy me.

"Fine. A-r-i-e-l-l-e," he said slowly, spacing out my name like he was sounding it out.

"So, are we going to do this or not?" McCartney asked, before I could lunge at Phin for being a major pain in my backside.

"Let's do it," I said, turning back to the computer screen. "I'm ready to be kissed."

And without hesitating, I clicked on the "Sell Item Now" box, and watched as my first kiss went to the highest bidder.

Chapter Three

I'D HAD THIS reoccurring dream ever since I was a kid, where I was at school and everyone around me was pointing and laughing. I had no idea what was so funny and couldn't remember how I'd gotten there in the first place. The room would start to spin as I turned around and around, looking into unfamiliar eyes that all seemed to be mocking me. The spinning always got faster, until I was so dizzy that I fell down. And that was usually when I woke up.

I was having that same feeling right now, only I wasn't asleep, and I wasn't going to wake up in a cold sweat in my bed. Because I actually *was* at school.

"Are people looking at me weird?" I asked, lowering my eyes to stare at the ground as McCartney, Phin and I walked down the hallway the next day.

"No," Phin said. "But if you keep looking at the floor you'll probably run into someone and *then* everyone will be staring at you for-sure."

I glanced up from my feet long enough to shoot an icy glare at him.

"Chill out, Arielle. We aren't even sure anyone knows about it yet," McCartney said with a frown. "Come on, we've got a few minutes before class. Let's go and check it out."

I fought to keep up with them as they sped to the nearest computer lab, which wasn't exactly easy to do with my eyes still downcast. It's also not something I'd recommend, even if you *are* in stealth mode.

Once we were safely in the nearly empty room, McCartney sat down in front of a computer and I waited silently as she pulled up my eBay account.

"Nobody's even looked at it yet," McCartney muttered after a minute, frustrated.

"Told you no one would want to bid on a kiss from me," I said, looking around to make sure no one was listening.

"Dude, you've got to turn that frown upside down," Phin said. "It's all about attitude. If you think something long enough, eventually you'll feel like it's true. So, just start thinking you're worth kissing and the kisses will come."

"I guess," I said, surprised to hear this come out of his mouth. "Since when are you all smart and stuff?"

"Gee, thanks," Phin answered sarcastically.

"I just mean that, well, that was sort of profound."

"I'm sneaky like that," Phin said winking at me. "You two don't know *everything* about me. I've got plenty of surprises up my sleeves."

I was about to ask him exactly what he'd been keeping from us, when we were interrupted by a voice behind us.

"Wow! You're seriously selling a kiss on the internet?" a girl said loudly enough for anyone within earshot to hear. I recognized her from fifth period geometry, but for the life of me, I couldn't remember her name. Not that I felt all that bad...it *was* only the second day of school after all. And I'd never really had a great memory.

"Uh, yeah, sort of," I said slowly.

"Huh. That's funny. Never would have pegged you to be the type," she said.

Wait, I'd only talked to this girl for about five seconds, and she already knew what "type" I was? I guess first impressions really *were* important. Did my plaid skirt and pink tank really scream, "I wouldn't sell my kiss on eBay?"

Before I had a chance to ask her this, McCartney had already jumped to my defense. "What does *that* mean?" she challenged.

The blond flinched as if McCartney had just hissed at her like a pissed off cat. I appreciated that McCartney had my back, but the girl needed to retract the claws just a little. I placed my hand lightly on her arm, and tried to smile at the new girl, whose own grin had faded away fast.

"Nothing. Just, you know, it's a pretty bold move," she answered, obviously intimidated by McCartney. "Don't get me wrong, I think it's cool. Er, let me know how it goes."

Then we watched as the girl practically ran out of the room.

"Well, that wasn't awkward at all," I said, turning to McCartney. "And if you're there to threaten everyone who brings up the subject, then I won't have anything to worry about."

McCartney ignored me as she turned back to the computer screen. "Forget her," she said, typing away at the keys furiously. "We've seriously got to do something about this whole 'no one knowing about your auction' thing."

"What are you gonna do, McCartney?" I asked nervously.

She hit a few more buttons, then announced triumphantly, "There! All done. People are *definitely* going to know about it now, which means you're that much closer to getting that kiss."

I looked at her, a sinking feeling growing in my stomach.

"I just sent the link to everyone in school," McCartney said nonchalantly, and got up to leave.

Frozen in place and now staring at a blank computer screen, I tried to process what she'd said. When I finally snapped out of it, I had to run to catch up to them.

"But," I sputtered. "The *entire* school? Was that really necessary? I mean, you could've just sent it to all the guys, because as you know, my first kiss isn't going to be with a girl...you didn't have to send it to everyone."

"Yeah, but some of those *girls* have other *guy* friends, or brothers or whatever," said Phin. "It's like networking."

"But now everyone's going to be all up in my business," I said, fidgeting uncomfortably.

"That's what you want," McCartney said. "The more people who know about it, the better chance you have of finding a totally kissable bidder!"

If I'd been worried about people staring at me before, I had a feeling I was about to be in for a strange couple of weeks.

By lunchtime pretty much everyone knew about my eBay posting. Walking down the hall to the caf was excruciating. I tried to pretend that I didn't notice the whispers and giggles as I walked up to the table we'd designated as ours. Collapsing into an open chair, I set my bag down on the table and then lay my head on my arms.

"You guys, I think this may have been a major mistake," I said, my head still down. "People are *laughing* at me. It's humiliating."

"Are you kidding? This is awesome!" Phin said, chomping on his double-stacked hamburger. "The more people who know, the more people will bid."

"He's right," McCartney said. "Now that we've gotten the ball rolling, the bids are sure to come in. And then, that kiss will be yours!"

I looked up at them stubbornly. "You guys would be feeling differently if it was *you* everyone was staring at. And judging ruthlessly," I said and then took a bite out of my banana.

Before either of them could respond, I heard a snicker coming from behind me. I turned to see one of the populars, Kristi Fern, standing there, sipping on her diet soda.

I blinked my eyes in surprise to see the Queen B herself, standing in our section of the cafeteria. As a general rule, the popular kids usually stuck to their own kind and rarely chanced being seen with civilians, so you could understand my confusion. Kristi shook her platinum blond hair off her shoulders and then placed her hand on her hip, leaning over to one side as if she were posing for a dozen hidden paparazzi cameras. The girl was like a walking shampoo commercial, and it totally made me want to barf.

Her two lackeys, June and Deb, trailed behind their leader, trying to copy her saunter but failing miserably. They each managed to slap on the same fake smiles, though, which was a feat unto itself.

"So, *Arielle*," Kristi purred. "It's really just *so* sad that you have to sell yourself to get a kiss! I mean, aren't you a little embarrassed that no one's wanted to go there, yet?"

I sat there stunned at Kristi's bluntness and felt my face begin to heat up. Suddenly it dawned on me what the "B" in Queen B stood for.

"Why don't you just shut it, Kristi?" McCartney shot back, giving her the famous McCartney stink eye. "I mean, if you had a penny for every kiss you gave, you'd be able to afford better highlights."

People around us had stopped talking as soon as Kristi had started to speak, and now they whispered as they watched the confrontation. You could tell they were all silently hoping for a catfight. And considering what Kristi had just said, I was almost willing to give her one.

"At least someone's going to *pay* to kiss me," I said boldly, before I could think of the consequences. Like ultimate social suicide. "You have to give yours away."

Kristi just smirked at me, unimpressed. "We'll just see about that," she said as she and her cronies walked away. "Really, who's going to want to kiss such a loser?"

"Whoa, Kujo, relax," Phin said as he pulled McCartney back into the chair she'd just jumped up from.

She glared at Phin. "Did you hear what she just said about Arielle?"

"Yeah. But it's *Kristi*. She's been evil since we were in middle school. Who cares what she thinks anyway?" Phin said, stuffing a few French fries in his mouth. "Besides, if Kristi's being a witch, it's just because she's mad that all the attention isn't focused on her. And that's because it's all on Arielle instead. That's revenge enough, isn't it?"

I looked around the room and saw that nearly every head was turned in our direction. Phin was right. The attention was definitely on us. Or more accurately, on me.

Before I could decide whether that was a good or bad thing, the bell rang and we started to pack up.

"You okay?" McCartney asked falling into step beside me.

"Actually, I feel great," I said and realized it was true. "Telling Kristi off actually made me realize that this crazy plan of yours might just work."

"That's my girl," Phin said smiling as he waited for a high five. Denied yet again, he stomped off to his next class.

McCartney and I walked into history, still talking about Kristi and her clones. We sat down next to each other and took out our books.

"Arielle?" Mrs. Beckett called out from the front of the room.

I looked over at the teacher surprised she already knew my name. Then I began to panic, because, well, why did she know my name?

"I have a note here that says Principal Howard would like to see you," she said, holding up a piece of paper for the whole class to see.

Around the room, people erupted into "ooooh's" like I was in trouble, and I stood up nervously, worried they were right. Looking at McCartney questioningly, I headed up to retrieve the note.

"Did he say what it was about?" I asked her quietly.

"Sorry, but no," she answered, already having lost interest in the situation.

"Okay. Uh, well, I guess I'll go then?" I said uncomfortably.

I grabbed my things and left the class, starting my walk of shame down the hallway. As I went, I racked my brain for reasons why Principal Howard might want to see me. Was it because of the argument with Kristi? Nah. I shook my head. Kristi caused scenes all the time. Whatever it was, my mom would kill me if I managed to land myself in trouble on the second day of school.

I took a deep breath as I arrived outside Principal Howard's door and then knocked on it three times.

"Come in," his voice boomed from inside the room.

Here goes.

Chapter Four

I SAT NERVOUSLY in a chair directly across from Principal Howard, who was planted sturdily behind his big oak desk. This was my first time inside his office and I *so* did not want to be there. Everything was intimidating. The furniture was all a dark shade of cherry or black, and every decoration screamed "scary adult." He didn't even have any family pictures on his desk or anything.

I started to bite at my nail, as he sat there staring at me with a blank look on his face. Like he was sizing me up. I'd never talked to Principal Howard before, but I'd had a chance to observe him at the opening day assembly. He seemed *suspicious* of the students, like at any moment we might start a riot or something. The guy never really smiled, in fact, his personality sort of screamed, "law enforcement." Before I could wonder any longer why I was in his office in the first place, he cleared his throat.

"Miss Sawyer. Do you know why I asked you to come down here?" he asked, his voice monotone.

Why do adults always ask that question? I mean, if we knew, why would we admit it, and if we didn't, you were going to tell us anyway. Seriously, I wished you would just cut to the chase, so I don't have to sit here ruining the nails I just polished last night.

But I just answered, "No, sir."

"Well, I wanted to speak to you concerning this little *eBay* situation," he said, his expression remaining the same.

I laughed nervously. "Oh. You saw that too?"

"Well, it *was* e-mailed to the entire school, Miss Sawyer," he answered with what I assumed was his attempt at sarcasm.

"Yeah, sorry about that," I said, silently cursing McCartney and Phin. Note to self: When you send out a mass e-mail regarding your plans to score your first kiss to your entire school, it's not such a good idea to *also* send it to the faculty. No matter how clever you think you are, they will *not* be impressed. You'd think this would be common knowledge, but here I was, having an incredibly embarrassing conversation with the principal. Not exactly my finest moment, I admit.

"I'm not sure if this is exactly a safe or smart thing for a young lady to be doing," Principal Howard continued. "Selling sexual favors on the Internet—in this day and age? It's not appropriate and I'm afraid that it will be a distraction for students."

"I don't think it's going to be too much of a distraction, sir. You know how teens are. By tomorrow everyone will be talking about something else," I said, although I knew this wasn't entirely true. This juicy bit of gossip had legs.

"Even so, I'm going to have to call your mother about this," he said, already reaching for the phone. "I can't imagine an intelligent woman such as herself would think this was a wise decision."

"Actually," I interjected as he began to dial. "My mom was the one who gave me permission to do the posting."

Principal Howard cleared his throat awkwardly and then continued to punch numbers into the phone. "I think I'd like to hear that from her, if it's all the same."

"Whatever you say, sir," I said evenly, leaning back in my chair and crossing my legs at the ankles. As I waited, I looked up at the ceiling and started to count the little holes in the tiles.

After a few rings, I could hear my mom answer through the earpiece of the phone. For a psychologist, she sure could raise her voice when she wanted to.

"Hello? Mrs. Sawyer?" he asked. "This is Principal Howard. I've got Arielle here with me in my office."

He paused and I could imagine my mom asking him a million questions all at once. Was I okay? Was I in the hospital? Had there been an accident at school?

"No, no, nothing like that," he answered quickly. "It's actually concerning an e-mail that was sent to the entire student body today."

Another pause.

"Actually, it was regarding her intention of selling a kiss on eBay?" he answered, looking straight into my eyes as he said it. "I told her I couldn't imagine that a professional, upstanding woman such as yourself would actually agree to something as potentially dangerous as this, but..."

I tried to hide the growing smile behind my hand as my mom cut Principal Howard off mid-sentence. Without saying anything, he turned his chair slightly to face the wall.

"You really condone this sort of behavior?" He tried his best to whisper, but I could hear every word. "You don't at all fear for her safety?"

Again, I heard my mom's squeaks coming from the phone and took this opportunity to reach into my pocket and apply some Chapstick to my dry lips.

"Oh. Well, I guess if you set certain *rules* for her, that changes things slightly," he sputtered, spinning around even further. "And I guess it *is* more like a school fundraiser if the money is going toward the new gymnasium."

Silence.

You could practically hear the crickets chirping outside the office window, it was so quiet in the room.

"No, Mrs. Sawyer, I'm not in the business of stifling young people's personal growth," Principal Howard said through clenched teeth.

I almost lost it then, but somehow managed to hold back my giggles. There was no way I was giving him another reason to make me spend more time in this stuffy room. In fact, I was starting to miss being in class—and I wasn't exactly student of the month if you know what I mean.

As the silence grew on Principal Howard's end of the convo, I knew my mom was convincing him that not only was this kissing thing not something to scold, but in fact, it was something that should be commended. And the truth of the matter was that I was beginning to think that myself. I was realizing that if I wanted something to happen in my life, I had to reach out and take the bull by the horns.

Or, the boy by the lips in my case.

I plastered a blank expression on my face and stared back up at the ceiling as Principal Howard turned back around and placed the phone back on its receiver.

"Your mother and I discussed it, and I suppose we don't have to take any disciplinary action today," he said.

You discussed it? More like Mom put the smack down on you, like those beefed up guys on WWE. But I kept my opinions to myself.

"And since all proceeds are going to the school, I guess I have no problem with it," he said. "Just let me in on these little 'fundraisers' before you do them in the future, okay?"

He actually used air quotes when he said "fundraisers," like we didn't both know what he meant.

"I will definitely do that, sir," I said. And then, drawing on all my acting skills, I kept my face looking as innocent as possible and added, "Thank you for looking out for my well-being. If only every school had a principal as concerned about his students as you, this world would be a much safer place."

I wiped away an imaginary tear and then placed my hand over my heart. He actually started to beam as I turned to go back to class.

And the Best Actress award goes to...

Chapter Five

AFTER SCHOOL THAT day, I found myself sprawled across McCartney's enormously oversized, round bed. We'd gone back to her house to hang out and check on the status of the auction. The three of us spent a lot of our free time at McCartney's place, mostly because her family was seriously loaded. "The Manor" as Phin and I had dubbed it the first time we'd seen it, had six bedrooms, seven bathrooms, a living room, a den, a huge kitchen, and a pool and hot tub in the back yard.

"Is this a new comforter?" I asked, pretending to make snow angels on her bed.

McCartney looked up from her laptop and nodded. "Yeah. I was sick of the old one."

"Didn't you just get that 'old one,' like, a month ago?" Phin asked, pushing me aside and then plopping down beside me.

"Yeah. But the polka dots just started to get…old," McCartney answered. "And don't even start lecturing me about my shopping habits."

Phin held up his arms in surrender. "Wouldn't dream of it," he said. Then he leaned over to me and whispered, "I couldn't handle it if she banned me from The Manor. The lack of pool access would definitely suck."

I giggled and then abruptly stopped when I caught McCartney's glare. Clearing my throat, I thought it best to change the subject.

"So, you won't believe what happened when Principal Howard called me to his office today," I said, quickly.

"Oh, yeah!" McCartney exclaimed, her annoyance disappearing as quickly as it had appeared. "What was that about, anyway?"

"Little Miss Perfect was called down to the principals office?" Phin asked, faking a horrified look. He tisked at me with his pointer finger and mouthed, "naughty, naughty," and only narrowly escaped being smacked in the side of the head with McCartney's pillow.

"Shut it, Phin. Besides, it was partly your fault I was down there anyway," I said, crossing my arms in my best you're-on-my-list way.

"How is it *my* fault?" he asked.

"Well, Captain Obvious, Principal Howard received the genius e-mail you two sent out to the *entire school,* and thought it would be a good idea to lecture me about my safety and what is, and is not, proper for a young lady like me to be doing."

"He did not!" McCartney said, her mouth hanging open.

"He most certainly did," I answered. "Then he made the mistake of calling my mom to see what she thought of the whole thing. And, well, you know how my mom is. By the end of the phone call, she had him believing that it was a great idea. Mostly, because she promised that any money I made on the kiss would go toward making repairs to the gym."

"Way to go, Mrs. Sawyer," Phin said, shaking his head in awe.

"Speaking of kisses and money," McCartney said, typing fast and furious on the keys of her laptop. "Let's take a look-see at how those lips are selling."

"There better be at least one bid, or I'm going to end it right here and now," I said in my best drama queen voice and fell back into the soft pillows on McCartney's bed. "Seriously though guys, these lips were made for kissing and I can't finish my freshman year without putting them to good use."

"Now, you're talking my language," Phin said. I watched as he began to smooch on one of McCartney's stuffed animals. I had to turn away from the perv as his animal hijinks began to get a little too animated for my taste.

"I just finally realized that it's time," I said still averting my eyes. "Time to join the rest of our class in the world of making out. I mean, it's fun, right? And why shouldn't I have a little fun every once in a while?"

"You're preaching to the choir, man," Phin said and threw his furry kissing buddy at me.

"So, I'm in this thing one hundred percent. Yep, I'm going to be a kissing machine before the end of the year," I said, making up my mind then and there.

"Well, you're definitely getting kissed this year," McCartney cut in and looked up from the computer screen.

"Somebody bid?" I squealed, kicking my feet up in the air.

"Not somebody," McCartney said slowly, and turned the laptop to face us. "Some*bodies*."

"Seriously? More than one guy bid on these lips?" I asked, pointing to my mouth.

"Uh, twenty seven guys to be exact," McCartney answered. "Your kiss is already up to $75!"

"Nuh, uh. No way," I said, scrambling off the bed to examine the screen. After I confirmed that it was true, I leaned back against the bed, slightly dazed—and confused. "Do they *know* what they're bidding on? Maybe they thought they were bidding on something else. Like a cool painting, or maybe a bike or something."

"Sorry sweet-thang," Phin said with a big grin. "They want those hot lips of yours."

"Ewwww. When you say it that way, it makes it sound so dirty," I said, making a face.

"Do you know what this means, Arielle?" McCartney interrupted.

"People feel sorry for the lame freshman?" I asked.

"No, loser," McCartney said, rolling her eyes. "It means, no more lip virgin for you. In exactly one month, you *will* be kissing one very lucky boy."

I stopped to think about what that meant. If I went through with this, I, Arielle Sawyer, would be locking lips with someone very soon. My stomach did a little flip-flop at the idea of finally kissing a boy. Then, another thought struck me, causing me to bolt upright.

"Who are the guys that have bid so far?" I asked.

"They don't give out their names, just a username," McCartney said. "You won't find out who the winner is until he's been picked. Then, you get a name and address."

"So, there's no way to see who I might be kissing in a month?" I asked, suddenly feeling a little sick to my stomach.

"Well, we could always take a look at the usernames and try to guess," McCartney offered. "I mean, they're boys, so they can't be all *that* bright, right?"

"Hey!" Phin exclaimed, acting offended.

McCartney and I ignored him as we sat down side by side in front of the computer. "Okay, the top bid right now is SoccerStud21," McCartney said out loud.

We sat there for a few moments before I finally broke the silence with a groan.

"That's got to be Calvin Brooks," I said. "He's on the soccer team and his number's 21."

Calvin was an okay guy. Just not the kind you want to smooch. He wasn't even the kind of guy you'd want to shake hands with. He was always running around and sweating. And I was *so* not digging the boy sweat. Unless we were getting sweaty because of the kissing, in which case...

"See, I told you guys weren't exactly the sharpest tools in the shed," McCartney said. This time Phin didn't bother trying to defend his gender.

"Okay, let's try another one," he said, pulling the computer onto his lap. "BigManOnCampus."

"Hmmm, that's more vague," McCartney said, scratching her head. "It could be someone who's a part of the populars, or it could be a really big guy. Like Chris Blaine."

"Please don't let it be Chris Blaine," I pleaded out loud, looking up and praying to the ceiling Gods.

"How about this one. RedMustang1," Phin read.

"That one's easy," McCartney said right away.

"Who is it?" I asked.

"It's totally Kirk Masters," McCartney said, as if she were explaining something to a child. "Kirk is the only one in school who drives a red mustang."

"But Kirk is one of the populars," I stated, shaking my head.

"I'm just surprised he took the time away from that precious car of his to get on the Internet," McCartney answered.

"All of this is starting to make my head spin," I said and closed my eyes. Suddenly the prospect of finding out the identity of my potential new kissing buddy seemed more stressful than when I hadn't known at all.

I stood up and walked over to where I'd dropped my book bag on the floor and placed it over my shoulder. "I'm going to head home. I think I've had more than enough excitement for one night," I said and headed for the door.

"Don't stress, Arielle," McCartney called out after me. "I'm sure that the final bidder will be someone worth it."

"Or you can always back out, like your mom said," Phin added, helpfully.

I turned back to look at my friends. "If I back out, I'll be back in the same situation. Kiss-less," I said. "And I don't want to be that girl anymore."

I gave them a weak smile before walking out the door.

Chapter Six

BY THE TIME Friday rolled around, so much was happening that I felt like I seriously needed a vacation from all the drama that had become my life. Nearly overnight, I'd gone from barely being a blip on anyone's radar to being the most talked about girl at Ronald Henry High. Which might sound pretty sweet in theory, but so far it was more trouble than it was worth.

Little had I known at the time, but the confrontation with Kristi and her clones wasn't an isolated incident. Ever since the e-mail had gone viral, the hallways had been buzzing with gossip—about me. I could hear the girls giggling and feel their stares as I walked by. And the guys—the guys just sort of gawked, like I was some sort of freak show. Not exactly the sort of attention a gal dreams about.

Figures that it would take me announcing my presence on the Internet for someone to notice I exist.

Despite the way it all made me feel though, I put a big, fat, fake smile on my face and walked down the hallway like none of it bothered me.

"You're the man, Arielle!" a voice boomed off to my side.

I watched in confusion as Aaron Breckinridge walked up and gave me a high five. I didn't even think Aaron knew my name.

"Seriously, dude, you rule," he added, before walking off in the opposite direction.

Stunned, I stared at the back of his letter jacket as he moved further away from me.

"Uh, thanks?" I said, unsure of how to respond. As I grappled with what had just happened, my gaze swept across the hall until I made contact with a pair of the bluest eyes I'd ever seen.

Eyes that were attached to Cade Jones—a junior, and one of the populars. He was one of those guys who belonged on a TV screen rather than walking the halls of a high school. His dark hair was cut just below the chin and it was always slightly mussed, like he'd just woken up, but in that perfect kind of way.

Wowza.

He smiled at me, a sort of sideways grin, and then leaned back against the wall. I glanced behind me to see whom he was staring at. But there was no one there. Yep, he was definitely looking at me.

I smiled back shyly, feeling my cheeks turning what I could only imagine was the same shade of red as my hair. Embarrassed about being caught mid-stare, I began to walk as fast as I could to class, leaving Cade staring after me.

I sat down at my desk right as the bell rang, thankful to be back in an environment where I felt comfortable. Trusty desk, typical slightly crazy teacher, school work—that was all familiar to me. What had just happened in the hallway, on the other hand, was not.

"Today, I'd like to start with a little writing exercise to get those creative juices flowing," Mrs. Glass said a little too happily. "I'd like you to create a fictional character and write a letter to yourself in that character's voice."

A few groans exploded around the room, but everyone was already opening up their notebooks and starting to scribble on their papers. I took one last glance around the room and then settled in to do the assignment.

Dear Arielle,

I cannot believe all the attention you've been getting these past few days! I mean, man, you were invisible before, but now you're everything but! It's crazy, because either you're getting glares from the girls, or getting high fives from guys you hardly know. You put one little ad on the Internet, and suddenly you're like those celebs on the cover of the tabloid magazines like Brangelina or Bennifer. If you'd have known all this was going to happen, do you think you still would have gone through with it?

"Okay, pencils down," Mrs. Glass called out from behind her desk, before I was able to get any further. "Now, I want you all to pass your papers to the person beside you. And that person will write back in the same voice."

"What?" I nearly shrieked. If I'd known anyone else was going to read my note to myself, I would've talked about food, or the weather, or Miley Cyrus. "Mrs. Glass, are you sure you wouldn't rather just read our papers instead?"

"I'll be reading them at the end. It *is* my writing assignment, you know," Mrs. Glass answered coolly. "Unless you have a better exercise in mind?"

As far as I was concerned, any exercise had to be better than having one of my classmates read my paper, but I held my tongue.

"No," I answered, finally. I looked to my left to see who I'd be sharing my embarrassing, personal thoughts with and felt myself grow faint. Passing out would've just been icing on the cake, given the circumstances.

Of course, of all the people I could exchange papers with, it had to be a popular like Dan Stevenson. I *so* didn't want him reading all about my freak out. I might as well stand up now and say, "Hi, I'm not only a member of the geek squad, but I'm also the club president."

"You ready to switch, Sawyer?" Dan asked, holding out his paper, and smiling at me.

"Uh, yeah," I said, even though I felt like doing anything but. "Just remember, it's totally fiction, okay?"

"Sure. Of course. Mine too," he said, smiling easily again. I found myself grinning back at him, despite my growing anxiety, and noticed how his hazel eyes crinkled in the corners.

The sound of shuffling papers around me snapped me back to earth, and I reluctantly broke my eye contact with Dan to begin reading his letter.

Dear Dan,

Yo, man, how've you been? Long time, no talk. Anyways, let's cut to the chase. Dude, have you heard about that chick at your school, who's selling a kiss on the Internet?

I felt myself begin to blush for about the tenth time that day. Did everyone know about this kissing thing? So much for fading into the background.

> You should definitely think about asking her out. She's totally cute, sweet and obviously has some balls, since she was able to put all that right out there. You've clearly been blind for not having noticed her before. So, buck up, man, and ask the girl out—before I do.
>
> Peace out, dude,
>
> Stan

I was confused—and totally flustered. Was this some sort of joke to play on the girl who had no play? Or was this his way of...*flirting*?

Glancing at Dan out of the corner of my eye, I saw that he was scribbling all over my paper, but still had that goofy grin on his face. Turning my attention back to Dan's paper, I quickly wrote some B.S. answer to his letter and then turned it upside down on my desk and waited—impatiently—for Mrs. Glass to collect it.

When the bell finally rang, I gathered my things as quickly as I could and booked it out of the classroom. I didn't even dare look at anyone as I headed straight for my locker. I deposited a few of my books on one of the shelves and then examined myself in my magnetic locker mirror. I looked into my familiar, pretty green eyes, and smoothed a few errant hairs, which had come loose from my ponytail. Then I applied a thin layer of Chapstick to my lips, before placing it back in my pocket.

When I slammed my locker door shut, Dan was standing beside me.

"Oh!" I exclaimed, surprised to see him so up-close-and-personal. I wasn't positive, but I had a feeling he'd been waiting for me.

"That's not exactly the reaction I was going for, but okay," Dan said with a smirk.

"Uh, you just...scared me, that's all," I said, and instantly realized how dumb that sounded. *Stupid, stupid, stupid*. "I mean, what's up, Dan?"

"Not much, Sawyer," he said and leaned his head against the locker door. We were both silent for a moment. Finally he added, "So, what did you think about my paper?"

That was a very good question.

I started to chew on my lip and tried to avoid looking straight at him. "Um. It was definitely…imaginative," I answered slowly. Was he trying to make me nervous or did he just have that affect on girls?

"Thanks," he answered. "I thought so."

I grew silent again. I still wasn't quite sure what he was doing here. At *my* locker. Talking to *me*.

"Well, I decided to take some advice from my friend, Stan, and see if you wanted to hang out Friday night?" he finally asked, lowering his voice a bit as if we were having a private conversation.

"Huh?" I asked, blankly.

Have I mentioned I'm a smooth talker?

"You know. Do that thing where I pick you up, we get some pizza, see a movie and then I take you home. That sort of thing," he said, playfully.

"Like…a *date*?" I asked, still a little slow on the pick-up.

"Yeah. Like, a date," Dan said, chuckling at my reaction.

I studied his face, and was surprised to find that he wasn't joking.

"Okay." I forced myself to sound calm, even though I felt a little like puking. "Sounds like fun."

"Sweet," Dan said, standing up straighter. "So, pick you up at seven?"

"Sure," I answered, grinning stupidly.

"Okay, then. See ya, Sawyer," Dan said as he turned and walked away.

I stared at him as he moved down the hallway. I couldn't help but admire how his shirt clung to his back and his jeans fit perfectly around his…

"Was that *Dan Stevenson* just talking to you?" McCartney asked, interrupting my Britney Spears-esque not-so-innocent thoughts.

"Yep," I answered, taking one last glance at Dan, before he disappeared around the corner. I turned to face McCartney and we began to walk to our History class. "He just asked me out. On a date. For Friday."

"No way!" McCartney squealed, jumping up and down and clapping her hands.

"Why is that so hard to believe?" I asked. She stared at me and raised a perfectly plucked eyebrow. I caved. "Okay. I can't believe it either."

As we walked, I told her everything. Beginning with the letter and ending with our date plans.

"That's wicked cool!" McCartney said, as we walked into class and sat down next to each other.

"Yeah, but do you think he's asking me out because of this eBay thing, or because he suddenly realized what a totally awesome catch I am?" I whispered as other students started filling in the desks around us.

"Who cares! Dan Stevenson just asked you out," McCartney hissed. "For once, don't analyze everything. Just enjoy it."

McCartney was right. Who cares why Dan asked me out? The point was he wanted to hang out with me—Arielle Sawyer. Nothing could ruin this moment.

"Pop quiz!" their teacher yelled out.

Except maybe for that.

Chapter Seven

"YOU'VE GOTTA HELP me find the perfect outfit," I said, nearing hysterics as I tore through my closet.

"We told you we'd help," McCartney said from her spot on my bed. "But first, you have *got* to calm down. You're running around like you're on fire."

"I'm going out with *Dan Stevenson* tonight," I said, stopping in my tracks. "I might as well *be* on fire."

"You are such a drama queen," Phin said from across the room. "He's just a dude. Like me. He puts his pants on one leg at a time like everyone else."

"Maybe so, but those pants he puts on look *soooo* good," I cooed as I thought of him. "And he's not like you. He's popular, remember?"

"Thanks for the reminder," Phin answered sarcastically.

"You know what I mean," I answered, going back to pacing around in front of my closet.

McCartney got off the bed and placed her hands on my shoulders forcefully. Girl was strong. "You go get in the shower and we'll find you an outfit," she said, pushing me toward the bathroom.

"Shower," I said slowly. "Right. Probably a good idea."

"Showering is definitely a good idea," Phin said, waving his hand in front of his face. "You don't want him smelling the *real* you."

I glared at him before disappearing into my bathroom.

Once the door was locked behind me, I turned the knob on the tub and watched as steam filled the room around me. I waited until I could no longer see my outstretched hand and then stepped under the hot stream. I let my thoughts slip away and concentrated on the steady thumping of water as it massaged my head. Before long, my nerves were nearly gone and I'd almost forgotten about my date.

Almost.

Eventually, I emerged from the room smelling considerably better than I had going in. Even girlie-like.

"Put these on." McCartney handed me a jean skirt and a shimmery black top that I didn't recognize.

"Where'd this come from?" I asked, eyeing the top.

"I figured you might need something a little un-Arielle," McCartney said, shrugging. "So, I brought it from home."

"Thank you?" I said, not sure whether my wardrobe had just been insulted or not. "Phin, can you turn around?"

"Not a problem," Phin said, holding up his hands and turning to face the wall.

I let my towel drop to the ground and stepped into the skirt after I threw the top over my head.

"I'm dressed now," I said to Phin and then modeled the outfit for them. "So?"

"Hello, Megan Fox-y!" McCartney said, nodding approvingly. "I knew you had it in you!"

"I don't know," I said checking myself out in the mirror. I wrinkled my nose and chewed on my lip thoughtfully. "You don't think there's too much cleavage?"

I pulled the top up a bit and then watched as it fell back down to its original place, exposing some of my nearly-flat chest.

"Um. As a guy, I can safely say there's no such thing as too much cleavage," Phin said. "Not that I want to see yours or anything."

"Good to know," I said and examined myself again. "Okay, so I've got the outfit, now I just need to do my hair and makeup.

"Already on it," McCartney said, holding up a hairdryer.

Thirty minutes later, my hair was blown out, my makeup was done and I was officially ready for my date. My stomach, however, wasn't quite as excited about the outing as my mind was.

"You guys, I feel sort of nauseous," I said, lying facedown on my bed. "I don't think I can go through with this."

"You're just nervous," McCartney said. "Once you guys start talking, you'll feel better."

"Yeah, Arielle, buck up," Phin said. "Stop being such a chick."

"Hello? In case you hadn't noticed, I *am* a chick," I said, standing up and placing my hands on my hips. "And I happen to recall a certain incident at school when you up-chucked while talking to Cindy Rossum, so don't even talk to me about 'bucking up.' "

"Dude, that was in fifth grade and I told you, I had the flu," Phin said, frowning.

"Yeah, the *crush* flu," McCartney said, smirking.

"You're such a brat," Phin retorted.

"At least I'm not a huge dork who pukes on girls," she responded in a sing-song voice. "Tell me, did the creators of 'South Park' base Stan after you? Or is that just a rumor?"

Before anyone could come to blows, the familiar chime of my doorbell rang and we all jumped up quickly.

"I've never been so happy to be saved by the bell before," I said, taking one last look in the mirror and then grabbing my jacket and purse. "Thanks for getting my mind off of things, guys."

"Anytime we can help you by fighting..." McCartney said with a grin.

I ran downstairs and headed for the door.

"Have fun tonight, honey," my mom yelled out from her place on the couch. "Any questions you have before going out?"

"No," I yelled, embarrassed. The last thing I needed was another "birds and bees" lecture from my mother. Talk about feeling sick. A convo like that would definitely send me over the edge and into barfsville.

I placed my hand on the doorknob, but hesitated before opening the door. I took a deep breath and closed my eyes. Was I really ready for this?

My thoughts were interrupted by the sound of the bell ringing a second time. Before I could stall any longer, I opened the door and plastered a huge smile on my face.

Five minutes later, I was sitting next to Dan in the front seat of his beat-up Corolla. Thankfully, the radio was on, because we'd just hit a lull in the conversation. We'd already made small talk for a couple of blocks and since this was foreign territory for me, I had no idea what I was supposed to say. So, I finally took to checking Dan out as he drove instead.

He was wearing faded blue jeans and an untucked, button-down blue and white checkered shirt. His blond hair was spiked up all over his head, but not greasy like some of the guys at school wore it. It looked soft, like you could run your hands through it...

Whoa, Nelly. The date hadn't even started yet and I was already thinking about getting to second base. I'd had no idea I was such a fantasy slut! I turned away from Dan and looked out the window.

The music faded out on the radio as the DJs told the audience what songs we'd been listening to.

"Hey, DJ Dave, have you heard about this teenager at Ronald Henry High School?" said one of the on-air personalities.

The mention of our school caught both of our attention, and Dan looked at me curiously before leaning over and turning up the volume.

"You mean the girl who's selling a kiss on eBay?" DJ Dave responded.

"That's the one," the other said.

"Arielle! Dude, you're famous!" Dan exclaimed, turning his head and smiling at me. "This is totally cool!"

"Cool" wasn't exactly the word I was thinking of at that particular moment. In fact, the words, "humiliating," "painful" and "please shoot me now," were repeatedly running through my head.

"Or totally embarrassing," I muttered under my breath. I silently begged the DJs to switch to a new topic, but luck obviously wasn't on my side, because they kept talking.

"It's gotta be kind of harsh being a freshman in high school and still not having had your first kiss," DJ Dave exclaimed. "I don't know about you, but I was about eight when I kissed a girl for the first time."

"Yeah, and I bet it was another five years before you got another chance, right buddy?" the first DJ chuckled.

"Ha, ha, wise guy. I just can't imagine being in this chick's position. I mean I've got to hand it to her for putting herself out there like that," DJ Dave said. "Sweetie, if you're out there listening to this, don't trip just yet. Guys like it when a girl takes matters into her own hands. I'm sure you'll be getting that kiss in no time."

Gee, thanks for the pep talk, DJ Dave.

"Don't tell me that you're going to be bidding on that first kiss of hers?" his buddy said in mock shock.

Ew, gross. Talk about dirty old men.

"With the amount of bids she's got so far, I don't think I could afford it even if I wanted to," he laughed and a moment later, music resumed on the station.

Thank God it was over, but now I was stuck in the car with Dan. In this awkward silence. As we both reflected on what had just happened. I couldn't bear to look over at him—I was too horrified to think of the look that might be on his face. Luckily Dan took his cue from me and didn't say anything else until we pulled into the movie theater parking lot.

Turning off the engine, he looked over at me and asked, "You ready to go?"

I nodded, still mortified over the radio incident.

"Hey," Dan said and placed his hand on mine. "You okay?"

"You seriously still want to hang out with me after all that?" I asked, looking down at my lap.

"Are you kidding? You're unlike anyone I've ever met before, Arielle," he said, a smile growing on his face. "Besides, it's like I'm going out with a *celebrity*."

Just what a girl wants. To be a celebrity known for being kissably challenged.

I laughed nervously as I got out of the car and followed him toward the theater.

"I've been waiting to see this movie for like, *ever*," Dan said once we were seated in the theater. He'd practically bought out the snack bar when we'd arrived. There was a giant tub of popcorn, nachos, M&Ms, Raisinettes and two extra large sodas resting on the seat beside us.

"Uh, didn't this movie just come out tonight?" I asked, as I watched Dan shove a handful of popcorn into his mouth.

"Yeah, but I've wanted to see it since I saw the previews *last* Friday," he said. A little bit of faux butter dripped down the side of his mouth and onto his chin.

"I can see how that would seem like forever," I said, jokingly.

"I know, huh?" Dan answered sincerely. "Do you like scary movies?"

I was surprised he was even asking me the question now, since he hadn't bothered to bring it up before he'd bought our tickets. I'd still been in such a surreal fog at the thought of being out with him and all, that I hadn't thought to mention my totally irrational fear of horror movies. I'd barely been able to make it through the first five minutes of *The Ring* and then had proceeded to sleep with my bedroom light on for nearly a month.

"Not really," I answered truthfully. "They kind of freak me out."

"That's cool," Dan answered, giving me one of his grins. "If you get scared, you can just grab onto me."

As tempting as that sounded—anyone with a pulse could notice how good Dan smelled—I was pretty sure I wouldn't be able to make it through the movie without hiding my head in the hoodie of my jacket. And what kind of impression would that make on a guy like Dan? Hiding in a hoodie wasn't exactly sexy.

When the lights dimmed, I immediately tensed in my seat. Dan glanced over at me, excitement flashing in his eyes. "You ready for this?"

"Ready as I'll ever be," I said honestly and forced a smile.

"Here," Dan said and held out his hand. "You can squeeze my hand whenever you get scared, okay?"

My fear melted away as I stared at his outstretched palm.

A boy was offering his hand to me. Dan Stevenson wanted to hold my hand! *Take it, you doofus,* I screamed inwardly as I continued to look at it.

I felt myself blush and wiped my sweaty palms on my skirt discreetly, before placing my hand in his.

I'd expected his hand to be rough like my grandfather's had always been, but it was soft and warm. I felt my heart begin to beat faster as Dan pulled our entwined hands back toward him and rested them on his thigh.

I ended up missing the first ten minutes of the movie, because I was still staring at our hands resting on Dan's leg. I was trying to memorize everything about the moment, so I could relay every last detail back to McCartney when she asked me about it later.

It wasn't until everyone around me screamed as the music in the movie hit its dramatic loud pitch to indicate something scary had just happened, that I remembered we were even in a theater. Watching a scary movie. Even though

I hadn't been paying attention, I jumped anyway, involuntarily moving closer toward Dan.

"Damn, girl. You've got a grip on you," Dan whispered through the dark.

I realized I'd been squeezing his hand so tightly that my knuckles were practically white. Embarrassed, I loosened my fingers and apologized.

"No worries," he said. "Like I said, I don't mind if you grab onto me. I mean, if you're scared and all." He added this part almost as an afterthought and turned his attention back to the screen.

Was that an invitation? Because if it was, I was definitely ready to RSVP yes. I bit my lip and stole a glance at Dan as he stared at the screen.

I tried to pay attention to what was happening in the movie after that, closing my eyes whenever I thought something was going to pop out, or somebody was going to get killed off. Suddenly, before I could realize what was happening, I was screaming at the top of my lungs and burying my face into Dan's shoulder.

I heard his faint laughter and then felt his breath in my hair, which had covered my ear as I'd turned around.

"So, you want to get right to it, do you?" he whispered. "I could tell you wanted me."

Huh?

"Huh?" I asked, pulling myself away from him.

"I knew I'd be your first," he answered.

"My first *what*?" I asked confused, beginning to feel slightly uncomfortable.

"Come on, Arielle," he whispered, pulling me back toward him. "You know. Your first kiss."

"What?!" I shrieked, right at the same time the audience jumped at another scary part in the movie.

"Hey, chill. It's cool. I'm up for the challenge," Dan said, laughing nervously at my reaction.

My mind whirled as I processed what Dan was saying. As the truth began to dawn on me, I stumbled up out of my seat and raced for the double doors at the top of the theater. I didn't bother to look behind me, but I knew that Dan was on my heels.

When I'd made it halfway through the lobby, I turned to face him.

"What *was* that?" I hissed at him.

"You know what it was about, Arielle," Dan said, placing one of his hands into his back pocket and smirking.

"No, I *really* don't. Why don't you enlighten me?" I said.

"You're looking to get kissed. I'm looking to get kissed," Dan said, his voice sounding innocent. "I figured it's a win-win situation."

"Is *that* why you asked me out?" I asked, a lump forming in my throat. "Because you thought I'd make out with you?"

"Well, not the *only* reason," Dan said sheepishly. "I mean, my friends and I thought it would be pretty cool to be the first one to kiss you, but..."

"Seriously?" I exclaimed, my voice growing louder. The anger I was suddenly feeling seemed to erupt out of nowhere. I was about to explode and I couldn't care less that the debris was about to hit one of the hottest guys in school. "Seriously? You brought me to some crappy slasher flick because you thought you'd bag the poor girl who's never been kissed?"

"Look, let's just go back into the movie," Dan said quietly, noticing that people in the lobby were starting to stare at us.

"Uh, uh," I said, shaking my head. "Why don't *you* go back in there and find some other skank to fulfill your make out needs, because you are *so* not worth my time."

I turned my back on him and started to stalk off in the direction of the entrance. A few feet later, I swirled around and looked straight at Dan and cocked my head to the side with an attitude I didn't know I had.

"And just so you know," I said, "you're *so* not worth my kiss either!"

People around me began to clap and I heard a woman say, "Tell him, girl!" as I continued to walk away.

Pushing open the door, I wandered off into the dark night, already reaching for my cell phone.

Chapter Eight

"THAT TOOL-BAG!" MCCARTNEY exclaimed, as I relayed all of the sordid details from my disaster date. We'd barely even stepped onto campus before I'd begun telling them all about it. Starting from the moment I'd opened the door and saw Dan standing there, straight through to the point when I'd called my mom to pick me up a couple of blocks away from the theater.

"Yep, pretty much," I nodded.

By the time I'd gotten home, I was practically shaking, I was so angry. After putting on my big, red, padded boxing gloves and punching the bag that was hanging up in the corner of my room for a half hour, I finally started to feel a little less homicidal. Not only was the punching bag a good workout, but it was one of my favorite ways to de-stress. And picturing Dan's face as I took each swing was a great motivator. It was a win-win situation.

"Wait," Phin said, his hands shoved deep into the pockets of his jeans. "He took you to the movies and just *expected* you to fall all over him? Even *I* know that you have to work a little for it."

McCartney and I looked over at him and made faces.

"Please! Not the evil death stare!" he said, shielding his eyes. "All I meant is that it doesn't matter if you're Dan Stevenson or Orlando Bloom...you still have to put some effort into a date if you think you're going to be able to make a connection that will end in a kiss."

"Nice save," McCartney said, sarcastically. Then she turned back to me. "And really? A horror film? That's about the most unoriginal idea for a date. They're all about some girl, running through the woods, half-naked. Then, she trips and falls over some imaginary branch or tree trunk or heck, maybe even over her own clumsy feet. And as the killer gets closer, she doesn't even bother to get up. Really, if you trip while running half-naked through the woods and don't get up, I'm sorry, but you deserve to be chopped to bits."

I laughed despite myself, as she vented. I'd heard this same complaint from her many times before, and didn't miss the irony in the fact that McCartney rarely missed a scary movie—no matter how awful or clichéd it was.

"I think you're missing the point of my story," I finally said. "The bottom line is: Dan only asked me out because he thought it would be cool to be the first one to *bag* me. Like, he'd win some prize or something for getting to me first."

"Well, he kind of would have," Phin said. Holding up his hands in surrender before we could glare at him again, he added, "I heard the radio spot with DJ Dave last night. You're becoming quite the local celeb. He may be high school popular, but being your first could've made him real-world popular."

"That's lame," I said.

"But it's also sort of true," McCartney said sympathetically. "Sorry, girlie, but some guys are only into what will help their reps, and right now you're the hottest thing at RHHS."

"Even *I* didn't think it would get this big," Phin admitted. "I looked up your listing last night and you're up to $175."

I was so shocked, I almost choked on my own spit, and then broke out into a coughing fit.

"What?!" I exclaimed when I'd regained control over my breathing and could talk again. "Someone wants to pay $175 to kiss me?"

"Yes, siree," Phin said, kicking at a rock and watching it skip over the concrete. "A hundred and seventy five smackaroos."

"It's gotta be a nerd," I concluded, shaking my head. I turned to McCartney. "I mean, only someone as desperate as me would pay someone else that much money to kiss them, right? I saw *Love Don't Cost a Thing*. I know how these things work."

"*Can't Buy Me Love* was so much better. Hello?! Have you *seen* Patrick Dempsey, a.k.a., Dr. McDreamy?" McCartney said, swooning. "And if I remember correctly, didn't the nerdy one end up with the dreamboat in the end?"

"Yeah, yeah, but this isn't a movie," I said. "Things tend to be a little more... *crappy* when it comes to real life."

"Way to keep it positive, Red," Phin said as we approached the school doors. "You've only got a few more weeks until that kiss is yours. And then all this drama will be over. We'll probably laugh over this whole situation."

Yeah, right. It will be hil-arious!

I pushed open the doors to the school and walked down the hallway toward my locker. I thought that after a week of everyone knowing about the eBay thing people would start to talk about something else. But everywhere I looked, I could see kids staring and whispering to each other.

"I *so* can't deal with this crap anymore," I said in a low voice as we walked past a group of three girls who were all chatting in hushed tones and glancing our way. I may not have had any proof that they were talking about me, but somehow I knew it was true. McCartney took a look at me and then followed my gaze over to the gossip girls.

"I'll take care of this," she said forcefully and walked right up to the group. "Hi, girls! Whatcha talking about?"

The blondest in the group gave McCartney a blank look and then put a fake smile on her face. "Nothing important," the girl stammered. "I mean, nothing at all, really."

"Well, I'd *really* like to hear what's got you guys buzzin' this morning," McCartney said putting on a sweet, southern accent to mimic the other girl.

The blond looked at her friends and then down at her shoes. Then she muttered something that I could barely make out. I found myself leaning forward, straining to hear what she was saying. Not that I was eager to confirm my suspicions or anything.

"I'm sorry, could you say that a little louder?" McCartney asked, her smile fading. "I couldn't quite hear you."

It was like she had ESP and could read my mind.

"We were just talking about how wrong it was that Dan's going around bragging to everyone that he was Arielle's first kiss," the girl answered quietly. Then, she looked sheepishly at me obviously nervous to be put on the spot. "Nobody likes someone who kisses and tells, right?"

The girl held up her arms and shrugged. I just turned away and stared at the wall, both shocked and embarrassed by the news.

"That's right," McCartney said, inching closer to the girl. "And I'd be careful about spreading rumors, especially when they're not even true."

"Oh, of course not, McCartney," the girl said trying to back away from us. "We weren't going to say anything to anyone else."

"I didn't think so," McCartney said, threateningly

We watched as the group of girls scuttled away, whispering again and glancing back over their shoulders at us before disappearing out of sight. I swear, as girls, we were our own worst enemies sometimes.

"So, Dan's telling everyone you two kissed," McCartney said.

"I heard. But he can't...we didn't," I said, at a loss for words. Then I confided in a whisper, "We only held hands."

"*We* know that, but as far as anyone else knows, that kiss we've been advertising is already gone," Phin said.

"We'll work this out," McCartney said. "Just meet me out here at lunch. I promise, we'll have your rep intact by the end of the day."

"Wouldn't it just be easier to let the rumor go?" I asked, my shoulders slumping a little. "Maybe even let the whole thing go?"

"No way! Then, he'd get all the glory when he didn't even earn it. And you'd still never have experienced your first kiss," McCartney said. "Besides, this guy's a creep. It's about time everyone else knew it too."

"I guess you're right," I said, still not feeling any better. In fact, the sinking feeling in my stomach took another dive.

"Hang in there, hon," McCartney said. "Trust me on this?"

I forced a smile and then rushed off to class as the warning bell rang.

Three and a half hours, and two soul-sucking classes later, I was standing next to my locker in the hallway waiting for McCartney so we could eat lunch together. Phin had already come and gone, explaining that his stomach was "practically eating itself," and that he promised to save us seats in the cafeteria.

Looking from one side of the hallway to the other, I willed McCartney to appear so I didn't have to keep standing around by myself like a total loser. Feeling a bit restless, I started biting my fingernails while I examined my feet nervously.

"That's a nasty habit," McCartney said as she walked up behind me, hooking her arm in mine. Then we began to walk toward the noisy cafeteria together.

"I was standing there by myself for*ever*," I said, frowning. "Where were you?"

"Don't you worry your pretty little head about that," McCartney answered with a devilish grin. "Besides, I figured Phin would be around."

"He was hungry."

"Want me to side kick that boy for ditching you?" McCartney asked.

"You can side kick *yourself* for making me wait for you," I said. "But seriously, what have you been up to? You've got that 'You can't see my devil horns, but they're there' look."

"Who? Me?" McCartney asked, feigning innocence. When I raised my eyebrows at her, she added, "You'll see soon enough."

"Should I be scared?"

"Have I ever let you down?" McCartney asked as we walked into the lunchroom. She paused mid-step. "Wait, don't answer that."

We stared around the room, trying to locate Phin. Instead, my eyes fell on Dan and the group of guys that were lounging around his table. They were talking in low voices and laughing. Every once in a while, one of the guys would slap Dan on the shoulder or give him a high five.

I suddenly got the urge to turn around and spend my lunch hour in the bathroom near the band room, but McCartney gripped my arm even tighter to make sure I stayed put. I could tell that she'd also seen Dan and his buddies.

Then McCartney started to pull me toward their table, even as I tried to get out of her tight grip.

"What are you doing?" I hissed through clenched teeth. "I do *not* want to go over there!"

McCartney ignored me and didn't stop until the two of us were standing right behind Dan. My cheeks began to burn red and I looked around helplessly trying to find the nearest exit.

"Daaaannn," McCartney said, in a sing-songy voice. "Heard you had a wild time Friday night."

"Yeah..." Dan answered automatically as he turned around. He stopped talking once he saw us standing behind him.

A few of the guys snickered and stared at us as if we were novelty gifts.

"Why don't you tell us about it?" McCartney asked, smoothly. "And don't leave out a single, juicy detail."

I thought he was going to break, admit he'd lied and maybe even apologize, but it didn't happen. Instead, he recovered quickly and let his mouth slide into his signature smile. "Well, a gentleman never tells," he said, folding his arms behind his head and leaning back in his chair.

"You know, that's what I've heard," McCartney said sweetly, a sparkle in her eyes. Leaning in to whisper the next part to the table, she added, "I've also heard you're not exactly a gentleman."

"Oh, really, McCartney? So what am I then?" Dan asked, chuckling and looking at the guys around him like this was the most ridiculous thing ever.

"Actually, I've heard that you're kind of the opposite," McCartney said, still smiling. "You know. The kind of guy who gets no action, but tells everyone that he did. Kind of makes you wonder how many other things you've lied about. Are you sure *you're* not the one with no experience?"

I looked around us and noticed that the whole caf had stopped eating and was hanging onto every word. I swallowed thickly as I turned my attention back to McCartney and the guys.

Dan's smile drooped into a frown as he noticed we had an audience too. "Why would I have to make something like that up?" he asked, his seat hitting the floor again. "She's the one who's all obsessed with kissing."

"It must have really freaked you out to have to make up a rumor like that, huh?" McCartney asked, pushing him even farther. "I mean, how often does Dan Stevenson get *turned down*? Was Friday night the first time, or have there been other girls who've realized what a tool you are?"

"Oh. I get it now. Don't worry, Janning, there's enough of me to go around," Dan said, tilting back in his chair again.

"You really should consider thinking a little *less* of yourself, Danny-boy," McCartney said, not missing a beat. "Besides, I just read an interesting e-mail that pretty much proves there are plenty of girls out there who are on to the jerk-wad you really are."

McCartney looked at me triumphantly, then back at the table of guys.

"Toodles," McCartney said, waving her fingers at them.

As we began to walk away, a familiar tune started up behind us.

"Sha, la, la, la, la, la...go on and kiss the girl," Dan sang softly. I stopped in my tracks and listened as Dan's friends joined in by humming the tune. Finally the guys erupted into laughter behind us, slapping high fives and patting each other encouragingly.

"Oh, *real* original guys. What, because my name's Arielle and I have red hair? Clever. Like I've never heard *that* one before. You guys are so *lame*," I said, growing annoyed.

What I didn't tell them was how close they were to the actual truth. That my mom had allowed me to choose my own name when I was old enough to do so—she thought that it was good for a person to choose their *own* identity. Unfortunately I was going through this whole Disney princess phase and my favorite movie at the time was *The Little Mermaid*...you get the picture. Naming yourself after a mermaid is cool when you're five, not so much when you're a teenager.

Then, Dan and his buddies were doing it again, singing the theme song, this time adding in obnoxious kissing noises into the mix. For his finale, Dan looked right at me as he sang, "I went and kissed the girl."

Before I knew it, I was stomping back toward the table. My fury from the night before came raging back, and I walked over to Dan until I was standing right over him again. Without hesitating, I reached out and pushed Dan back in his chair, until it toppled over with him still in it.

"Oh, *I'm* sorry!" I exclaimed, covering my mouth dramatically, before leaning in toward him. "I guess your chair just couldn't hold your big ego anymore. Might want to get that checked out...and maybe work on your dating skills, too, while you're at it. I was *so* not impressed."

Dan jumped up from where he'd landed on the floor and took a few steps forward like he was going to get up in my face. Before he could reach me though, somebody stepped in between us.

"Hey there, Dan. Why don't you go take a walk," a voice said, sharply from out of nowhere.

"You think I'm gonna let some wi-atch talk to me like that?" Dan asked.

"I think she just did," the guy replied. "Now, trust me. Go. Take. A walk."

Dan squinted his eyes at us a few seconds before silently stalking off.

Suddenly, the cafeteria was buzzing again, and I realized I'd been holding my breath through the whole embarrassing confrontation. Letting it out deeply, I tapped on the shoulder of the guy who was still standing with his back to me.

"Hey, thanks for that," I said.

The guy turned around and I was surprised to see who it was.

"No problem," Cade Jones said, tucking his dark locks behind his ear. "It's guys like him who give the rest of us bad reps."

"He *is* kind of a jerk, isn't he?" I agreed.

Cade smiled at me, and let out a little laugh.

"What?" I asked, starting to feel defensive again.

"I was just thinking of the look on his face when you pushed him over," he said. "It was seriously priceless."

"Oh. That," I said, suddenly very self-conscious.

"Yeah. *That,*" he answered.

Cade started to walk away, but then stopped and looked back at me. "If it's any consolation, I never believed the rumors."

I was surprised to find it actually was a consolation, but before I could tell him that, he was already out of earshot. Shrugging, I walked over to the table where McCartney and Phin were now sitting and eating their lunches.

"Now, *that,*" Phin said, between bites, "was awesome!"

"Did you ever know that you're my heeeerrroooo," McCartney sang to me.

I began to blush again as I took out my lunch. "Cut it out, guys," I said, chewing slowly as I replayed what had just happened in my head. After a minute, I leaned in toward them.

"That *was* kind of cool, huh?" I asked.

"Totally!"

I couldn't help but beam, even while Dan and his crew continued to glare at us the rest of lunch.

Chapter Nine

"IT WAS JUST like, 'Wham' and the jerk went down," McCartney exclaimed, toppling backward onto the floor of her room. She had the radio turned on to her fave alterna-rock station and we were all lounging around. "God, Arielle, it was like, all of a sudden you were this crazy-strong, totally Buffy'd out girl. I think everyone in the cafeteria thought you were gonna kick his sorry butt all over that room!"

"Yeah, right," I said sarcastically, but smiling at the memory. After standing up for myself that afternoon, I'd felt a surge of power go through me. Like I was part superhero—or at the very least, that I was taking my cues from the superheroes I'd seen in movies and on TV. It was strangely exhilarating, and I was surprised—but happy—to notice that the feeling hadn't faded yet.

"All this excitement has made me hungry!" McCartney said, hopping up from her place on the floor, and walking over to the speaker that was built into her wall. "What do you guys feel like?"

"Taquitos," Phin said, laying on his stomach on McCartney's bed.

"Chips and salsa," I answered with my usual choice.

"And sodas," Phin added.

McCartney nodded as she pushed the button on the bottom right of the speaker.

"Yes, Miss McCartney?" a sweet voice filled the room.

"Hi, Teddy! How are things going today?" McCartney asked the voice in the box. "You hear anything from that Latin boy of yours yet?"

Theodora had been working as the Janning family maid since the three of us had started middle school. Before then, McCartney'd had another maid—a little, old, crotchety woman, who got a little too old to chase after McCartney anymore.

After having lived with the Janning's for the past three years, Teddy (this was our nickname for her) had become more of a friend to us than hired help. I smiled as I pictured Teddy's cheeks flushing pink at the mention of her latest crush.

"Nothing yet, my little gossip monkeys," Teddy answered jokingly. "I'm playing the situation 'cool' as you kids say."

"Please, Teddy, unless he's blind, the guy's gotta be jonesing for you by now. Really, you're like, a hottie." Phin said. Teddy was exotic-looking. Wore her dark hair in waves around her face and actually was a total babe. Plus, she was only in her late twenties, so she totally had youth on her side.

"If he doesn't make a move soon, Teddy, you may just have to take matters into your own hands," I piped up.

"This, coming from Miss Kissy Face herself," Teddy said, challengingly.

"Okay, okay, we give up!" McCartney said, finally. "Actually, we're just so hungry that we can't argue with you anymore."

"What can I get you kids?" she asked. I could hear her rumaging around as she took out a scrap of paper and found a pen.

McCartney rattled off a list of snacks and then thanked her, before turning her attention back to us.

Running back over to McCartney's bed, I did a forward somersault onto the mattress. I narrowly missed kicking Phin in the face as I settled into place and stared up at the ceiling.

"Whoa, Xena," Phin said, covering his face with his hands. "You may be a badass, but you've gotta put in some extra training if you're gonna be pulling moves like that."

"Oh, I've got moves you've never seen before, Phin-ster," I said in my best flirty voice.

"And suddenly I'm not hungry anymore," Phin said, clutching his stomach in mock disgust.

I punched him playfully in the arm and pouted a little.

"Omigosh!" McCartney exclaimed suddenly. She crossed the room, laptop in hand, and sat down between the two of us.

She turned to me as she fired up the computer. "You remember when I told Dan this afternoon that I'd read something that proved what a slimy slug he is?" she asked, her eyes growing mischievous.

With everything that had been going on at the time, I guess my brain had glossed over that part of the convo. I shook my head and McCartney continued.

"Well, I was sort of telling the truth—and sort of not," she said. She typed on a few keys and then swiveled the computer so both of us could read the page. The website was called "HesAJerk.com" and on the main page were a few pictures of guys around our age, as well as little bios on each of them.

"Type Dan's name in the search box," McCartney prompted.

I did what she said and then watched as another page popped up with a picture of Dan and his name in bold black letters. I began to read aloud.

> "This is Dan Stevenson. He's a junior at Ronald Henry HS. And he is a dog. Look out for this jerk, girls. He's been known to take ladies out for the sole purpose of trying to lay his not-so-smooth moves on them, and then spread false rumors about them around school.
>
> To this creep, accepting an invitation to a movie or a bite to eat means that you, in turn, are expected to make it worth his while. And we're not talking just buying the tub of popcorn and soda at the theater. We're talking—well, use your imagination.
>
> So, if you're asked out by this slimeball, I'm warning you—Just. Say. No. Otherwise, before the date's even begun, you might have agreed to something you never signed up for. Oh, and he also has bad breath."

I looked up from the screen, my jaw dropping open as I stared in disbelief at my friend.

"You wrote this?" I asked, incredulously. "How did you even find this site?"

"I'm going to plead the fifth to your first question, on account of not wanting to incriminate myself," McCartney answered slowly. "But if I *were* to have something to do with this, I may have heard about the site from a cousin of mine who had a run-in with a player at *her* school last year."

"Can you *really* do this?" I asked, feeling a tad bit guilty at the thought of tarnishing someone else's rep. Even if the victim in question *was* a dirt bag like Dan. "I mean, is this sort of thing legal?"

"Freedom of speech," she replied, shrugging. "Besides, more than one girl left messages under Dan's profile. So, it's not like I'm making it up."

I scrolled down the page and sure enough, there were at least another half a dozen entries by different girls recounting their negative experiences on dates with Dan. A few of them even said things I would have been embarrassed to read out loud. After reading all the testimonies, I didn't feel quite so bad about what McCartney had written.

"But, bad breath? I never told you that," I sputtered, scrolling back up to the top of the page.

"I never said I was a *nice* girl," McCartney said devilishly. "Besides, no one trashes on my girl."

"Have I ever told you that you're a great friend?" I asked, leaning over and giving McCartney a tight hug.

"Yeah, but it never hurts to hear it again," McCartney answered, laughing.

There was a knock on the door and Teddy came in with our snacks. She placed the tray of goodies down on McCartney's desk where her computer had been a few minutes before, but now lay between us.

Phin jumped up and practically attacked the food. "Thank God, Teddy. I think the estrogen in here was beginning to kill off my total manliness," Phin said, shoving the food into his mouth.

"You were manly before?" McCartney asked, raising an eyebrow.

"Why do you think we keep you around, Phin?" I added. "You're like one of the girls."

"Take it back," Phin said, stopping mid-chew.

I smiled at him innocently.

"I hope you two know that I have guy muscles, and guy sweat, and plenty of girls don't think of me as 'just one of the girls,'" he said, narrowing his eyes at us.

"Okay," McCartney answered.

"Whatever you say," I said, nodding my head.

Phin could hear the sarcasm in our voices. "You guys suck."

Teddy snickered as she left the room, closing the door behind her. We made our way over to the food and brought it back to the bed.

"Now, on to more pressing matters," McCartney said, dipping a chip into the salsa and popping it into her mouth.

"Such as?" I asked.

"Well, the Homecoming dance is coming up," she answered. "It's our freshman year, so we have to decide whether we're going to be making an appearance or not. And if we're going as a group or with dates."

"Sorry to burst your bubble, girls," Phin said, quickly. "But there's no way I'm not getting asked. And as I've learned by hanging out with you two today—three's a crowd. And so is four."

"You know we were just joshing you before, Phin," I said. "You're the manliest man around. Really. You're more guy than Bradley Cooper. Man sweat and all."

"Now say it once more with a little *more* feeling," Phin answered, crossing his arms and puffing out his chest.

"So, does that mean, we're voting on the side of going to the dance?" McCartney asked, ignoring Phin's show of masculinity.

This was a good question. On the one hand, going to a high school dance had been something that the three of us had been talking about ever since Phin's older sister had bragged about it while we were in grade school. But on the other hand, who needed the added stress of finding the perfect dress, bagging the perfect date *and* having the perfect time while trying to dance around in heels?

Still, I already knew what Phin and McCartney were thinking, so I sighed loudly.

"Okay. I'm in," I said. "I'm not promising I'm going with a date, though. It's enough that I have to deal with this whole kissing thing. There's no way I want Homecoming to turn out to be like another date with Dan."

"Fair enough. Let's just agree to go, with or without dates," McCartney said. "We'll all share a limo no matter what, and no one's ditched or left behind."

"Sounds like a plan, Stan," Phin said, hopping up from the bed. He crossed the room and picked up his bag and slung it over his shoulder. "Gotta jet. Mom's cooking lasagna tonight. See you two chicks later."

And before we could say goodbye, Phin had ducked out of the room.

I shook my head and laughed as we listened to him lumber down the stairs.

"So, we're Homecoming-bound?" McCartney asked me, holding out her hand.

I rolled my eyes and then shook her hand. "We're Homecoming-bound," I answered with a groan.

"This is gonna be awesome, Arielle. Just wait," she said, tossing a chip in the air and catching it in her mouth. "Totally *epic*."

Chapter Ten

BY THE TIME I got home that night, the table had already been set and dinner was beginning to cool.

"Sorry I'm late, Mom. We were hanging over at McCartney's," I said and let my bag fall to the floor before slipping into one of the empty seats.

"And how are things over at the Janning's?" Mom asked, placing a heaping spoonful of what appeared to be tuna noodle casserole onto my plate.

"Fine. The usual," I answered and poured myself a glass of milk.

"And where are McCartney's parents this week?"

"Um, I think Paris, maybe," I said, scratching my head. "Or maybe it's China. I can never keep track."

"Well, you guys let me know if she needs to stay here for a few days," she answered, taking a bite of her food.

"Thanks, Mom, but it's not exactly like McCartney's *alone* in the house," I said, my mouth full of cheesy goodness. "She's got Teddy, and like, three other housekeepers hanging around 24/7."

"I know, but it's not the same as having family around," Mom started to lecture.

"Mom. That *is* her family," I tried to explain for about the hundredth time. We were constantly having this same conversation. Mom feeling bad over the fact that McCartney was basically raising herself, and me insisting that not only was McCartney used to it, but she preferred it that way. Changing the subject, I added, "Speaking of family, how are things going with you?"

If all else failed, ask people about themselves. People *love* talking about themselves.

As I thought this, Mom smiled at me as if I'd just announced that I decided to run for Daughter of the Year.

"Thank you for asking, Arielle. That is so *thoughtful,*" Mom said, placing her fork down on her plate. "I just got another client today. And this couple is a doozy. I can't tell you who it is, but I *can* tell you that they're in the entertainment industry. It's going to be a challenge with these two, because neither have really had successful relationships in the past and their lives are *so* public."

My mom must have thought I never turned on the TV or walked past those gossip mags, because if she did, she wouldn't be giving me such easy clues as to who her newest famous clientele were. I was already making a mental list of who she could be talking about as she continued to chatter on distractedly.

"I mean, after my book came out and I started doing guest appearances on talk shows, I began to realize what these celebrities' lives must be like. To lose your anonymity like that…" she said thoughtfully. "But, oh well, that's the life that I chose—I guess giving up some of my privacy to the public is a small thing compared to *helping people.*"

I began to tune her out, since this was also a conversation we'd had before—that is, if you could call my mom rambling on while I stared off into space a conversation. My attention was piqued though, when I heard my name.

"I just want to make sure that you understand what being in the public eye could mean for you. Before you decide whether to agree to this or not," Mom was saying.

"Huh? Agree to what?" I asked, my forkful of food stopping halfway to my mouth.

"The interview. With *The Kennedy Daily?*" she said. And then she narrowed her eyes at me like she was just realizing I hadn't actually been listening to her after all. This was her biggest pet peeve and I wasn't about to endure another lecture about being a mindful conversationalist. So I played along.

"Oh, yeah, that," I said and coughed a few times.

My mom sighed, like she wasn't up for the lecture either. "I was just telling you that a reporter from *The Kennedy Daily* left a message, requesting an interview with you for her column," she explained for the second time. "But I want you to *really* think about it before deciding what you want to do. If you say yes, it would mean making your personal life public knowledge. Everyone in town would know everything about you. And I mean, *everyone*. Your neighbors, your teachers, the kids you like, the kids you hate—they would all know your personal business. Your life would be on display."

Though I wasn't exactly thrilled to know that my loogi-snorting math teacher might read all about my non-existent love life in his morning paper, I had to admit, I was intrigued.

"Who wants to do the interview?" I asked, running through a mental list of the columns that were usually published in the paper.

My mom got up and walked over to the pad of paper we kept near the phone, so that we could write down messages for each other. My mom of course, was the only one of us who ever remembered it was there. It was like I had this strange mental blank spot when it came to passing things along. Somehow my mom's Obsessive Compulsive side hadn't extended to me. Thank God.

"It's a woman named Sylvia Longood," Mom read off the scrap of paper. "She writes a column called..."

"Sylvia's Secrets?" I asked, surprised. Sylvia's column was basically our town's equivalent of "Sex & the City." Only with a lot less sex and even less city. McCartney and I had been reading the column since we'd discovered it back in middle school.

"Yeah. She says she's doing a piece centered around dating and wants to talk to you about your fundraiser," Mom said, handing the slip of paper over to me.

"It could be cool to at least *meet* with her, I guess," I answered, trying not to sound as excited as I felt. "I mean, it would be rude not to."

"You know I'll back up any decision you make, honey," my mom began, "but I don't want you to feel at all pressured to bend to the will of the media. And if you *do* choose to meet with her, I need to know you understand what you're getting into."

"I appreciate that Mom, but my privacy was sort of taken away the day I decided to put my first kiss up for auction on the Internet," I answered. "People at school already know what's going on, and I was mentioned on the radio the other day, so I'd say the word is already out. Maybe it's time I told my side of the story."

My mom was silent for what seemed like an eternity. Finally, she smiled and resumed eating.

"Then I'm behind you one hundred percent," she said, with a firm nod. "Would you like me to come with you? I have had a bit of experience in this arena myself."

"I think I can handle Sylvia on my own," I answered. Seeing my mom's slightly hurt expression, I added, "But if anything comes up, you're my first call."

Happy to hear this, Mom began to clear the remnants of our dinner from the table. As soon as she was distracted, I took the note with Sylvia's phone number on it and snuck up to my room to give the reporter a call.

I agreed to meet Sylvia Longood for coffee at *The Roast* the following morning before school. It was 6:30 am and I was running late. It was hard enough for me to get up on time for the ungodly hour that school required of us, but to have to be coherent before the sun had barely begun to shine, was practically torture.

Wishing I was more awake, I stumbled into the coffee house and looked around for my interviewer. I'd studied her picture in the paper the night before, but as I searched the place, I didn't find anyone that resembled the journalist.

Finally, I noticed a woman wearing black-rimmed glasses, her hair pulled back into a tight ponytail, waving at me enthusiastically from the corner. Turning around and finding no one else behind me, I realized the enthusiastic greeting was, indeed, intended for me.

I smiled nervously before shuffling over to the table where the woman had set up shop.

"Arielle, right?" she asked. "Hi. I'm Sylvia Longood. Well, aren't you just the cutest thing!"

She looked me up and down, nodding her head in approval, but it just made me feel self-conscious. So I hurried to sit down, landing awkwardly on my butt before settling into my seat.

Great first impression, Arielle. Really stellar.

As Sylvia flipped through the pages of her little notebook, I snuck a glance at her. Take away the glasses, shake out the hair, apply some serious makeup, and she'd *almost* look like the woman I'd seen in the newspaper. My guess was that photoshop was her friend.

I was still studying her when a waitress came by to ask if I wanted to order. Sylvia insisted that our breakfast was "on the newspaper," so I ordered a chocolate chip muffin and a coffee.

I'd never actually had coffee before, but I didn't want this big-time journalist to think of me as a kid. Even if I technically was. I wanted Sylvia to see me as a young lady on the verge of womanhood. Someone worthy of the attention of her readers. Not that drinking coffee would do all that, but hey, it didn't hurt. When the steaming mug arrived in front of me, I took a small sip and instantly resisted the urge to spit it back into the cup.

Who would drink this foul-tasting stuff willingly?

All too aware of Sylvia's eyes on me, I forced myself to gulp down another mouthful, thus proving my adult-ness. Then, as nonchalantly as I could, I reached across the table and began dumping bag after bag of sugar into my cup in an attempt to make it taste better. As I did this, Sylvia gave me a Cheshire Cat grin.

"So?" I fished, trying to take the focus away from my coffee-flavored sugar water.

"Soooo," Sylvia purred. When neither of us said anything else, Sylvia cleared her throat and fiddled with her pad of paper. "Well, I guess you know why I asked you here, right, Arielle?"

She pronounced my name oddly, putting a lot of emphasis on the "L," and then letting it trail off at the end. I hadn't even been there for five minutes and the woman was already irking me.

"I'm guessing you want to ask me about the whole eBay thing, right?" I asked, stirring my coffee methodically. I figured if I was stirring it, I wouldn't be expected to drink it.

"Exactly," Sylvia said, pen poised above her paper.

There was another uncomfortable silence.

"Well, what do you want to know?" I asked finally.

Geez. Was I supposed to do her job for her or what?

"Why don't we start off at the beginning," Sylvia said, her smile practically taking up her whole face. "How did you get the idea to sell your first kiss on eBay?"

"Um, well, I'm a freshman this year, and haven't, you know, kissed anyone yet, or anything," I said, staring into my mug and feeling my cheeks turn red despite myself. I wasn't sure why I was still embarrassed to talk about it—it wasn't like everyone didn't already know the deal. Pressing forward, I told Sylvia about how McCartney and Phin had gotten the idea to solve my "problem," and how things had developed since then.

"I think the bid's up to two hundred bucks or something," I finished, shrugging.

Sylvia nodded as I spoke. "That's *fascinating*. People sell stuff on eBay all the time—why not a kiss?" she said almost to herself as she scribbled something furiously on her paper. I picked up my mug of coffee to give myself something to do while I waited for her to finish.

"Is there someone you hope wins?" Sylvia asked finally.

No one had bothered to ask me that before, and to be honest, I hadn't given it too much thought. Until right now. Was there someone at Ronald Henry that I wanted to kiss? Had I already met him or would my first kiss be from the person I least expected? I had no idea how to answer Sylvia's question. Eventually I spit out the first thing that came to my mind.

"Really, at this point, I just want to get it over with," I answered.

Sylvia grinned as if I'd just said exactly what she'd been hoping I'd say. This, of course, made me nervous. Had I done something wrong? Should I have not answered at all? Before I could ask to take it back and start all over again, Sylvia reached across the table to shake my hand and then placed a few bills on the table and stood up.

"That's it?" I asked, surprised. We'd been talking for less than twenty minutes.

"I think I've used up enough of your time, Arielle," Sylvia said, letting the "L" linger even after she'd started walking away. "The piece will probably be in tomorrow's paper, so be sure to keep your eyes peeled. Ta, ta."

Then she left me to sit at the table by myself, staring after her and wondering exactly what the heck had just happened.

Chapter Eleven

"**IT'S OUT! IT'S** out!" McCartney screamed at the top of her lungs.

I turned to see her running after me as I navigated my way through the school parking lot, and cringed as everyone near us shifted their focuses our way. It was way too early for this kind of enthusiasm. Especially from McCartney, who was typically the morning crank. But when I saw how excited she was about Sylvia's article, I couldn't exactly burst her bubble.

The only problem was: I didn't know how *I* felt about it. In fact, I still wasn't sure whether the feature even portrayed me in a positive light. Until I figured that out, I didn't exactly want to publicize it to everyone I knew.

Clearly, McCartney had found no problem with it though. So, I put a smile on my face and joined in my friends' enthusiasm. "Do you really think it's good?" I asked her.

"Duh! You're mentioned in our favorite column ever!" she exclaimed. "How much better can things get?"

"What's going on, ladies?" Phin asked as he slipped in beside us.

"Sylvia Longood wrote her *whole article* about Arielle!" McCartney practically screamed and then waved the paper around for Phin to see.

"Awesome!" Phin said, and paused. "Who's Sylvia Longood?"

"You're dead to me, you know that?" McCartney said, her face serious.

"She's this reporter at *The Kennedy Daily,*" I explained to Phin. "She's got her own column about people living in Kennedy and stuff."

"Sounds *fascinating,*" Phin answered sarcastically. "So, why did she write about *you*?

"Thanks for the vote of confidence," I snapped, before explaining, "She wanted to know about the whole eBay thing."

"Here, listen to this," McCartney said, opening up the paper to Sylvia's article as dramatically as one could.

> "Dating isn't just tough for single adults in Kennedy—teenagers are even feeling the stress of finding a partner. More than a few times, I've vented about how difficult it is to meet people in this town, let alone find someone that you want to see past the first date.
>
> But after talking to Arielle Sawyer, a freshman at Ronald Henry HS, I realized that we're all in the same boat—no matter what age we are. This 14-year-old is so bothered at the fact that she hasn't kissed a boy yet, that she's resorted to putting her first kiss up for sale on eBay! "I really just want to get it over with," Sawyer said about the posting.
>
> With bids well over $200, it's starting to look like this young lady had the right idea. Which leads me to wonder—Are we so starved for love that our only choice to find it is to sell it online?"

McCartney shut the paper and turned to hug me tightly around the neck, cutting off my air supply in the process. "Girl, you have officially arrived!" she squealed.

"Whoa, calm down, Cart," I said, dislodging myself from my friend's embrace. "Being mentioned in a local newspaper is definitely not a sign that I've *arrived.*"

I felt my cell vibrate in my pocket just as McCartney began to argue with me. Looking down at the screen, I saw that it was my mom. Uh-oh. She rarely called me at school, so of course my imagination immediately went to worst-case scenerios. There'd been an accident and she was lying in a ditch somewhere. She'd been kidnapped and was being held by a crazed lunatic in some out-of-the-way cabin in the woods. Gramps had died. All these thoughts flashed through my head as I flipped the phone open.

"Hey, Mom. Everything okay?" I asked, plugging my other ear with my finger so I could hear.

After a few minutes of just listening to her, I closed the phone, and gently placed it back in my pocket. The silence grew around us, but I barely noticed it.

"Hello?! Who was that?" McCartney asked finally, searching my face for some kind of answer.

"My mom just got a phone call," I said, slowly. "A news station in New York wants me to be on their morning show. Tomorrow."

"Shut *up*!" McCartney screamed, and started dancing around in a circle.

Phin whistled loudly and patted me on the back.

"Now," Phin said. "I think it's officially safe to say that you have *arrived*."

I could barely concentrate throughout the rest of the day, settling for walking around, my head in a fog, oblivious to the hustle and bustle that was happening around me. And classes? Forget about it. I know I went, but I have no idea what we learned.

When my miserable math teacher, Mr. Haan made a comment on my paper, calling my handwriting, "worse than chicken scratches," I muttered, "thank you," and slunk back to my seat without putting up a fight. It was only later when my classmates began snickering, that I even looked up and acknowledged that he was there.

"Huh?" I asked, forcing my attention back to the subject I was supposed to be working on.

"If you spent as much time studying as you do daydreaming, Miss Sawyer, you might be passing my class," Mr. Haan said, clucking his tongue as he walked back up to the front of the classroom.

If I weren't already so freaked out about the phone call with my mom, I might've been embarrassed. Or annoyed. Possibly both. But even Mr. Haan's usual bullying tactics couldn't take my mind off the fact that in less than 24 hours, I was going to be on live TV.

And yeah, it may only be local news, but it was still TV.

Suddenly, I felt a headache coming on, and lay my head in my hands, allowing my forehead to touch my desk. A few moments later, I heard a noise. More specifically, a coughing sound, like someone clearing his throat.

I looked up, to see Mr. Haan standing over me again.

What now? I grimaced as I looked at the frown on his face.

"Hi, Mr. Haan..."

"Miss Sawyer, if it's not too much of an inconvenience for you," he started, "you may want to wake up long enough to go home."

I looked around and noticed that everyone had already left the room. The bell must've sounded and I hadn't even heard it.

"Let me try this again: The period's over, Miss Sawyer," he said, sighing. "Do us all a favor and try to get more sleep before class tomorrow, or don't bother coming at all."

"But," I started and then let my voice trail off. There was no point in arguing with the guy, when he was already halfway out the door.

I pulled my bag from the floor and packed up my stuff slowly. All I wanted to do was go home and take a nap.

Maybe if I was asleep I wouldn't stress about being seen by hundreds of strangers on TV. I placed my bag over my shoulder headed home.

Chapter Twelve

I WAS HOPING that my after-school plans would consist solely of sleeping and dreaming of anything other than embarrassing myself on live TV, but I realized too late that I was mistaken. Instead, my mom ambushed me as I walked in the door. And from the look on her face, it was clear I wasn't getting out of whatever she had planned.

"I thought we could go through your closet and find an outfit that would be appropriate for your television debut," Mom said. She already had her "serious therapist" glasses on, and was using the soft tone she usually reserved for her patients.

I groaned and tried to make my way toward the stairs, hoping that if I acted like I hadn't heard her, I could make it to the safety of my bed. Or maybe if I stalled long enough, she'd forget about it completely.

No such luck. As I passed by, she grabbed the bag from my shoulder and set it down near the stairs, steering me toward the couch. Gently pushing me down onto its comfy cushions, Mom squinted her eyes and studied me. I began to squirm as she stared, wishing, for once, that I wasn't an only child.

"Now, given the topic of the segment, you should dress nicely, but still look your age," Mom said, putting her fingers to her mouth thoughtfully. "A nice pair of slacks and a cardigan should do nicely."

I made a face. No kid my age wore slacks and a cardigan. Outside of private school at least. And that look certainly wasn't going to earn me any bidders, despite whatever my mom thought.

I opened my mouth to say as much, but was interrupted as the front door burst open, and McCartney and Phin charged inside. Our living room was a descent size, yet almost immediately I began to feel claustrophobic. Like the walls were closing in on me. My heart started to race, and my breath caught in my throat, causing what I could only describe as sheer panic.

Looking around at everyone, I realized that it wasn't the walls that were closing in on me—it was them.

"She's gonna be talking about *kissing*, Mrs. Sawyer," McCartney argued with my mom as respectfully as she could. "We can't have her dressing like a nun. She needs to wear something that's gonna make the guys *want* to bid on her. Like a jean skirt and a halter."

"What's a halter?" Phin asked, confused.

"A top that goes like this," McCartney said, gesturing in a V-motion around her neck and chest.

"Oh, yeah, we *like* those," Phin said, nodding enthusiastically.

I scrunched up my face as he agreed. I *so* didn't need Phin looking at me that way. It was just too...weird. And kind of gross. The halter was officially out.

"Any other ideas?" I asked, crossing my arms and sighing.

"The important thing is to feel confident in whatever you wear," McCartney said, pushing forward. "Confidence is *sexy*."

"Kids, I'm not sure if 'sexy' is the vibe I want my daughter to put out there on national television, given the slightly scandalous topic," Mom said, frowning.

"My mom just said 'vibe' and 'scandalous' in the same sentence," I said, shaking my head in disbelief. "Do you even know what those words mean?"

"You know what guys *really* like to see girls wearing?" Phin interrupted and moved over to my side. He placed his hands in the air with a flourish. "Sweats and a T-shirt."

Phin smiled as he pictured whatever girl he was currently crushing on, lounging around in bummy housewear.

"You know, I've never really understood that," McCartney said, curiously.

"I'm not going on TV in sweats!" I exploded, throwing my hands up in exasperation. None of this was helping. In fact, it was just making me more stressed out. Part of me didn't even want to go anymore.

Willing myself to calm down, I took a few deep breaths with my eyes closed. When I finally opened them, I looked from one surprised face to another. I rarely had outbursts, so this had caught them all off-guard.

"Listen, guys," I tried again, more calmly. "I really appreciate all your suggestions, and I know you're just trying to help... but I think I'm going to figure out what I'm wearing on my own."

"Just remember that this outfit is even *more* important than the first-day-of-school look," McCartney said solemnly. "And you didn't exactly ace that one. Just saying."

I bit my tongue to keep myself from screaming. When I was sure I could move without freaking out on her or the others, I slowly turned away and walked over to the stairs. Without looking behind me, I climbed the steps. Once in my room, I shut the door and let out a sigh.

I'd never wanted to be alone so much in my life.

I dragged my tired butt over to the bed and collapsed face-first on top of its covers. Burying my head in my pillow, I let my whirring mind go still, until the only sound I could hear was the steady beat of my own heart. Before I knew it, I was asleep.

It was a little bit after six in the morning and I was fully primped and standing just offstage on the news station set. I watched as the two morning anchors bantered back and forth, trading jokes every few minutes. The man seemed older than my mom, the woman younger, though they were both so done up that it was hard to pinpoint their exact ages.

"You're on after the next break," a man whispered, appearing next to me from behind the stage. Before I could thank him he was gone, off to carry a cheese platter over to a table set up with snacks in the corner.

I watched as the lights dimmed slightly on set, signaling that we'd gone to commercial, and then snuck a peek around the curtain. Glancing at the audience, I tried to locate my mom and friends. Every face was unfamiliar though.

I *so* wasn't prepared to do this alone.

My stomach started to twist into knots, but then the lights were bursting back on, forcing me to turn away from the action on the set. A familiar voice began to talk again, this time with heightened enthusiasm. It was the female anchor and we were back on the air.

"We mentioned earlier that we had a special guest for you today, and boy, is this one *special*," the woman said, chuckling to herself.

"Boy, is she," the man next to her answered, and let out his own fake laugh.

My stomach lurched and I frantically searched for the nearest bucket in case I threw up.

"Lets all welcome to the show, *Arielle Sawyer*!" the orange-faced anchorwoman called out like a game show host on a sugar rush.

Both reporters turned to face me, cartoonish smiles plastered across their faces, expectations wafting off them in waves. Only, I hesitated. I wasn't sure whether I was ready to go out there. Suddenly I was having trouble breathing.

As I struggled to catch my breath, someone shoved me hard from behind and before I knew it, I was staggering onstage, tripping over my own feet. Then I froze. Right in the middle of the walk to the set. I thought about how everyone was watching me back at home, waiting to see my segment, and here I was failing *epically*. But hard as I tried, I couldn't seem to get myself to move toward the guest chair.

"Arielle Sawyer, everyone," the female anchor repeated, clapping her hands politely but raising her eyebrows at me. The audience applauded a second time, assuming I just needed more encouragement. But that wasn't it.

Confused by the noise and the bright lights, I remained where I stood, my mouth opening and closing like a fish out of water.

"Arielle," the man said, smiling stiffly. "Why don't you come over *here* and sit down?"

He motioned to the chair next to the big desk they shared.

Smiling uncomfortably, I took one hesitant step and then another, until I was finally sitting in the chair next to them.

"Well, now," the woman said, looking relieved that I wasn't going to be a problem after all. "Why don't we start off the interview by talking about this *outrageous* outfit you're wearing? What kind of *statement* are you trying to make today?"

I looked down to remind myself what I'd actually put on that morning. "Uh, I don't know, I just..."

My heart dropped into my stomach as I saw that my top, which had been tied tightly behind my neck just a few minutes before, was now hanging loosely around my waist, the thin strap ripped at its seams. The strapless nude bra that I could barely fill out, was fully exposed for everyone to see.

I let out a strangled scream as I frantically attempted to cover up my "Girls Gone Wild" moment. But it was too late. I could hear some of the audience members start to snicker while others gasped in disgust. Like I had *planned* it or something.

I wanted to yell out, "Hello?! I'm not Miley Cyrus, people!"

"Oops, sorry there folks," the female anchor said with a light chuckle. "If I'd known it was going to be a 'wardrobe malfunction' kind of morning, I would have warned ya."

She said it as if it wasn't a big deal. The way you'd apologize for pronouncing a guests' name wrong. Not the way you should respond when your guest *flashes the entire country*! I was pretty sure that underage nudity was a big television no-no. Maybe they were just planning on editing it out later.

But wait—the show was live, wasn't it?

"I'm *so, so* sorry," I gushed as I fumbled to hold my shirt together. My upper half was flushed with embarrassment by now, which just brought more attention to my miniscule chest. "I don't understand how this happened. Can I just get another shirt and maybe come back to do it again?"

"I'm sorry, but that's all the time we have for today," the male anchor replied, gesturing in my direction. "And remember, you saw Arielle here first. *All of her.*"

"What?" I asked, stunned. "No! But I didn't even get to say anything yet. We can't be finished!"

The lights dimmed seconds later and I was once again left in the dark, feeling sick to my stomach. I was horrified, shocked, and confused, and I just wanted to die. Didn't matter how it happened—it could be because of blood loss due to thousands of little paper cuts and I wouldn't care.

I just wanted *out.*

Exhausted and gasping for air, I shot up in bed, my hair stuck to my face and neck. I'd been having a nightmare. As my chest heaved up and down, I realized I'd sweat completely through the shirt I'd been wearing when I passed out after school. I pulled the damp top over my head and tossed it onto the floor beside me. Glancing at the glowing clock across my room, I saw that it was 3:30 in the morning.

Still groggy, I tugged at my shoes and yanked off my jeans and then laid back down onto my bed in a heap, my heart still beating a mile a minute. I groaned as

I recalled my dream and pressed my fingers to my eye scokets, willing myself to forget where my head had gone to.

But as hard as I tried, I couldn't get the horrifying images out of my mind. So, imagination still spinning from the dream, I got up and turned on my bedside light. Sighing, I moved over to my closet and surveyed my clothes closely. Then, I began to throw outfit after outfit off its hanger and onto my bed.

I knew the only way I was going to be able to get any sleep was if I found the perfect outfit for my interview later that day.

One that didn't fall off mid-interview, preferably.

Chapter Thirteen

IT WAS JUST after 4 am when I reluctantly dragged myself into the passenger side of our car, my favorite snuggly fleece blanket pulled tightly around me. The last time I'd been up this early was years before, when mom and I decided to take a road trip to Disneyland. She'd wrapped me up in a blanket, carried me out to the car, and buckled me in before the sun had even started to peek out. Of course, then I'd promptly gone back to sleep until Mom announced that we were at the park.

This morning however, was different. There was no way I'd be getting any more sleep. Partly because of the topless dream I'd had, which had only added to my existing nerves. But also because I wouldn't be on this drive alone. We were on our way to McCartney's house to pick her up. And that girl could *talk* no matter how early it was.

I yawned as we pulled out of the driveway, shaking a bit with sleep. Then, I reached down and pulled a Red Bull out of my bag. Popping the top, I began to guzzle it down, barely breathing as I crushed it.

"I don't know how you can drink that stuff," Mom said, glancing over at me as she drove. She made a face. "It smells like cough syrup and makes you all jittery."

I finished off the rest of the can and then placed it in the cup holder next to my mom's thermos. "Still tastes better than coffee," I said, shuddering as I remembered that first cup with Sylvia. "And it's four in the morning. I could use a little hyper activity, don't you think? Nobody likes a guest who puts them to sleep."

My mom sighed, but didn't argue any further. I leaned over and turned on the radio, scanning the channels until I found a country station. Taylor Swift's voice suddenly filled the car.

"I love this song!" I exclaimed and started to sing along. "As far as I'm concerned, you're just another picture to burn!"

I started to dance the best I could while strapped into a seatbelt. If anyone were out on the road this early, they'd probably think I was crazy. And I wouldn't be able to blame them. Pointing to an imaginary ex-boyfriend as I recited the lyrics, I channeled my inner angry girl. I tapped my toes on the dashboard to the beat of the song and closed my eyes as I let loose.

"Okay Shania," my mom said, turning the volume down when she'd had enough. "Lets try not to wake the Janning's or their neighbors at this hour."

I rolled my eyes as I watched the massive houses fly by. "I'm not even sure the Jannings are in town," I muttered as we pulled into my friend's driveway.

Before the car had even stopped, McCartney was already out of the house and running towards us. She jerked open the car door and tossed her things into the back seat before climbing in herself.

"Have fun," McCartney's mom said from the front porch where she was standing in a blue fluffy robe. "Thanks for taking her, Karen."

"We're always happy to have her, Rita," my mom answered.

I heard McCartney buckle her belt and then open a can with a "pshhh" sound. She tapped me on the shoulder and without looking, I reached back and took the drink she was offering.

My mom stared first at me, and then back at McCartney, who was already chugging her energy drink like a thirsty man in the desert. She shook her head at us and then muttered something under her breath that I was sure ended with, "kids these days." I turned to look out the window again before taking another sip of the tangy liquid.

An hour and a half later, McCartney and I had managed to sing our way through Miley Cyrus' latest CD—four times—and catch up on what was going on in the entertainment world thanks to the copy of *Life & Style* that McCartney had snagged from her mom's secret rag-mag stash.

"The Teen Queens caused another scene," McCartney announced to the car, even though Mom had lost interest in our conversations by the time we'd hit the highway.

"Surprise, surprise!" I said, making a face. "They think they're so cool." I looked at the page McCartney was holding up and pointed a finger at the leader of the current celeb brat pack. "I think he might actually *be* the devil. All that shaggy blonde hair just covers up his horns."

"Totally," McCartney nodded in agreement. "When you become famous, please, please, *please* don't turn out to be like them."

"That so won't be a problem," I answered. "And don't you think you're getting a little ahead of yourself with the whole famous stuff? This is just a local news station. I'll be lucky if a dozen people are up to see it."

"Yeah, but this is the local news for *New York City*. It's not exactly Podunk, Alaska," McCartney said. "Do you know what you're going to say yet?"

"Um, I could barely sleep last night because I was trying to figure that out. Then when I finally did close my eyes, I had nightmares. So I decided I'm just gonna wait for them to ask me a question, and then I'll answer it."

"What was your nightmare about? Sharks again?" McCartney asked.

"No. And I'm sort of sick of thinking about it, to be honest," I mumbled, remembering my nearly-naked experience from the night before. "Let's talk about what we're gonna do *after* the show, instead."

I could tell McCartney wanted to push the subject further, but after a moment, her face softened, and she handed me the magazine she'd been reading. "Can we go by the MTV studios in Times Square? Apparently you can see the guests from the street, and if they think you're rowdy enough, they may even bring you up into the studios!"

"Mom?" I asked, looking over at her expectantly.

"We can stop by *if* we have enough time," my mom agreed.

"Yes!" McCartney said, pumping her arm into the air and doing a little victory dance where she sat. "Thanks, Mrs. Sawyer!"

As we neared the city, McCartney and I both pressed our faces up against the windows, mouths hanging open slightly as we stared in awe at the large buildings that lined the city streets. I'd been to NYC a few times when I was younger, but hadn't been in years. It was so much bigger than I remembered it.

There were so many people walking around, even at this early hour. Men wore tailored suits and checked their Blackberries and iPhones for e-mails from their clients as they walked to work. Women were dressed in smart dresses and sneakers, so they could pull double-duty as they power-walked to the office. Nannies herded their charges down the street to daycares, playdates and pre-school before hurrying home to start the mountainous list of to-dos that had been left for them.

"Okay, so maybe more than a dozen people will watch the show," I said, gulping nervously. I sat back in my seat and closed my eyes, the nerves building back up in my stomach.

"Deep breaths, Arielle. Deep breaths," my mom said gently. "Try and think about something else. Keep telling yourself, 'This too shall pass.'"

Yeah, it'll pass... but will I survive the aftermath?

Still, I did what she suggested and concentrated on my breathing. After a few minutes, my pulse went back to normal and I felt myself calm a bit. I'd never had a panic attack before, but I was pretty sure I'd just narrowly missed having my first.

"Okay, I think we're here," my mom said as she pulled the car into a parking garage.

As we found an empty spot and parked, I grabbed my bag that held my outfit and makeup for the show. I'd figured it would be pointless to get ready before we left, considering the hours we had to be in the car. My clothes would've ended up wrinkled and my makeup would've disappeared to the place where makeup so often goes. On my hands and shirt. So, I'd neatly packed everything away and figured that I'd just get ready at the studio.

"Got everything?" my mom asked as we clambered out of the car and made our way to the street.

"I guess," I mumbled.

"This is so exciting!" McCartney practically shouted. "Are you excited? I can't believe you're going to be on TV. *My friend* on TV!"

I could think of a word that described how I felt, but excited wasn't it. In fact, I couldn't help but feel sort of like I was headed to my own execution.

Dead girl walking. Wasn't that how the saying went? It felt incredibly appropriate at the moment.

We crossed the street during a lull in traffic and found ourselves smack-dab in front of a large television studio. The outside of the building was made up entirely of glass and I squinted as the morning sunlight bounced off the windows and hit my eyes. The whole thing was blinding. And impressive. With a tentative look up, I realized with awe that the structure was the tallest in the area. I tried to count the stories, but gave up at floor 17 and turned my focus back to the spacious lobby we were about to enter.

Following my mom and McCartney through the revolving doors, I clutched my bag closer to my body and joined the throngs of people who'd just started showing up for work. Strangers pushed past me, grasping their jumbo cups of coffee and giant purses, flashing their passes to the security guard off to the left of the check-in desk. My mom talked to the woman sitting behind the counter for a few minutes, before we were handed day passes and told to follow the crowd to the elevator banks.

It was so busy that we had to wait as four elevators came and went before all three of us were able to fit inside together. When we finally saw an opening, we shuffled into the metal box and pushed the button for the thirty-third floor. In the corner, there was a small TV screen, posting news bytes. Nobody looked at each other as they studied the screen, hoping for a glimpse of what had happened in the world since they'd left for work.

A TV in a TV station. How original.

When we arrived at our floor, we quickly made our exit, and found ourselves in yet another lobby. As mom checked us in at the counter, I wandered over to the nearest wall and studied the photos hanging in my eyesight. Every frame held a picture of one of their anchors interviewing a different celeb, each one more famous than the last.

Scarlett Johansson. Ashton Kutcher. Jennifer Aniston. Kim Kardashian.

"I wonder who'll be on the show today. Do you think it'll be someone big? Like Zac Efron?" McCartney asked, sneaking up behind me as I checked out the pictures. "Please let it be Zac Efron…"

"God, I hope it's *not* Zac Efron," I said. I so didn't need the extra stress that a celebrity encounter would add to the day.

"Bite your tongue!" McCartney said, horrified.

"Come on, guys," my mom called out, ending what was probably the beginning of a fight.

A woman stood next to Mom in the lobby now, wearing a headset and carrying a clipboard; a clear sign that she worked on the show. Which meant that she was a very important person. To me at least.

We walked over to where the woman and Mom were talking, and I attempted what I hoped was an I'm-super-excited-to-be-here smile, despite the fact that I was probably going to throw up at any moment. She didn't smile back. In fact, her face seemed to fall even more as we made eye contact.

"You Arielle?" Miss Snippy asked me, the annoyance in her voice loud and clear.

"Uh, yeah. That's me," I answered, raising my hand slightly before letting it drop to my side again.

"Uh, huh," Miss Snippy said, then sighed. "Walk with me."

She abruptly turned and began to march down a nearby hallway, making turns without giving us any notice. I looked back a few times, trying to keep track of where we were going, but after a while it was useless. We were like Hansel and Gretel minus the tasty treats to mark our way back home. Or in this case, out of the TV station and back to our car.

How was I supposed to make a speedy getaway if I didn't know where I was getting away to?

"Wait here until someone comes to get you," Miss Snippy said, before disappearing from the room she'd just deposited us in.

"But how long will we—" my mom began, but the girl was already gone. "Well she was rather...brusque."

"More like a bit—" McCartney said.

"*McCartney,*" Mom warned before she could finish her sentence.

"Sorry Mrs. S."

I busied myself by getting ready, since none of us knew exactly how long it would be before they'd bring us to the set. I dumped my makeup bag out onto the empty counter, which was surrounded by ten tiny lightbulbs. Then I went over to my bag and retrieved the outfit I'd finally decided on—Free from any possible malfunctions...trust me. I checked. Twice—and skipped over to the bathroom in the corner to put it on.

A few minutes later, I walked out in a pair of jeans and a pink iridescent tank top. I pulled on my favorite pair of cowboy boots and wrapped a beige belt around my waist.

No way anything was falling out of this.

McCartney opened her mouth to say something, but I cut her off.

"I don't even want to hear it," I said, both hands up in the air defensively. "I don't need to dress like I'm going clubbing at the buttcrack of dawn. This is what I'm comfortable in and at least I know everything will stay put. You're gonna have to deal with it."

McCartney snapped her mouth shut again as I finished my speech, but she continued to eye my tame outfit wearily. Finally, she stood up and made her way across the room until she was standing right in front of me.

"Fine. But *I'm* doing your makeup," she said, picking up my mascara and twisting it open.

"Deal," I answered relieved, and sat down on the stool in front of her.

I may not trust her to dress me, but I had to admit that McCartney was a genius when it came to wielding a makeup brush. She had a natural touch and the uncanny ability to pick *the* perfect shade to match your complexion and compliment your outfit—all without making you look like a clown or a drag queen. I was always trying to convince her to go to cosmetology school, but she insisted it was more of a hobby of hers than a calling.

"If you become famous, do you think you'll move to New York? Or maybe LA would be better. I'm not sure I could handle you being so far away. Unless, I move to Cali with you, in which case..." McCartney chattered on distractedly as I tuned her out.

There were so many things that could go wrong during the interview. I'd already come up with over a dozen scenarios that would lead to the demise of the rep I'd managed to create at school so far. A few of these included, but were not limited to: The reporter finding the idea of me selling a kiss so funny that she literally laughs me off the stage; Being interrogated and questioned about my views on child prostitution; And me getting so nervous that I start to hyperventilate and then pass out on live TV. At least the last one ensured that I would be unconscious for most of the humiliation.

A knock at the door interrupted my obsessing session and I glanced over to see who it was. Luckily Miss Snippy had been replaced by a tiny blonde with a black headset of her own. Only, unlike her predecessor, this one seemed friendly.

"Arielle?" the girl asked, enthusiastically.

"That's me," I said meekly.

"Cool! If you're ready, I can take you to the set now," she said.

I wanted to tell her that I might never be ready to go out there. That I would rather be stranded at the bottom of a pit-full of flesh-eating cockroaches than chance the social suicide I was about to walk into. I knew it sounded dramatic, but well, wasn't TV all about drama?

But instead, I said, "Sure," and stood up to follow the new girl.

As I walked by the mirror, I paused to check out my reflection. McCartney had added a little shimmer to my eyes, making them pop more than usual. Despite her pushiness, I *could* always depend on McCartney to make me look good. Makeup-wise at least.

"Here," she said, shoving a lip gloss into my hand. "Finishing touches for when you're right about to go on."

"Thanks," I said, and gave her a clumsy hug.

After waving goodbye, I nervously followed the stage-hand out of the room and down the hall. As we walked, she explained to me that while Mom couldn't come to the studio with me, she and McCartney would both be able to watch the interview from the holding room. I just nodded and tried not to trip as I trotted along behind her.

"I think it's so cool what you're doing," the girl said as she pointed me to a door with a sign that said, TO WAKE UP. "I wasn't nearly as clever as you when I was your age."

I murmured to let her know that I was listening, but the truth was, I was too distracted to think of anything to say. When I didn't answer, the girl just smiled knowingly and then pointed to the door.

"Just head through that door and wait at the side of the stage until someone mics you," she said. Then she gave me a wink. "And good luck, Arielle."

"Thanks," I managed to say.

I was going to need it.

Chapter Fourteen

I HAD TO practically force myself to walk over to the door and push it open. Last night's dream was still fresh in my mind and I couldn't help but worry it was a warning of what was to come. Still, it was too late to back out now. Even if I wanted to. Even if everything in me was screaming to head back the way I'd come and convince my mom to take me home.

Nope, this was happening.

As I inched my way into the room, I could hear two people talking from a spot I couldn't see. Walls were built up around what I assumed was the set, blocking my view. I looked around quickly and spotted an opening and tip-toed over to it. Peeking around the corner, I caught a glimpse of a pretty, young brunette, and a guy about my grandpa's age sitting on stools behind a desk. As they spoke, a dozen other people moved around the room, fiddling with cords, aiming cameras, whispering into headsets, and otherwise taking care of all the things that had to do with taping the show.

"Here's a new twist on the old kissing booth fundraiser, folks. When we come back from break, we'll be talking to one local teen who's really putting her money where her mouth is," the woman read off the teleprompter near the camera.

She and the old guy looked at each other and smiled before the lights dimmed in the studio and someone yelled, "We're at commercial!"

I started to have a major déjà vu moment as a guy with choppy hair and highlights made his way onto the set and began to touch up the anchors' makeup (Yes, even the old guy wore makeup. And if it was supposed to help hide the wrinkles, it wasn't doing its job.), while an older woman fussed over their hair.

"Who are you?" a male voice demanded from behind me.

I turned around, startled to see a slightly balding man in glasses, staring at me with his hands firmly planted on his hips.

"Arielle?" I said, blinking at him. Then, realizing that my name probably meant nothing to him, I added, "Um, I'm supposed to be interviewed next?"

"Ahhhhh," he answered, a smirk creeping onto his face. "You're the Kissing Queen."

"Well, I wouldn't exactly say that..." I started.

"A kid makes out for money and it's called a fundraiser, but you try to do that as an adult and suddenly you're jailbait," he muttered, shaking his head. "Come with me."

I was too shocked by this to actually say anything, so I just scurried behind him as he soared across the room and onto the stage where the anchors were finishing with their touchups. Baldy pointed to the only empty chair and commanded me to "sit" the way someone would scold a dog. I did what I was told, because frankly, I was too nervous to worry about some middle-aged d-bag on a power trip. So, I sat there silently until the anchors noticed that they were no longer alone.

"Well, hello there, Sweetheart!" the male anchor greeted me brightly. "I'll take one box of the Thin Mints and one of the Samoa's. My wife's thrown out all the cookies at home—she says that I've gained a few pounds—but I have a mini-fridge in my dressing room that I can hide them in."

I stared at him blankly for a few seconds, before realizing that he thought that I was a Girl Scout. In what world could anyone mistake me for one of those sweet, little ankle biters? I felt myself start to sweat with embarrassment. When he started fishing through his pockets for what I imagined was the money to pay for the cookies I wasn't selling, I finally spoke up.

"Um, I'm not selling cookies," I said, in a much quieter voice than I'd intended. Suddenly shy, I looked around to see if anyone else was listening to the exchange we were having.

"What was that?" he asked, scrunching up his face in confusion. His wrinkles were so baggy that it was possible they were actually covering his eyes and he couldn't make out who he was talking to.

"I'm—"

"For Pete's sake, Gary, the kid's not a Girl Scout," his co-anchor said dryly. The brunette rolled her eyes at the older man, and gave me a sympathetic look. "You're Arielle, right hon?"

I could tell she wasn't saying it to make me feel like a kid, but instead as a term of endearment. She oozed coolness and was easily one of the most beautiful women I'd ever seen…in real life at least.

"Yeah," I stammered, nodding like a bobble head doll.

"I'm Kara," she said, a genuine smile on her face. Then she leaned across the old guy as if he weren't even there and shook my hand firmly. "You excited to do this?"

I started to lie and tell her that I was super-psyched to be there, but then opted for the truth. I had a feeling Kara wasn't going to judge me.

"Actually, I feel like I'm gonna throw up," I said, looking down at my lap. "I don't know how you get up here and do this every morning. Doesn't it freak you out?"

Kara bent forward and rested her elbows on top of the table. Her deep chocolate brown hair fell over her shoulders, framing her heart-shaped face like a piece of art. I found myself wondering why in the heck she was a reporter when she could've easily had a nice cushy career as a supermodel.

"You bet it freaks me out," Kara said, her eyes wide. "The first three months I worked here, I threw up in a garbage can right off set, every night before we went on air. I'm pretty sure people thought I was either pregnant or had an eating disorder, but it was really just good, old-fashioned nerves."

"Why did you keep doing the show then?" I asked incredulously. It was hard to imagine that a pretty, put together woman like Kara would do anything unladylike, but it sort of made me like her even more.

Kara shrugged. "I fell in love with it," she said simply. "Not the throwing up part of course, but being in front of the camera, bringing people the news…there's just no other feeling like it. It's such a rush. And to be honest, I sort of feel like, in a little way, I'm making a difference in other people's lives. And doesn't everyone want to know that they're here for a reason, that they did *something* to impact the world in some way or another?"

I nodded my head, totally understanding what Kara was saying. Ever since I'd gotten to high school, I'd felt a little like I had no idea who I was or where I fit in. Add to that, the fact that everyone else around me seemed to have connected with someone on an intimate level, and it was hard not to feel like a total loser. How was I supposed to leave my mark on the universe if I had nothing to offer?

"I wish I had something I was good at like that," I admitted. "But I think the only impact I'm going to have on people today, is by being their comic relief."

"Or," Kara chimed in, "Maybe by talking about how you took your life into your own hands instead of just sitting around depressed or unhappy, you'll inspire other women to do the same. *I* think you're very brave. Your story actually makes me feel motivated to take a stand myself."

I started to blush under Kara's stare. Sheepishly, I looked away. "What do *you* have to take a stand on?" I asked softly, thinking she was just humoring me.

"Honey, you're not the only one with *man* problems."

I couldn't stop myself from giggling, and we both sat there laughing together for a moment. It was exactly what I needed to hear in that moment, and for that, I was immensely grateful.

I was still smiling when a guy in jeans and a baseball cap standing near the biggest camera in the room yelled for everyone to be quiet. The lights flashed back on and I squinted as my eyes adjusted to the brightness. Sweat began to pool under my arms, across my stomach and at my hairline, causing me to fidget in my seat uncomfortably. It was so freaking hot underneath these lights! Like being stuck in an over-sized tanning bed. Thank God I'd opted for a tank top instead of the sweater I'd been considering.

"Okay, Arielle, we're about to start. Here's the deal. I'll do a little intro, ask you a few questions and then that's it. Relax, have fun, and try not to think about the camera. Just act like you're chatting with one of your friends and you'll do just fine," Kara explained, tapping her papers on the top of the desk absently. "Any questions?"

If I pass out, will you cut to commercial or just let me lay there while you try to fill the dead air?

But I answered, "I don't think so."

"Alright. Here we go," Kara said, as the guy behind the camera counted us down from three, then two, then one.

Showtime.

"That was *epic*!" McCartney exploded as I walked through the door of my changing room. "I mean, seriously. I've never seen you like that before! You were funny and totally chill...you couldn't tell that you're totally a freak over public speaking."

I shot her a look. "Gee, thanks."

"Don't act all shocked. You know it's true," McCartney said, brushing off my response. "Anyways, the point is, you were great. *I'd* totally kiss you."

My mom and I both stopped to stare at her.

"If I were a *guy*," McCartney finished. "I'd kiss you if I were a *guy*. Sheesh, get your mind outta the gutter, perve."

I shook my head and started to stuff my things back into my bag. As I retrieved my makeup from the counter, I replayed the interview in my head. And I had to admit, McCartney was right. Once the camera's red light had started to blink, it was like someone turned a switch on inside me, allowing my inner rock star to shine through. My head had cleared, and before I knew it, I was smiling at Kara and the old guy like I'd been on the show a million times before.

I had to give most of the credit to Kara though. She'd been gentle with me, remaining just as nice on the air than she'd been when we were talking one on one. Any other reporter might've asked me inappropriate questions or treated the segment like an interrogation rather than an early morning entertainment piece. But Kara had done the opposite. She'd been *kind*.

"Yo, Space Cadet," McCartney said, snapping me back to reality.

"Huh?"

"I was asking if we were still heading over to Times Square...because I sort of told Phin we'd bring him back something from MTV," she said as the three of us headed out the door.

I looked over at my mom questioningly.

"It's fine with me, but we need to leave in about an hour," my mom said, pulling out her phone which had just begun to ring.

McCartney gave me a high five and started to rattle off all the things she *had* to do while we were walking around 42nd street, including singing with the Naked Cowboy, taking a picture with a NY cop and eating a hot dog from a street vendor.

"I don't think you're actually supposed to eat those things," I said, making a face. "I saw this thing on TV once and they found all sorts of gross stuff in the street meat. They even found a rat in one of the hot dog bins."

"Why do you want to ruin my dreams?" McCartney said dramatically.

My mom flipped her phone shut and rejoined us as we walked toward the elevators.

"Was that Grandma? Did she see me on TV?" I asked her.

"Nope, and there may be a change of plans," she answered slowly. "That was the booker at the *You Snooze, You Lose* show. They saw your segment and want you to fill in for a cancelled guest they had today."

"You said yes, right? Please tell me you said *hell yeah,* Mrs. S," McCartney blurted out, eyes wide.

My mom raised her eyebrows at McCartney's choice of words, but didn't say anything else.

"I thought you wanted to go to Times Square?" I asked my friend.

"I want to go where the stars are, and it sounds like that's going to be next to you," McCartney said. She turned her attention back to my mom. "When do we go?"

My mom hesitated before answering. "They'd need us over there within the hour if we want to do it," she said, looking straight at me. "But we can always skip it and go to Times Square like we'd planned. It's up to you, Arielle. What do *you* want to do?"

I looked from McCartney to my mom, and then down the street as I thought about my options. A few feet away, a girl exited her tiny NYC apartment and strutted down the street like her life was a walking photo shoot. She was young, confident and clearly going places. Suddenly I knew my answer.

"Let's do it," I said, turning back to them. "It's not like a little spotlight ever hurt anyone, right?"

Chapter Fifteen

WE WERE BACK in another waiting room—same deal, different network—and I was frantically getting dressed for my second TV appearance of the day. We hadn't had to wait long for the car they'd sent over once Mom had called them back and told them we'd do the show. As we made our way across town though, I realized we had a problem. In a world where celebrities never wore the same outfit twice, it would be embarrassing to make two public appearances while wearing the same thing. So, before heading into the studio, we ran into the nearest store and picked out a different top to go with my jeans.

Presto change-o!

Fifteen minutes later, I was ripping the tags off my new pink shirt—I figured hot pink would stand out on TV—and slipping it over my head. Admiring my quick change in the mirror, I plopped down in an empty white chair and started to pull my hair back into a ponytail.

"I can't believe we're going to be on *You Snooze, You Lose*!" McCartney squealed as she clapped her hands excitedly.

"*We're* not going to be on the show. *I'm* going to be on the show," I said as I studied my reflection.

"Same dif," McCartney answered.

"Not exactly. You'll be back here where you're safe from making a fool of yourself in front of millions of people."

I fished my cell out of my pocket as I felt it buzzing and read an incoming text.

PHIN: I SO hate you right now for going on SNOOZE without me! Can you ask Big Johnson how he could break up with his super-hot girlfriend? Is he insane? Good luck, A!

"McCartney?" I asked slowly, looking up from my phone.

"Yeah?"

"How does Phin know that I'm gonna be on *You Snooze, You Lose*?"

McCartney instantly looked guilty. "I don't know."

"McCartney..."

"Okay, okay. *Maybe* he found out because I tweeted about it while you were in H&M?" she answered sheepishly.

"McCartney!" I screeched. "You know I don't like that whole social media stuff. Nobody needs to know what I'm doing every single moment of *every single day*. It's like we're creating a world of voyeuristic gossip-mongers. And trust me, no good will come of it."

McCartney looked at me bored as I rattled on. "Okay, first off, I don't even know what that means, but I hardly think that Twitter is the root of all evil. Second... you're in the public eye now! And that public is going to want to know what you're doing," she said, taking out her phone and punching on the keys furiously. "So, I started a Twitter account for you."

"*McCartney*," I growled, sending a glare her way.

"You won't even have to worry about it. I'll take care of *everything*," she insisted.

That was what worried me.

Before I could force her to delete the profile, a young guy popped his head into the room to let me know that I had five minutes until my segment. Once gone, I turned back to the mirror to make a few touch-ups to my makeup and then smoothed my hair back with my hands. In the reflection, I could see McCartney looking at me expectantly, her hands on her hips, waiting for some kind of response from me. I sighed and spun around to face her.

"Fine," I said. "But nothing too personal and keep the updates to a minimum. There's no reason why people need to know my every move. I's like saying, 'Hey stalker guy, let me make things easier on you. This is where I am. Come and get me!' No, I prefer my weirdo's to do their own leg work."

"That's not something to joke about, Arielle," my mom piped in from her spot on the couch in the corner. "Stalkers can be dangerous."

"I was *kidding,* Mom," I answered. "Besides, I highly doubt anyone cares what I do on a daily basis. So if McCartney wants to waste her time writing about me," I said, glancing her way and shrugging my shoulders, "She can be my guest."

I stood up from my seat and smoothed down my new shirt. You'd think that pink would clash with my red hair, but I had to admit the pairing just made my eyes look brighter and my skin look extra sun-kissed.

"We're ready for you now," the cute, possibly-an-intern guy said, as he popped into my doorway again.

I made a face that I was sure matched how I was feeling on the inside: nervous, slightly sick and just a little bit excited.

"Wish me luck," I said to no one in particular.

"Good luck," they both sang out in unison. Then my mom added, "Break a leg."

I took a deep breath and followed the cute intern out the door and down the hallway toward the *Snooze* set. We were only about fifteen feet from the door that would bring us to the where we'd be taping, when I heard voices.

Nope, it was just one voice, and a whole lot of laughter. The noise got louder as we got closer.

"What's that?" I asked in a whisper.

"Live audience," he responded.

"Oh," I whispered again.

The cute intern shot me a lopsided grin and lowered his voice to match mine. "Why are we whispering?"

"I thought..." I started, my voice still low.

I stopped when I realized that the adorable guy in front of me was teasing me. My cheeks began to burn and I promptly turned my attention to the ground.

Maybe if I embarrassed myself enough now, God would cut me some slack and let me get through the interview without completely effing it up. Or was that just wishful thinking on my part?

I cleared my throat. "So, do you like working here?" I asked, recognizing how dorky the question was almost as soon as I'd said it. Of *course* he liked his job...it's not like he was working at McDonald's or anything. He was working for a friggin' TV station. He probably got to hang around celebrities all day, and go on awesome trips, and eat all the free food he wanted from that gourmet restaurant, Kraft Services. I'd overheard some people talking about what was on the menu for lunch and it sounded *amazing*. Yep, he'd hit the job jackpot.

"Working here *is* pretty sweet," he admitted, smiling as he fiddled with his headset. Then he turned his head and spoke into the empty hallway loudly. "We're on our way." Pause. "Like two minutes." Pause. "Gotcha."

We started to walk again, and I listened to his side of the conversation as we passed door after door. Our feet began to make a rhythmic beat as they hit the tile, and after a few seconds I was able to forget where we were going. And what I was about to do.

"You ready?"

"Huh?" I asked, not sure whether he was talking to me or the guy inside his headset. "Sorry. Were you talking to me?"

"Yeah. You ready to go out there?" he repeated as he held the door open for me.

"I guess. Any advice?"

The cute intern stopped for a second and thought. It was clear this was the first time anyone had bothered to ask him that.

"Marc's cool and really likes it when you joke around with him, so keep things light," he answered. Then, choosing his next words carefully, he added, "How old are you, anyway?"

"Fourteen," I answered, cringing at how young it sounded, even to me. "Why?"

He shoved his hands into his pockets then and took a step away from me. "Damn. Guess that takes me out of the running for that kiss."

I began to blush as he turned around and walked steadily away from me.

"Okay folks, as you know, you can pretty much buy anything off the internet nowadays—hell, last week I ordered myself a crate of spider monkeys to be delivered next day air," host Marc Johnson, AKA, Big Johnson said.

I rolled my eyes from my place just off set, as the audience erupted into laughter that wasn't really worthy of the joke. Apparently, this was what the cute intern had meant by "live audience." The little room was packed with about forty people, all crammed into these tiny plastic chairs seated right in front of the stage where the taping was taking place. A girl stood in front of them, holding up a sign that said "Laugh" in big black letters.

At least it made the gut-busting laughter make sense.

"But when I heard what our next guest was selling, I knew I'd officially seen it all," Big Johnson said enthusiastically. "Please welcome my first guest, 14-year-old Arielle Sawyer!"

The audience began to clap for me as I walked out onto the stage and headed toward the show's host. As I put one foot in front of the other, "This Kiss" by Faith Hill began to blare from unseen speakers, startling me at first. Recovering quickly, I sped up my walk to match the beat of the music.

I eased myself into the chair next to Big Johnson's desk, which was considerably more comfortable than the first news show's had been. I tucked my legs up underneath me and turned my upper body to face the large man. Up close, I was surprised to see how much makeup it took to make him not look so... *old.*

Phin's gonna die when I tell him that his hero wears eye liner. Maybe that was why he broke up with his model girlfriend... he caught her stealing his makeup!

I forced myself to focus as the commotion around us began to die down, and the studio became quiet again. Not sure what to do with myself, I reached over and took a sip of the water that had been placed on the table in front of me. I wasn't actually thirsty, but I remembered that most celebrities used their mugs as accessories when they were on talk shows too, so I figured it was just what you did.

"Great to have you on the show, Arielle," Big Johnson said, leaning across his desk to shake my hand.

"Thanks for having me," I answered, smiling at him and then at the audience.

"Now, Arielle, you've got a pretty interesting story." I nodded my head. "You're fourteen and you've never been kissed." He wasn't asking me. He was making a statement, and didn't even wait for me to confirm it before continuing. "Well, I think we've all felt like we were the last of our friends to do *something.* Do you mind telling us what you decided to do about it?"

"Uh, sure," I said, sneaking another glance at the audience. But instead of seeing a sea of faces, I was blinded by the bright lights shining back at me. At least this way, it was easier to ignore the fact that I had a crowd of people hanging on my every word. "Well, my friends thought it would be a good idea to sell my first kiss... on eBay."

I watched as the woman standing off-stage raised one of her signs, prompting people to hoot and holler in response.

"Wait, let me get this straight," Big Johnson said, holding up his hands to silence the audience. "You're *selling* a *kiss*? What, you just woke up and thought, 'I think I'll kiss someone today—I might as well make a buck doing it?'"

More laughter.

I tried to fight off the rising blush in my cheeks, and forced myself to chuckle along with Big Johnson. Remembering what the cute intern had told me, I decided to push back a little. "And what's wrong with that?" I joked, breathing a sigh of relief as I got the response from the audience that I'd been hoping for. "Nah, it wasn't really like that. Basically, I was sick of being the last one I knew to have that experience. That's when my friends came up with G.A.A.K..."

"Gack?" Big Johnson asked, raising an eyebrow questioningly. "Is that some sort of new aphrodisiac the kids are using these days?"

I had no idea what an aphrodisiac was, but based on the audience's reaction I had a feeling I didn't want to know. I breezed over that question and continued to explain.

"It stands for Get Arielle A Kiss. And I know it's dorky, but my friends, McCartney and Phin, wouldn't stop calling it that. Anyway, my mom told us about how her books were selling on eBay and my friends started to freak out."

"Now, we should mention that your mom is an author and a celebrated marriage counselor. So, what did *she* think when you told her you were selling yourself on eBay?" Big Johnson asked, leaning toward me imposingly.

"Not myself. Just my *kiss*," I corrected him like I was scolding a precocious little kid.

"Is there a difference?" he asked, looking to the audience for support.

"Of course. First off, I got permission from my mom to do the eBay thing and she even helped come up with the parameters for it," I said, picking up my mug and taking another sip of water.

Geez, it was awful hot under these lights. Or maybe I was sweating because of the round of questions that were being thrown at me. Either way, I was glad I'd gone with the extra strength deodorant.

"What *are* the rules of selling a kiss on eBay?"

"First off, I can't kiss anyone that is more than two years older or younger than I am," I said, ticking off pointer finger on my right hand. "Number two is that the money I make off the winning bid has to go to a charity or an organization of some sort. That way I'm not taking money in exchange for, well... kissing services."

Big Johnson threw his hands up in the air like I'd just said something crazy. "You don't actually get to *keep* the cash? What's the point in selling a kiss in the first place if you don't even get the money?" he asked genuinely curious.

"The point is getting that kiss. Not the money. I think the allure to the whole eBay thing is that people like competition by nature. So, by giving people the chance to bid on something, they're going to be more intrigued and involved with the whole thing, which brings me one step closer to getting what I want," I said sweetly. "My first kiss."

I hadn't really thought of it this way before, but as soon as it came out of my mouth, I realized it was true.

"And we all know that guys like a girl who goes after what she wants," Big Johnson said as he raised his eyebrows suggestively at the camera.

More than a little creeped out now, I quickly moved on. "And the last thing is: if I end up not wanting to kiss the guy who wins, then I don't have to, and I don't accept the money."

Big Johnson shook his head as he took all of this in. "I guess the only thing left to ask is, what's the bid up to?"

That was a good question. I really had no idea where the numbers were at. I started to panic slightly at not being prepared for such an obvious question.

And things had been going so well, too!

Just as I was about to admit that I didn't know how much my kiss was worth, my cell phone buzzed in my pocket. I sneaked a peek at the screen and saw I had a text from McCartney.

"Uh, well..." I stammered, trying to buy myself some time. I smiled as I closed my phone without anyone being the wiser. "I think we're up to around... $483." As I actually began to comprehend what those numbers meant, my eyes widened with shock.

"Whoa!" the host exclaimed before whistling loudly. "That's some serious money for a first kiss."

"No kidding," I answered before I could stop myself.

"Why do you think people are willing to pay that much to be your first?" he asked.

I looked at him blankly and then turned toward where I knew the audience was seated. "Honestly? I don't really know," I answered. "Insanity maybe?"

This got just the right amount of chuckles before the show's music started playing, signaling that the interview was coming to an end.

"Well, thanks for coming on the show Arielle, and I wish you lots of luck on your next big sale," Big Johnson said, shaking my hand before turning back toward the camera. "When we come back, Ryder Diggs, from *Night Light* will be here."

Are you shitting me?

My mouth dropped open just as the camera panned my way. But I couldn't help it. Ryder Diggs was here. Back stage. At this very moment. Maybe I could watch his segment from the side of the stage?

Cheers, far louder than the ones I'd received, exploded around us at the mention of the TV star's name. And to be honest, I was barely able to keep the screams from escaping my own throat.

As I started to plan out what I would say if I ran into him backstage, the studio lights went out, making it difficult to see anything in front of me. I had to blink a few times before I could focus again, and when I finally could, my vision was littered with spots.

"Good job, kid," Big Johnson said, not nearly as over-the-top as he'd been when we were taping. "You got guts and I respect that. Why don't you stick around for the rest of the taping? You know this Ryder kid?"

Suddenly losing all ability to speak, I just nodded my head like a cheerleader on speed.

"Good deal. Janine! Can I get a mocha latte, stat!"

I watched as my new favorite talk show host walked off the set in search of his girlie coffee drink. Then I sat there, stunned, thinking about how much my life had changed in just a single day.

I was about to meet the hottest guy on television. The guy whose poster was currently hanging above my bed, and whom I frequently imagined myself marrying whenever I daydreamed. Which was pretty much *all the time*. I was about to have a close encounter of the celebrity kind and I had no idea how I was going to stay conscious long enough to enjoy it.

Chapter Sixteen

I WAS AFRAID that if I left my seat, they wouldn't let me back on the stage. Either I'd get locked out of the studio or Big Johnson would take back his invitation for me to stay on through the next segment. And then I'd never get to meet Ryder. So I just sat there, alone.

At least the seat was cushy.

Still, I started to get antsy, and I knew myself well enough to recognize that hysteria wasn't far behind. So, I did the only thing I could think of to keep myself from totally freaking out. I texted McCartney.

> **ME:** Thanks for saving my @ss back there. I almost froze.

I pressed send. I didn't have to wait long before she responded.

> **McCARTNEY:** No problemo. And *ALMOST* froze? Hahaha, kidding. U were awesome! It's like u grew a pair this morning. I'm impressed.

I smiled, appreciating the compliment. Then, running my fingers quickly across my phone's keyboard, I got to the real reason I'd texted.

> **ME:** Thanks! I ate my Wheaties this morning. Now, on 2 more pressing issues...I was just invited to stick around & watch Ryder's interview!!!! On the stage!!! In the seat next to him!!!! OMFG!!! What do I do?!?!?

I sent the message and looked up as I heard the audience begin to murmur excitedly. Only, when I glanced around, I was still the only one there—except for the dozens of crew members running around, of course—so I turned back to my phone as I got an incoming text.

> **McCARTNEY:** I. Hate. U. Seriously, y isn't any of this happening to me?!?! OK, pity party over. Don't forget to breathe, memorize everything about him—the way he smells, what he's wearing, any weird quirks—and see if you can get him to sign an autograph for me. Or steal something from him. We can always sell it on eBay later. I'm fine with either.

I knew that McCartney was a little crazy, but she was in rare form today. I rolled my eyes before answering.

> **ME:** I'm not stealing from Ryder Diggs. If you want something of his, you're going to have to go all grand larceny on your own. But I'll be sure to tell him you say hi when we're on our honeymoon.

I sat up straighter in my chair as Big Johnson sauntered back to his desk, a steaming cup of something foamy in his hand. He took a sip of the liquid and closed his eyes like he was savoring something delicious. I hadn't been able to get myself to try the stuff again. A beverage that tastes like dirt just wasn't my idea of a good time.

I felt my phone buzz again and flipped it open one last time.

> **McCARTNEY:** You're the devil. And P.S. I'm already searching for Ryder's room. I *will* get a keepsake.

"You're gonna have to scoot on over, so the kid can sit in the interview chair," Big Johnson said, cutting through my thoughts before I had a chance to text McCartney back.

"Oh. Yeah. Sure," I said, scrambling up out of the chair and sitting down in the one right next to it. It wasn't quite as comfy, but it could have been made out of needles and glass, and I still would've sat in it if it meant getting to be *thisclose* to Ryder.

"We're on in ten, Marc," a woman yelled out.

Seconds later, the bright lights flashed back on and I was once again blinded to anything that was happening in front of me. But this time I wasn't worrying about it, because I knew that any second Ryder was going to come out and sit down next to me.

You know those defining moments in your life where all the stars align and you just know that nothing is ever going to be the same? Well, I was pretty sure this was one of those moments.

When the music started back up, my stomach erupted into a lava-flow of nerves and I suddenly had the urge to throw up. Clamping my mouth shut, I kept my butt glued to my seat and hoped for the best, as Big Johnson introduced Ryder.

"Girls go crazy over him and guys secretly want to *be* him. He plays a brooding vampire on the teen drama, *Night Light,* please help me welcome, Ryder Diggs!" Big Johnson said energetically.

I looked to my left and then panned right, but couldn't seem to find Ryder. I wasn't the only one either, because when I glanced at the few audience members I could see, they were searching for the TV star themselves.

Were we being punked?

And then we saw him. Ryder seemed to explode from between the crushed velvet drapes off to the right of the stage and then glided over to us as if he were walking on air. It was super sexy and sort of ethereal all at the same time. And clearly, the reason Ryder was cast in the supernatural show in the first place.

I watched, slightly slack-jawed, as Big Johnson shook Ryder's hand before they both sat down in their respective seats. Losing my breath for a second, I studied my dream crush as he elegantly lowered himself into the chair beside me. He continued to smile as the crowd screamed for him uncontrollably. I, however, was too busy trying not to drool to join in. Instead, I stared, as non-stalkery as I could, memorizing the smell of Ryder's cologne as it hit my nostrils.

When the crowd finally died down, Ryder turned his back to me and faced the host, as if he wasn't fazed at all by the fact that half the audience probably wanted to rip his clothes off.

Or maybe that was just me.

"Ryder, thanks for coming by," Big Johnson started.

"It's great to be here," Ryder said, coolly.

I felt myself unconsciously leaning toward Ryder to catch every word he said.

"Geez, I've never heard an audience go that crazy over a guest before. Do you always get that kind of response from people?"

Ryder smiled sheepishly as he looked down at his lap. He opened and closed his hands as he nodded lightly. "Not always like that, but yeah, it's sort of hard for me to go anywhere lately without a crowd following me."

"I read last week, that you were actually *mobbed* by a dozen private school girls while shopping downtown and the cops had to be called to get you out of there safely," Big Johnson said. "Now, I always knew teenage girls were dangerous, but *that's* ridiculous."

Ryder laughed right along with Big Johnson as he chuckled at his own cleverness. I laughed too, but only because of nerves. The truth was, Ryder was the most beautiful guy I'd ever seen and sitting next to him was quickly turning me into a blithering idiot.

I studied his face as he looked around the room, taking note of his super-long eyelashes, bright green eyes, soft blond hair and sharp cheekbones. He wasn't exactly skinny, but he wasn't uber buff either. The pair of fitted jeans he wore were the perfect compliment to his blindingly white button down shirt and sparkling pair of Keds. A black skinny tie hung loosely around his neck as if it were an afterthought, a last-minute accessory that pulled the whole look together.

"Aw, well, my fans are great, but sometimes things can get a little...*crazy*," Ryder said, shaking his head in disbelief.

"What's the craziest thing a fan's ever done?" Big Johnson prompted.

Ryder scrunched up his face as he searched for an answer. Finally, he began to laugh, suddenly looking embarrassed.

"One girl hid in my hotel closet for fourteen hours until I came home from a shoot," he recalled. "I found her asleep on the floor wrapped up in a pile of my clothes. When I asked her to leave, she told me that she wouldn't unless she got a kiss from me."

"What did you do?"

The whole audience, including myself, were hanging on his every word. As much as I didn't want to hear about my crush kissing other girls, I couldn't pull my attention away.

"I kissed her," Ryder said, with a shrug.

We all let out the collective breath we'd been holding in anticipation of his answer, and then people started to laugh and some even cheered, as if he'd cured cancer and not just lip-locked with girl.

"Hey, that doesn't sound all that bad," Big Johnson teased him.

"Yeah, but then she stole my favorite hoodie."

The whole room erupted in synchronized, "Awwww"s, as everyone sympathized with him. I, on the other hand, was sort of jealous of the super-fan's moxie.

"Speaking of kisses, did you hear Arielle's story? She's actually selling her first kiss on *eBay*," Big Johnson said, gesturing in my direction. "What do you think about that?"

For the first time since Ryder had come out, he turned to face me straight on. We locked eyes, and I swear I felt electricity, fireworks, *love*. And then he smiled at me and my whole world dropped out from underneath me.

"Yeah, I was watching from backstage. That's pretty intense," he said, not breaking our gaze. "I couldn't have *paid* someone to kiss me back when I was your age."

Ryder continued to stare at me, which surprisingly, made me uncomfortable. Like staring straight into the sun. Feeling my mouth start to twitch from all the smiling, I forced myself to look over at the audience. Then I giggled along with them, nervously.

"Hey, now *here's* an idea," Big Johnson said, as if the words were just coming to him instead of from the teleprompter. "How about *you* give Arielle that kiss she wants so badly and we'll all call it a day."

What the—

Within seconds, the room had erupted into pandemonium. I couldn't tell whether people were excited by the idea of Ryder being my first kiss, or if they were outraged that they wouldn't be cozying up to the star themselves. Either way, I was too busy panicking to care.

Don't get me wrong, getting a kiss—make that my first kiss *ever*—from Ryder Diggs, would be beyond wild. But having that kiss on live TV? In front of millions of people? What if I was a terrible kisser? That would be horrifying in its own right, but to have the whole world witness my ineptitude? I'm not sure my fragile ego could handle it.

And it wasn't like I could say, "Sorry, Ryder. Can I take a raincheck on that kiss?" Well, I could, but then I'd forever be known as "The Dumbest Girl Alive," and I didn't exactly want that to be my legacy.

"I have to admit, it's *tempting*," Ryder answered, turning to look at me again, this time checking me out. "But I really *do* prefer to get to know a girl before I kiss her."

The audience laughed and I joined in nervously.

On the one hand, I was grateful that Ryder had gotten us out of a very public, and potentially embarrassing, display of affection. In fact, he'd said the exact right thing. However, I couldn't help but feel a tad disappointed that Ryder *didn't* go for it.

As I tried to decide if I should slink offstage while the camera was on Ryder because I'd just been rejected in front of the whole world, the Hollywood heart-throb gave me a funny look.

Good, God, you don't have to spell it out. I get it. You don't want to kiss the weird eBay girl. Can we move on before I spontaneously combust?

"But I'll tell you what...let's talk after this, and we'll see where it goes," Ryder said, suddenly flirty.

And then he winked at me.

I blinked back at him, wondering if everyone else had seen what had just happened or if I'd passed out and dreamed the whole thing. As whistles filled the air, I felt a wave of lightheadedness hit me and I had to pull my eyes away from his to stop the room from spinning.

Had Ryder Diggs just said that? In front of everyone? He'd said we should talk...did that mean he wants my number? And if he wants my number, did that mean he wants to ask me out?

I wasn't sure I could date a celebrity. I'd seen how the paparazzi followed famous couples around, trying to catch them when they were looking all scrubby in their sweats. And the rumors that always got started? It was no wonder why so many Hollywood relationships ended, what with all the different magazines reporting false information on a couple's status.

When I looked up after steadying myself, I saw that Big Johnson and Ryder were both staring at me, waiting for a response. I turned to the camera blankly. What the heck was I supposed to say to that?

Holy crap, Arielle, just say *something*!

"I'm game if you are," I said finally, surprising even myself.

"Well, there you have it. Once again, history has been made on *You Snooze, You Lose*!" Big Johnson yelled out to the camera.

Once the hysteria died down again, he continued. "But, let's get back to your show, Ryder. *Night Light* just began its second season and you play a vampire, right? But you're a good vampire? What exactly does that mean? Are you like, a vegetarian or something?"

"Actually, my character still drinks blood, but it's strictly animal blood...." Ryder explained, taking the subject change in stride.

With the spotlight finally off of me, I found myself able to breathe again. My heart started to slow to a semi-normal pace and I was officially able to sit back and enjoy the whole experience. I listened to the two banter back and forth like the interview was a tennis match, proving they were both pros at the talk show game. A few minutes later, the music signaled the end of our segment.

"Let's thank Arielle and Ryder for being on the show tonight," Big Johnson said, clapping from behind his desk. "And tune in tomorrow when our guest stars will be Kirsten Bell and The Jonas Brothers."

We all smiled as the camera took one last sweep across the stage, and then I tried to listen in as Big Johnson and Ryder talked in hushed tones just below the music. Then the lights shut off and the audience members were standing up in their seats.

It was over.

I rised along with everyone else, tugging down on my shirt awkwardly, not quite sure what to do next. Was I supposed to say goodbye to Ryder before heading back to my dressing room? Or was that too cheesy? What if I just played it cool and said nothing, leading him to think I was this totally mysterious girl who he just *had* to get to know better. Forget the fact that he was three years older than me and completely out of my league.

Instead, I just watched as my celebri-honey walked over to the audience and began signing autographs and taking pictures with the gaggles of teenage girls—and a few middle aged women—who had stuck around just to meet him.

I found myself swooning as Ryder reached up into the stands to hug a little girl who was on the verge of a meltdown. She was wearing a T-shirt embossed with a picture of Ryder as his vampire alter ego and was periodically using it to wipe at her eyes. As Ryder pulled her into his arms, she started sobbing, all the while telling him how much she loved him.

Ryder held onto the girl until she calmed down, and then took a few pictures with her before turning away to leave. I still hadn't moved from my spot, but now began to hastily gather my things as he headed my way.

Pivoting around, I tried to search for an escape that would lead me back to where my mom and McCartney were waiting for me, but lost my footing and smacked right into Ryder.

Literally.

My face slammed into his chest, and then I stepped down hard on his foot, letting out a little screech of surprise as it happened.

"Omigod, I'm *so* sorry!" I apologized. Awkwardly patting his chest, I briefly worried that I'd bruised him with my big head. "I'm seriously the clumsiest person ever. I mean it. Look up 'clumsy' in the dictionary and I bet it will say, Sawyer comma Arielle. See why I have to do the eBay thing?"

Ryder started to laugh as I rattled on nervously, still standing close enough for me touch him. Not that I did...again, anyway. He cocked his head to the side, eyes shining as he studied me the way you might a peculiar animal at the zoo. Like you're curious, but also glad that there are metal bars separating you and the freaky beast.

"You're a funny girl," he said finally. "And no. I don't see why you have to do the eBay thing. Have you even *tried* getting a kiss the old fashioned way?"

Although I adored the compliment, I was simultaneously offended that he would think that I hadn't tried absolutely everything I could to *not* have to sell my kiss to the highest bidder. This was more of a last resort solution to my problem.

"Not all of us are *gorgeous* superstars who have people sneaking into our rooms just to get a kiss," I said, playfully. "Besides, correct me if I'm wrong, but don't *you* technically get paid to kiss girls too? Your co-stars I mean? How is that any different than this?"

"Touché," Ryder said, letting out another laugh. "But seriously, I hope you weren't offended by what I said up there. It's not that I *didn't* want to kiss you. It's just—well, I remember my first kiss—and I wouldn't have wanted half the world witnessing it while it was happening. And now, with the digital age…well, you could end up watching the awkwardness of your first time *forever.* Trust me, you don't want to be haunted by your past on YouTube."

He had a point. Wait. Rewind. Had he just admitted that he would've kissed me? Because I was fine with that. In fact, we could still make that happen. There were no cameras on us anymore. Maybe if I just leaned in a little bit closer…

But just as I started to go for it, Ryder took a step backward. Shrugging to try and play off what I'd been trying to do, I said, "You're probably right. It would've totally been weird. Besides, then the school wouldn't have gotten the donation money. And you should see our gym. It's more of a disaster area than a fitness center."

"I really admire that," Ryder said, folding his arms across his chest and nodding his head. "You know, I'm really big into charity work. I feel like it's everyone's duty to help out where they can. It's so nice to find a young person who thinks of someone other than themselves for a change."

I didn't bother admitting that it was actually my mom's idea to donate the money to the school. Nor did I point out that the only reason I was doing any of this at all, was because I wanted that kiss. If my focus had simply been on giving back to my school, I would've just helped out at a car wash like the band did each summer.

"Mmm-hmm," I said, biting my tongue. "It's important to give back."

Not sure what else to say, I smiled at Ryder. And then he smiled back at me. And then we were just standing there, less than a foot away from each other, grinning like idiots. The thing was, I knew why *I* was smiling, but I had no idea what he was smiling about.

I *wish* I knew what he was smiling about.

"Ok. Well, it was great meeting you, Ryder," I said, feeling like it was time to make my exit.

Smiling one last time, I forced myself to turn on my heel, and then headed toward the doorway I'd walked through earlier. But leaving was the last thing I wanted to do. I wondered if I'd just squandered the one chance I'd ever have to be that close to a celebrity.

I'd only gotten a few steps before I heard Ryder clear his throat.

"Hey, Arielle?"

I swung around to face him. He looked so cute, standing there, hands in his pockets, hair hanging messily over his forehead. It took everything in me to keep myself from running back to him and jumping into his arms and acting out that famous scene in *The Notebook*.

"Yeah?"

"So, I was thinking, maybe we could exchange numbers or something?" he said. I couldn't be sure, but he almost looked...nervous. "I mean, so we could keep in touch. Hear how things are going with the eBay thing and everything."

Had I entered the "Twilight Zone" or had Ryder just asked for my phone number?

I must've looked as startled as I felt, because he added, "If that's cool."

"Yeah. Sure. Of course," I said, giving him my number shakily. Then, I programmed his digits into my phone and saved it under "Future Husband."

"Awesome. So, talk to you soon?" he said, slipping his cell into his pocket and patting it protectively.

By this point, I could barely talk, so I settled for just nodding. Then, before Ryder could walk away—and before I lost my nerve—I closed the space between us and threw my arms around his waist.

Completely surprised by my sudden display of affection, Ryder tensed up, but then relaxed, before finally squeezing me back. For a second I imagined what it would be like to hug him on a daily basis and not just when we were saying goodbye after having just met.

And it was epic.

I pulled away from Ryder just as suddenly as I'd attacked him, and then walked slowly backward and in the direction of my dressing room as if in a trance. In a moment of sheer nerdiness, I tried to wave goodbye but ended up tripping over a stray cord that was taped to the floor instead. Recovering as gracefully as I could, I turned and rushed out of there. I could hear Ryder chuckling as I left.

When I was sure that he could no longer see me, I took off running down the labyrinth of a hallway, eventually collapsing against a random wall breathlessly. I closed my eyes and replayed the last ten minutes in my head, praying that I hadn't made it all up.

Catching my breath, I took out my cell and looked through my phonebook.

Future Husband.

Nope. Definitely didn't make it up.

Chapter Seventeen

BY THE TIME I hit the school hallways on Monday morning the news of my appearances on not one, but *two* talk shows had gone totally viral. If I'd been a disease, they would've had to declare an epidemic.

Girls I'd never met gushed over how cute Ryder was and begged me to spill on what he was like in real life. Of course, there were also those who were downright bitchy about the fact that it had been me, and not them, who'd gotten to spend time with the *Night Light* star. But it's not like I could blame them. I'd have been just as jealous if I were in their position.

Surprisingly, the guys were just as bad. For some reason they felt the need to fill me in on everything that was wrong with Ryder. Ricky Telman claimed he was "a total douche who wasn't as cool as he thought he was." Chad Ferguson smirked as he said, "Ryder's definitely into dudes." And Ted White glared as he said, "That turd is such a chick, he might as well be wearing a tutu."

I was getting the vibe that my classmates of the male variety were feeling just a tad bit...*threatened* by my new friend. And the girls? Well, they were somehow under the impression that dating a superstar was *actually* an attainable prospect. Which was *so* not true.

After riding the wave of euphoria that kicked in upon leaving Ryder at the *Snooze* soundstage, I'd tried to stay busy. Subconsciously, though, I was really just waiting for Ryder to call me. Or text me. Either would've been fine, I swear.

It started with me just checking my phone when I woke up in the morning, hoping he'd called me after I'd already gone to bed. Then, it escalated. In the past, I'd left my cell in my room when I was at home, only checking for messages if I needed to call someone. But suddenly I was carrying my phone with me everywhere: when I was in the kitchen making breakfast; as I went out to retrieve the mail; and even into the bathroom with me when I went to take a shower.

In other words, I became a *tad bit* obsessed. Mom finally had to take my cell away from me and hide it where I couldn't find it. This was torture, but at the same time, I was grateful to quiet the crazy.

And now, it was Monday morning and still no word from Ryder. I was a little disappointed, but not totally surprised. I'm not sure what I'd been thinking. That this big-time actor was going to trade in his celeb friends and all the bright lights and fame, just to play the role of average Joe and hang out with me? Yeah, not so much.

Still, no one at school knew that Ryder and I weren't talking, and I wasn't about to tell them. For now I just tried to ignore the glares, answer people's questions as honestly as I could ("Yes, Ryder's as nice in person as he seems on the show" and "No, he wasn't wearing lifts in his shoes to make him taller") and enjoy the positive attention I was getting from my brush with fame.

Unfortunately, this did nothing to impress Kristi, who happily continued to rain on my popularity parade. And in Kristi's world, when it rained, it poured.

"Saw you on *Snooze* this weekend," she said, all perky and peppy.

The tan and toned girl squeezed herself down next to me, nudging out Phin, who just rolled his eyes before moving to the other side of the table. Then Kristi smiled at me as if we were buddies. Like she *hadn't* been torturing me nonstop since third grade. People passed by, glancing over at us as they attempted to figure out what was going on. It probably even looked like we were having a friendly conversation. But I was close enough to see the evil in Kristi's eyes.

Well, okay, so maybe the purple contacts she was wearing weren't helping. But still. She was pure evil.

"What do you want, Kristi?" McCartney asked, not falling for her nice act either.

"Now, now, now, McCartney. What's with all the *anger*? Haven't you heard that frowning causes major wrinkles and premature aging?" Kristi tisked.

"And haven't you heard that having a stick up your butt all the time can cause constipation? I bet *that* causes wrinkles, too," McCartney fired back. "What do you think, Arielle?"

"Yeah, I read that somewhere, too. I'd watch out for that if I were you, Kris, I think I already see a few forming," I added, seriously.

Kristi looked from McCartney to me, and then frowned as if she were trying to decide whether to keep up her act or not. It didn't take long before she chose, and we both watched as she went from sweet to Satan right before our eyes. It was like watching the wolf change out of its sheep's clothing. Which is really gross if you think about it, because that wolf is actually wrapped up in a sheep's carcass.

"Cut the crap, losers," Kristi spat under her breath. Then she turned back to me. "Couldn't you have picked a more suitable outfit to meet a totally brilliant guy like Ryder in? Now he's going to think that everyone from our school dresses like they can't afford a closet in a trailer park. Really, Arielle, can't you think of anyone other than yourself for like, two seconds, and instead focus on how your actions affect the rest of us?"

Had Kristi gone mental? Or was she just completely devoid of normal human emotions and actions? Like a robot. That would at least explain why she thought it was acceptable to talk to people the way she did. I glanced around the table and saw that, like me, everyone's jaws were practically grazing the table.

And before I knew what I was doing, I stood up from the table slowly until I was towering over her. I mimicked Kristi's earlier smile, as we locked eyes.

"Huh. That's funny. Ryder didn't seem to mind my outfit when he was asking me for my phone number after the show." As I finished my sentence, there was an audible gasp from nearly everyone around the table. I even caught a look of surprise on Kristi's face, but it was gone just as quickly. "But I'll be sure to ask him about it the next time we talk." Then, I pulled out my cell and opened it up like I'd just gotten a text. "Whoops, there goes my phone. We're done here, right?"

Not bothering to wait for an answer, I slung my bag over my shoulder and turned my back on my frenemy, doing my best to confidently walk away. Rustling started up behind me, and knew without looking, that McCartney and Phin would be catching up with me any second.

I could always count on them to have my back.

Once we'd successful left the caf behind us, I finally let out the breath I'd been holding. Spotting an opening, we slipped into an empty classroom. Collapsing into the nearest desk, I put my warm face down onto the top of the cool surface, trying to calm my nerves.

"I've never heard anyone talk to Kristi like that," Phin said, looking surprised. "I think I saw the actual moment she shit herself."

"Wait. Did Ryder *really* ask for your number?" McCartney cut in.

I nodded. "Sorry I didn't tell you before," I said, feeling terrible that McCartney had found out the same time as everyone else. "I just sort of wanted to keep it to myself for a while. In case he never called. Which he hasn't, by the way."

McCartney stared at me, her face curved downward in an exaggerated frown, and I waited nervously to see how she'd react. I couldn't handle it if my friends were mad at me, too. Especially after probably having just started a war with the wickedest witch of the west—west of Ronald Henry, I mean. And I'm not exaggerating. Kristi made Blair Waldorf look like Barney.

Of course, McCartney could be just as lethal, so staying on her good side was paramount.

Luckily, she broke her silence by sighing loudly. "You're lucky I'm such an awesome friend, Arielle Sawyer," she scolded lightly. McCartney was officially letting me off the hook. For now. "So, did he ask you for your number or did you go all Angelina Jolie and put your sexy mojo out there to reel him in yourself?"

I smiled at her, grateful to finally have someone to talk to about Ryder. After surviving what felt like the longest weekend of my life, I'd come to the conclusion that I wasn't meant to be a secret keeper. I liked to talk about things to other people too much. How were you supposed to get different perspectives on a situation if you were only listening to your own brain? Yep, secrets are bad.

We sat down on top of the nearby desks, ignoring the fact that we weren't supposed to be doing so. But when you had to discuss the possibility of starting a secret affair with a big-time celebrity, there were obviously more important things to think about other than where to park your tush.

I promptly began to spill. I told them everything that had happened from the time the cameras stopped rolling, all the way until I reappeared in the dressing room. I could see McCartney's eyes getting wider as I talked. Phin just kept shaking his head. Both wore the funniest expressions on their faces, though I couldn't exactly tell what they were thinking.

"And he still hasn't called," I said, finishing up with a pout. "I don't know why I thought he was actually interested. I mean, this is *my* life after all. And in *my* life story, famous hot guys don't pursue geeky girls like me."

"Oh, *shut up*!" McCartney exploded, rolling her eyes. "Look what you've experienced so far. Maybe it's not a Blockbuster hit, but face it, A, it's at least a movie-of-the-week situation that you've got going on."

"Yeah. At least you're the one *living* all of it. McCartney and I have to just sit back and live vicariously through *you*. So, now who's the lame one?" Phin added.

"*You* sort of are for wearing that shirt," McCartney muttered.

"Oh, har, har, McCart," Phin said loudly as he glared at her. "You'd be the first person killed off in *my* movie."

"Oh, please, like yours would even be a movie," she snorted. "More like a 15 second commercial."

I looked back and forth between my besties as they fought like brother and sister. I debated letting them keep at it, but if they were verbally sparring it meant that they weren't actively trying to solve my boy problem. And I was desperately in need of their advice.

"Guys? I hate to break up your very amusing WWE smack down, but I really need you to tell me what to do here," I pleaded.

They stopped mid-fight and both turned to face me. The classroom we were in grew silent and I waited quietly as they brainstormed. I hoped their lack of response was due to the fact that they had so many ideas running through their heads that they didn't know where to start.

"He gave you his number, right? So why don't you just call him?" McCartney said finally.

That was her answer? Call the super hot and famous superstar? And say what, exactly? Why haven't you called? Did you come to your senses and realize that you don't feel like slumming it right now? Why don't you like me? Yeah right. Talk about your stalkerific moves.

"I can't do that," I answered bluntly. "Phin, please tell McCartney why calling a guy I only met once is *so* not a good idea."

I waited for Phin to answer, but he just raised his eyebrows at me. "Actually, it's not...totally bad. Guys love it when girls pursue them. It lets us off the hook for a change," he said. "But flext him instead. That way you can figure out what you're going to say first. Let's be honest here. You don't exactly give good phone."

"Ooooh, yeah! Flext him! In fact, do it right now. We've still got a few minutes until the bell rings."

They mean flirting by text, a term we'd made up back in middle school when everyone in our class had begun to get cell phones. Flexting. I hadn't done a lot of it myself, but it seemed to work for McCartney. And for Phin. Maybe it wasn't such a bad idea to send Ryder a little message, after all.

"Are you guys serious about this? He won't think I'm a freak for texting him first?"

"No way."

"Nuh uh."

"Where's your cell? Start off by saying something like, 'Hey, stranger, miss me?'"

"I am *not* saying that, McCartney. Ryder knows I'm not the kind of girl to mac on a relative stranger with some totally lame pick-up line."

"But you *are* the kind of girl who sells kisses over the internet?" Phin asked pointedly.

"It's not the same thing," I argued, annoyed that he was trying to throw his plan back in my face.

"Fine, don't say that, but for hottie's sake, say something!" McCartney begged.

Exasperated, I pulled out my cell and started a new text, muttering multiple four-letter words under my breath. As I typed, McCartney and Phin both shut up, allowing me to focus on what I was doing. Only, I had trouble finding the right words, because I wasn't totally convinced I should be texting Ryder.

Was I the kind of girl who made the first move? Could I let a guy know what I wanted and then go after it (or him)? Would Ryder think I was a boy-crazy, celebrity whore for reaching out to him? It was clear that the answers weren't going to come as I stood in an empty classroom with my friends hovering over me, so I hurriedly pressed send and listened to the wooshing sound as the message left my outbox.

"What did you say?" McCartney asked, as she bounced around excitedly.

"Whatcha up to?" I said.

Silence.

"*That's* your idea of flexting? No wonder you're kissably challenged..."

"Thanks, Phin. But I think I've been doing fine on my own so far—he asked for my number, right?"

"You could've at least said 'Whatcha up to, *hot stuff*?' What you said makes you sound like you're his sister. Or worse... his *friend*!" McCartney exclaimed, horrified at the notion.

"And that's a bad thing?" I asked.

"There's nothing worse than finding yourself in the *friend zone*. It's the quickest way to ensure that nothing sexy will happen between the two of you in the future," Phin said. "Ever."

I shook my head in disbelief. "I can't listen to this crazy talk anymore or my brain is going to start leaking out of my ears."

McCartney began to argue with me, but was interrupted by a knock on the door. We all turned to see a blond standing in the open doorway, looking apologetic but eager. She looked familiar, but I couldn't place her name or what grade she was in. By the look of her outfit though—she was wearing a fitted black jumper with pink and gray gingham tights and platform Mary Jane's—she was a prepster. My guess was she was on the student council or the debate team. Either way, I was curious to see what she wanted.

"Arielle?" she asked timidly.

I blinked at her, surprised to hear that she was there to talk to me. Not because I was too cool for school, but because I wasn't exactly the girl people went looking for. I glanced over at my friends questioningly. McCartney just shrugged before turning her focus back on Preppy Patty.

"Um, yeah. That's me. Can I help you?" I asked slowly, dragging out the words as I spoke them.

The thought briefly crossed my mind that the girl might've been sent by Satan's Spawn to deliver my punishment for the unfortunate incident at lunch. But as I continued to study her, I couldn't help but get the impression that wasn't the case.

"I hope so!" Preppy Patty answered excitedly.

Her shoes click-clacked their way across the floor as she closed the distance between us, stopping just a few feet away from me. She pulled herself up onto one of the desks and crossed her legs daintily.

"You probably have no idea who I am. My name's Bree!" she said, waving her hand at me. "And you're Arielle, right?"

I smiled and nodded politely, still confused over what was happening here.

"Awesome!" she exclaimed, clapping her hands together enthusiastically. "I'm so excited to *finally* meet you! You have no idea how much I admire you!"

"For what?" Phin asked loudly.

I turned and glared at him before focusing back on Bree. Although I was wondering the same thing myself, there was such a thing as tact, and Phin was severely lacking in it.

"Duh. She's like the bravest person I know in real life," Bree answered. Then she lowered her voice and looked at me seriously. "I would've been too scared to put myself out there like that. You wanted a kiss and you did something about it. You're totally badass... like Angelina Jolie, only younger and less freaky."

"Um, thanks?" I answered, letting what she was saying sink in. I was surprised that she was focusing on what I was doing to get my kiss, instead of the fact that I was so lame that I needed to put my kiss up on eBay in the first place. The truth was, nobody had wanted to kiss me before. Nothing cool about that.

"So, why were you looking for me exactly?" I asked, still confused.

"Oh, yeah. Sorry. I'm just so excited, that I'm not making any sense. Okay, so I was looking for you, because I was hoping you could help me out with something," Bree said. "See, I'm on the Homecoming dance committee and we're in desperate need of a few more members to pull off the greatest party in Ronald Henry history. And of course... I thought of you! Please say you'll do it!"

What the frack was going on here? This girl I barely knew was practically *begging* me to join her club. Me. Arielle Sawyer. The girl who, up until a few weeks ago, was non-existent. I couldn't get over the fact that, for some reason, this girl thought I was way cooler than I actually was.

"No offense, but *why* did you think of me? I've never even been to a dance before, let alone helped plan one," I said honestly. "I'm not saying no—but what makes you think I'd be any help to you anyway?"

A look of guilt crossed Bree's face as she realized that she'd been caught. Caught doing what exactly, I wasn't sure. Sheepishly, she looked down at the floor and began to explain.

"Well, I saw you on *Snooze* and you were really cool and funny... and you were just sitting there, chatting with Ryder Diggs, like he wasn't the hottest thing since Twitter, and I just thought, 'that's who we need planning our dance.'"

I stared at her, stunned by the admission and completely unsure how to react. I had to appreciate her honesty. Bree could've easily made up some kind of BS about how she admired my entrepreneurial skills or something, but she'd respected me enough to lay it all out there. There was something refreshing about that.

Bree stood there in front of me, looking both hopeful and unabashedly grateful at the same time. It dawned on me that this was what it must feel like to be popular. People wanting to be around you just because of who they thought you were. Not because of who you *actually* were.

"It's really nice of you to think of me, Bree, but I might end up doing more damage to your dance than help. See, I'm a little accident-prone," I admitted, looking over at my friends for support

"It's true," McCartney piped up for the first time since we'd started talking. "Arielle managed to break my iPhone, and its case was supposed to be indestructible."

"I told you that wasn't my fault. That fat guy hit it out of my hands, and there was no way for me to catch it before it hit the escalator. So, technically, it was that fat man and the escalator that broke your phone. Not me."

McCartney rolled her eyes and mouthed, "It was her," to Bree.

"I'm not blind, McCartney. I can see you." I was growing irritated.

I turned back to Bree and tried to bring the conversation to a close. "Anyway, I'm just not sure I'm the right girl for the job. You'd be better off getting someone else to help. Someone who's more of a party girl, maybe. Why don't you ask Kristi? She probably lives for that stuff."

"Can I be honest with you? I feel like I can tell you anything." Bree looked around the room as if there might be a spy hiding under a desk just waiting to hear her dirty little secrets. "When Kristi was on the dance committee last year, she was a total control Nazi. She pushed for the polka dots theme when she knew they'd make the rest of us look fat. So this year, we black-listed her." She paused, thinking over what she'd just divulged. "But Kristi doesn't know that, so please don't tell her, okay?"

I was shocked to learn that there were other people at RHHS who weren't Kristi fans, either. I was even more floored that the list included other popular kids.

"Besides, if you came, I have a feeling it would be the best turnout for a dance ever. And the money we make fully goes to some Orphanage in the city, so I just figured you'd want to help out...."

"Okay, Bree," I said, worrying that if I didn't agree soon, the girl might pass out from lack of oxygen to her brain due to all the talking. And even though I'd just met her, I didn't want that on my conscious. "I'll do it."

Bree's face lit up like a 100-watt bulb, and she jumped up and down, clapping her hands like a cheerleader. Then, she scurried over to me and pulled me into a tight hug. I was caught off-guard by the act and my arms remained at my side limply as she squeezed me like a stress doll.

"This is so great! I can't wait to tell *everyone*!" she exclaimed. "So, our first meeting is tomorrow after school. We meet at 2:15 in the student lounge. Start thinking of themes!"

"Great," I answered.

I watched as Bree bounced out of the room, wiggling her fingers goodbye as she disappeared.

"Whoa. That girl's got a *whole* lot of spirit, doesn't she?" Phin asked, letting out a low whistle. "Think she'd go to Homecoming with me?"

"No," McCartney answered. "Besides, we're all going together, remember?"

"I just figured, now that Arielle's gonna be Queen of the Party People, she could just find us people to go with."

"I'm not going to force people to go with you to the dance, Phin," I answered, picking my bag up off the floor. "Not that I have that power anyway. Nobody's gonna care that I'm helping out with the dance. The only reason I said yes in the first place was because I figure it'll look good on my college apps later on."

"You should ask *Ryder* to go with you," McCartney blurted out. I turned to look at her and saw that she had her trouble-making face on. Whenever she was planning something devious, she got this grin on her face—sort of like the Grinch who stole Christmas—and her eyebrows shot up into the shape of little tiny devil horns.

"You've officially gone mental," I said flatly. "You either need to go on some sort of medication or check yourself into the loony bin, because you're twelve kinds of crazy right now."

"You *would* look great in a straight jacket," Phin agreed.

"Just think about it," McCartney implored as she followed me out the door.

The scary thing was, I already had.

Chapter Eighteen

THE NEXT DAY, I dragged myself to the student lounge to meet Bree and her crew for our first Dance Committee meeting. I'd been kicking myself ever since I'd agreed to do the thing in the first place. But now that I was actually on my way, it was taking everything I had to keep from turning around and ditching the whole thing.

It also didn't help that McCartney and Phin had both given me a hard time about heading to the meeting instead of hanging out with them like usual. They even made up a song about it and sang it to me before first period. And again at lunch. And in between every break. As annoying as the lyrics were, I had to admit that the tune was pretty catchy. And now I couldn't get it out of my head, which meant that I was effectively torturing myself for them.

"We're hanging alone now, our little Arielle is busy dancing around. She's making the plans now, she'll pick the color, theme and a hip-hop sound." I sang the lyrics softly to the tune of Tiffany's "I think we're alone now," as I neared the lounge. Realizing that I was doing it again, I shook my head to clear it. "Damn you McCartney and Phin!" I cursed under my breath.

I walked into the student lounge, which was everyone's go-to spot whenever they weren't in class. It was exactly what you'd think a teachers lounge would be—except way cooler. And only for students. Once two large rooms that had been separated by a flimsy folding wall, the student lounge was now one big open area, filled with couches, bean bags, tables and even a hammock.

The lounge had been the Class of 97's gift to the school and every senior class since then had added another accessory to the space. In the last three years, graduating classes had donated a popcorn machine, cappuccino station, flat screen TV, Nintendo Wii and a pool table.

The area was more impressive than your local arcade and 100% free to students. I had to assume that ours was the only school where the students didn't actually *mind* being there. Not in here, at least.

I spotted Bree right away, and made my way over to the corner where she and about six others were lounging around. There were three other girls with her, all whom I recognized, but didn't know personally. A bunch of guys sprawled around, looking all different levels of bored. I smiled as I recognized one of the faces.

Cade Jones.

The good-looking, brooding, hunk of a hero who'd come to my rescue after I'd given Dan the old chair tip-over. As happy as I was to see him, I was confused by it, too. I wouldn't have thought this was his scene. Not that it was exactly mine, either.

"Hey guys," I said, sitting down on a beanbag breathlessly. "Sorry I'm late."

"No problem, A," Bree chirped happily.

A? When did we move into nickname territory?

"Okay, so now that we're here, I'd like to call our Homecoming meeting to order," Bree said, taking her role as committee president seriously. "The dance is only three weeks away and we don't have a theme. In case you weren't aware, the theme we choose can totally make or break the dance. If the motif sucks, then no one will come, and that means the dance will suck. And I will *not* throw a sucky Homecoming."

"Because *that* would suck," Cade whispered just loudly enough for me to hear.

I glanced over at him and saw that he was looking at me out of the corner of his eye. I smiled at his comment before forcing myself to focus on Bree as she continued.

"So, any ideas?" she asked the group, looking from one face to another expectantly.

The brunette closest to me raised her hand and then lowered it back down when she realized we weren't in class. She covered this up with a blinding smile and pushed forward. "How about 'Star-Crossed Lovers?' People can dress like their favorite doomed couples. Romeo & Juliet. Bonnie & Clyde. Brad & Jen."

"Sounds a little…depressing. I don't want anyone going home after the dance and offing themselves," Bree said. "Think more upbeat."

"Depending on who it is, that *could* be upbeat," Kyle Gambit joked. He erupted into laughter and leaned over to hi-five his friend whose name I couldn't place.

Ugh. Boys were so disgusting sometimes.

"Not funny, Kyle," Bree said in response. "Next."

A bleached-blond with pink streaks in her hair, popped her gum loudly to get our attention. "Rock & Roll," she said with a devilish smile. "Lots of black, pleather and spikes. It'll be *hot*!"

"Not everyone looks good in skin-tight gear and I don't want to have to stare at some girl's jelly-rolls because she thinks it's her right to wear spandex. Next." Bree was getting frustrated now.

"Ooh, ooh, ooh!" Kyle's hi-fiving friend said as he jumped up and down in his seat.

"Yes, Jake?"

Jake Pritchard. For some reason I remembered that he was on the wrestling team. And that he liked to hit the bong on occasion.

"Let's do 'Pimps & Ho's!' It'll be so cool. Guys dress up like pimps—like my man Snoop Dogg—and chicks dress up in tiny, little…"

"Absolutely not," Bree said cutting him off. "As much as I'd like to channel my inner Britney, Principal Howard has already made it clear that the theme can't be clothing optional. Anyone else?"

"Heaven on Earth?"

"Been done."

"Under the Sea?"

"Are you kidding me?"

"Secret Lovers?"

"Come on, guys! We have to come up with something that's actually *good* and *won't* get us kicked out of school. It shouldn't be this hard," Bree said, gripping the bridge of her nose like she was getting a headache. "Think, people! We just need one good idea."

"Opposites Attract?" I said, surprising myself when it rolled past my lips.

Bree looked like she was thinking this over. I waited for her to shoot down my idea just like she had all the others. Instead, after about thirty seconds, she reached over and gave me a squeeze.

"Opposites Attract...it's *brilliant,* A!" Bree squealed. "Thank God you're here, otherwise we'd have absolutely nothing."

I saw the others roll their eyes as Bree threw out the backhanded comment. If this had been class, they'd all be calling me Teacher's Pet right about now. And from the looks of it, they wouldn't be wrong.

"Okay, so now that we've got the *perfect* theme," Bree announced, turning to me and winking, "we need to assign people to teams to make this dance happen. Let's see...we'll need a group on decorations, someone to book the music, another person to figure out refreshments and a few to get the word out to the student body."

"I'll handle the music!" Kyle shot up out of his seat excitedly. "My cousin has a sweet music collection and he can do this thing with his computer that will blow your mind—"

"Fine. Kyle, you're on music," Bree said. "But no country or rave."

"No problem," he answered, a smirk on his face. "What kind of loser listens to that stuff anyway?"

I frowned. I loved country. Well, okay, so maybe I mostly liked pop-country, like Carrie Underwood, Jessica Simpson and Taylor Swift, but still. What was so wrong about that?

"I'll take refreshments," the pink-streaked girl said.

"And since I do the morning announcements, I guess I could spread the word," Jake chimed in.

"Good. And since I'm out there talking to the student body anyway, I guess I can make sure everyone knows the details of the dance, too," Bree said. Then she turned to look in my direction. "I guess that just leaves Cade and A to manage the decorations. That cool with you two?"

"Uh, yeah. Sure," I answered, surprised to be partnered up with Mr. Tall, Dark and Handsome. "Happy to help out wherever."

I looked over and watched Cade shrug easily. "It's cool with me."

"Great!" Bree said, stepping down from the director's chair she'd been sitting on. "Why don't we meet again on Friday to touch base about how far we've all gotten. Now let's get going. We've got less than three weeks to get this together. And failure is *not* an option."

The group broke up then and I gathered my stuff slowly, trying to time my exit with Cade's. I was secretly hoping for a chance to talk to him. As I watched the last of our group leave, I fell into step beside my new dance partner.

"So, guess it's just you and me," Cade said softly as we exited the student lounge and started making our way down the nearly-empty hallway.

"Looks like it," I said, hoping I was coming across as somewhat cool.

"So…can I get your number?" he asked me.

I nearly tripped over my own feet as he said it. Was it possible that he was feeling the same butterflies I was?

I must have looked as surprised as I felt, because Cade broke out into a sheepish grin before turning forward again. "I mean, we should exchange numbers so we can set up a time to meet to talk decorations."

"Oh. Right…yeah, okay," I said, embarrassed. Somehow I managed to give him my number and programmed his into my phone, too.

"So, I'll call you," he said as we arrived at a crossroads in the hallway.

I nodded and studied him as he walked away. When I was sure he was gone, I let out a shaky breath. "God, I hope so."

When my cell phone went off a few nights later, I raced across my room before my mom could hear it. We had a phone curfew in our house, one of the few things my mom was strict about. She claimed that electronics led to restless sleep at night. I was supposed to turn mine off after 8pm. It was totally weird, but you have to pick your battles.

I put the phone to my ear as I looked over at the door for any sign that my mom had heard it ring. I hadn't even bothered to look at the caller ID to see who was on the other line before picking it up. Which meant I was answering blind.

"Hello?" I whispered.

"Is this Arielle?" a guy's voice asked.

I blinked. The voice wasn't Phin's. So who was calling me this late at night?

"Yeah," I answered curiously. "Who's this?"

There was a pause on the line.

"Hey…it's Ryder. Ryder Diggs? We met on *Snooze* back in—"

I rolled my eyes. This *had* to be Phin playing a prank on me. He'd imitated others before. Well, fool me once, shame on you, Phin. Fool me twice, shame on me.

"Yeah, *right*. You're such a butt-munch, dude. Why don't you call McCartney and bug her? Maybe she'll fall for your crap."

Silence fell over the phone line again, as I waited for Phin to fess up. I was just about to hang up, when I heard a voice chuckle on the other end.

"Um, I'm not sure who you think this is, but I actually *am* Ryder. You gave me your number, told me I could call you to get an update on your *Plan de Smooch*?"

Frack. Frack. Frack.

I couldn't believe I didn't recognize his voice before. And now I was going to have to kill myself because I'd just called Ryder Diggs a butt-munch. Holding the phone away from my face, I screamed loudly into my pillow. It didn't change what had happened, but it did make me feel better. Brushing my hair out of my eyes, I placed my cell back up to my ear.

"Oh, hey, Ryder," I said as breezily as I could. "Sorry about that. My friend's been pranking me all night. It's this whole silly thing he does. Kind of childish if you think about it... anyway, it's so good to hear from you!"

He let out a chuckle that vibrated through the phone, and I silently thanked the universe that he hadn't hung up on me yet. Because I would've understood if he had.

It would've broken my heart, but I would've understood.

"I just thought I'd give you a call, say hi, see how the whole eBay thing's going," he said. His voice was low and soft, and I imagined he was serenading me as he spoke. I couldn't believe I'd thought for even a second that it was Phin I'd been talking to before.

"Well, 'hi' to you, too," I said, grinning. I began to pace around the room to try and get rid of some of the nervous energy I was feeling. Walking over to the window, I glanced out at the street below, and then turned around and walked back toward the other side of my room. "To be honest, I haven't even checked my account lately. I've been so busy at school. Suddenly everyone knows who I am, and wants to hang around me all the time. And there's this girl, Kristi, who's pretty much the Devil incarnate and thinks it's her job to humiliate me as much as humanly possible. Oh, and I was talked into being on the Homecoming dance committee, which is ironic because I've never been to a school dance before."

I took a deep breath, and realized that I'd just basically unloaded all my stress onto this beautiful boy who'd been calling just to say 'hi.' I faintly recalled that an article in *Seventeen* had mentioned that guys weren't into girls with too much baggage. Well, if that was true, this might be my first and last phone conversation with Ryder.

"Okay, let's see if I can help you out here. First off, I have to admit that I just checked your eBay listing and you're up to $879," he said, sounding impressed. "Second, I've totally been in your shoes with the newfound popularity thing. After my first movie came out, people started stopping me on the street, asking me to take pictures with them and autograph stuff. It really freaked me out at first, but after a while, you sort of get used to it. Just be polite, and keep your *real* friends around you to help you stay grounded. Next, it sounds like this Devil-girl—Kristi—is just jealous. I mean, I can see why, but I'm sure that's all it is. Ignore her and it will drive her nuts," he said.

"Wow. I'm impressed," I said. And I was.

"Don't be. I memorize stuff for a living," he said easily. Then he laughed. "And lastly, Homecoming committee? What are you in charge of?"

"Decorations."

"Isn't there usually a theme for those things?" he asked.

"Yep," I answered. "It's 'Opposites Attract.'"

Ryder laughed again. "Seriously? Who the heck came up with that?"

I grew silent. Ryder noticed this and after a moment he coughed uncomfortably.

"*You* came up with it, didn't you?" he asked sounding embarrassed by his faux pas.

I didn't want to admit that I was responsible for the lame theme and give Ryder yet another reason to think I was a super dork. But I also didn't want to lie to him.

"Guilty as charged," I finally answered. Okay, so I was Queen of Dorkonia. If we were going to be *talking*—or whatever this was—Ryder was just going to have to deal. And if I was too outside-the-box for him, well, then better I find out now, right? "But in my defense, the other suggestions were way worse."

"I'm sure they were," Ryder said with mock seriousness. "So, I'm assuming since you're the brains behind the operation, that you'll be attending the ball, too?"

I rolled my eyes, but my heart was fluttering at the same time.

"I'm going with my friends, McCartney and Phin. And it's not a ball or anything like that. It's a *Homecoming* dance. It's a big deal to some people, though."

"Is it a big deal to you?"

I stopped and thought about his question. Despite the fact that I'd already agreed to attend, I'd never actually asked myself if I *wanted* to go. On the one hand, it seemed like a lot of work to put in for what could potentially be a lame night. But on the other, it meant I might get the chance to dance with a boy. Or boys. And wasn't slow dancing practically a step away from kissing?

"Yeah, I guess it *is* sort of important to me." As I said it, I knew it was the truth.

"Man, you're so lucky," Ryder said, sounding genuinely jealous.

"You're kidding, right?"

"Nah. I've never been to a school dance," he said. "By the time I was old enough to actually go to things like dances, I was already acting full time. I've had tutors on set since the seventh grade, so all this stuff you get to do, well, I never did. Whenever I hear people talk about going to Prom or to football games on Friday night, I always kind of wish I knew what it was like."

There was a longing in his voice that took me by surprise. How could Ryder possibly be sad over missing out on something as boring as public school? Especially when he'd had it so much better than the rest of us.

"Yeah, but you get to go to the *Teen Choice Awards* and the *MTV Movie Awards* and Hollywood parties. That's *so* much cooler then a silly high school dance," I said, plopping down onto my bed.

Our conversation had started to flow more easily now that we'd been talking for a while. We weren't quite strangers anymore. The thought made me feel braver, so I continued on.

"And, *hello*?! You play a high school student on TV. Granted, your character's a vampire, and it's all for the cameras, but you get to experience most of the same things as us. You go to the dances, you have the breakups, you try to survive high school. Sure it's not quite real life...but who wants to live that anyway?"

"I get what you're saying," he said as I finished. "And don't get me wrong... Diddy's parties are unbelievable. But going to those things—the award shows, the parties—it's still *work*. I'm bored out of my mind half the time. It's not the same as going to a gymnasium with a hundred other people my own age, having fun and dancing with cute girls."

I didn't remind him that we weren't exactly the same age either.

"And as for my character on the show," he continued with a sigh. "Try having a true high school moment with a dozen cameras pointed at you, and someone telling you where to stand, when to cry and how to hold a girl's face when you kiss here. Not exactly the stuff memories are made of."

Hearing him talk about everything he was missing out on left me feeling sort of bad for him. As bad as I could feel for someone who frequently rubbed elbows with people like Seth Rogan and Jennifer Lawrence, and probably had Miley Cyrus on speed dial.

"Well, if you're in the area two weekends from now and feel like seeing what a real dance is like, you can be my guest," I said, jokingly.

Now it was Ryder who grew quiet. It dawned on me that if he hadn't taken what I'd said as a joke like I'd intended, he was probably weirded out by my invitation. My invitation to a *high school dance*. With *me*. I was just about to explain what I'd meant, when he beat me to it.

"Yeah, okay. That would be fun."

"Huh?" I asked, wondering if he was joking with me now.

"The dance sounds like fun," he repeated, sounding genuinely excited. "Just text me the details and I'm there. Do guys still get corsage's for their dates?"

Date? Ryder was actually considering going with me to Homecoming? My head started to spin as I tried to keep up.

"Um, I'm not really sure. Maybe? I haven't really been to a dance before," I stammered.

"So, it'll be a night of firsts for both of us then," he said, with just a hint of flirtation in his voice. "Well, since we're each sort of clueless on how this is supposed to work, and all I know about this stuff is what our writers come up with, how about I bring you the corsage anyway. Then, if we see that no one else is wearing them, you can just toss it."

Toss it out? Was he kidding? That baby would be placed in a see-through, airtight box, and prominently displayed on my trophy shelf where everyone would be able to see it.

"You don't have to get me one if you don't want to," I said, blushing. Thank God we weren't having this convo in person. "Are you sure you really want to go to a high school dance in Podunk, nowhere?"

Ryder responded with a laugh. "Are *you* sure you want to go with *me*?"

"Is that a trick question?" I asked before I could censor myself. "I mean, I hope you're not just doing this because you feel bad for me or anything. It's not everyday that a TV star asks me to a dance. You've gotta see how this would throw me off, right?"

"I get your point. But really, I think we'll have fun. We'll go as friends so there's no pressure or anything, and I'll forever be in your debt for giving me the gift of a normal teenage experience."

I nodded my head and then realized Ryder couldn't actually see what I was doing. "Well, when you put it that way…then yeah, it sounds like fun!"

It sounded like more than fun, but I couldn't tell *him* that. Not during our first phone call anyway.

A little later, we said our good-byes, and Ryder promised to call me in a few days after he'd let his agent, manager, publicist and parents in on the plans. It was so weird to think that someone like Ryder had to get the approval of more people than I did to go out.

I lay back on my bed and stared up at the ceiling, replaying our conversation over and over again. Nobody would believe me if I told them what had happened tonight. Hell, *I* barely believed it myself. As I began to drift off to sleep, my phone started to ring again.

I lunged across the bed to answer it, annoyed that I'd forgotten to put it on vibrate before. Smiling, I brought the phone to my ear, hoping it was Ryder calling back to tell me that two weeks was too long to wait to see me and that he was hopping on a plane to visit. Or something like that.

"Hello?" I asked quietly, hoping my mom was already asleep in her room.

"Hey, Arielle. Sorry to call so late," a guy's voice said.

It wasn't Ryder calling me back. But the voice *did* sound familiar, and I racked my brain to attach a face to the caller. Only, I came up blank.

"It's Cade," he said, solving the mystery for me.

"Oh, yeah, hey," I said stupidly.

I'd gone fourteen years without so much as a 'hi' from anyone besides Phin—and he didn't really count—and now in one night I'd received phone calls from two *ridiculously* hot guys. And they weren't pranking me. Was it a full moon or something? I walked over to my window to check it out.

"I was calling to see if you wanted to meet up after school tomorrow to work out the decoration details?" Cade said as I looked up into the sky.

No full moon. Guess it was just my lucky day then.

Forcing my focus back on Cade, I tried to process what he was saying. Tomorrow was Friday, and surprise, surprise, I *didn't* have plans. But what was weird was that Cade didn't have any either. I started to wonder what he did in his spare time.

"Sure," I said, trying to sound like I got phone calls from cute bad boys every day. "Do you want to meet in the Student Lounge?"

Cade paused and I could hear him shuffling around as we talked. "I was thinking maybe we could hang at your place? The Student Lounge can get a little... distracting sometimes. I'll bring food."

"Well, if you're bringing food..."

I gave him my address and told him I'd meet him an hour after the last bell. After hanging up and remembering to put my phone on vibrate, I turned off my lamp and snuggled underneath my covers. I yawned loudly, suddenly exhausted from all the excitement of the evening.

Man, was I going to sleep well tonight.

Chapter Nineteen

"YOU'RE GOING TO Homecoming with *Ryder Diggs*!"

I covered my ears as McCartney let out the first of several high-pitched shrieks. Glancing around, I was embarrassed to find that everyone was staring at us with annoyed looks on their faces. I immediately regretted my decision to tell my best friend about Ryder while we were in public. We'd stopped at the smoothie shop to get an early morning pick-me-up, but after hearing McCartney's screeching—which I was convinced only dogs and other small animals could hear—I think it was safe to say that I was officially awake.

"Jeez, Cart. Way to make a scene," I said, before apologizing to those around us.

"That's *your* fault, sister soldier. You can't drop a bomb on me like that and expect me to act like it's not *the* biggest news I've ever heard in my entire life," she said. Placing her hand up to her mouth and faking a dramatic yawn, she looked at me tiredly. "Oh, you're going to Homecoming with the hottest celeb in the universe? You think that's impressive? Try going Han Solo like me."

McCartney's sarcasm was not appreciated, though I could kind of understand her point. This thing with Ryder was certainly the highlight of my fourteen years so far. I probably would've reacted similarly if I'd been in her shoes. Possibly even worse.

"Okay, okay," I said, giving in and smiling. "I admit, it's pretty freaking cool."

McCartney shook her head, squinting her chocolate brown eyes at me accusingly. "You little mother humper," she swore under her breath. "How did this happen? More importantly, why isn't it happening to *me*?"

I knew she didn't really mean it, but I stepped ahead of her in line and paid for both our smoothies to try and "smooth" things over anyway. We both ordered the "Monkey Business," a drink we'd been getting since the second grade. It was a combo of chocolate, peanut butter and banana, and it was delicious. I watched as McCartney immediately shoved the straw into her mouth and slurped away at the mixture like she was mad at it. Only, I knew her annoyance should've been directed at me. When she still refused to speak to me, I launched into my explanation.

"He called me up out of the blue, Cart. I didn't even think it was him at first. I mean, I called him a *butt-much,*" I said, recalling this horrifying bit of the story. "Anyways, we ended up just shooting the breeze, talking about the eBay thing and Kristi being a be-yotch, and then I mentioned that I was on the Homecoming committee. He started to talk about all the stuff he'd missed out on because he was so busy getting famous, and so I jokingly told him he should go to the dance with me and...he said *yes.*"

"You're shitting me, right? All you had to do was *ask* him and he said yes? And you weren't even being serious about it? This is so unfair! Where's *my* celebrity Prince Charming?" McCartney whined. Suddenly her face softened and she turned her head sharply to look at me. "Do any of his super-hot, super-famous friends want to go to Homecoming with me? I would be excellent arm candy, you know."

I burst out laughing, almost snorting "Monkey Business" out of my nose in the process. "I don't know, McCartney. Part of me doesn't even believe he's actually gonna show."

"Just ask him next time you talk, okay? Promise me you'll put it out there," she pleaded. If she could've gotten on her knees to beg at my feet without getting her white jeans dirty, I was pretty sure she would've done it, just to prove how much the request meant.

"I promise," I answered.

At school, we walked down the hallway in silence, both of us distracted with thoughts of Ryder. We'd only made it a few feet before McCartney turned to me, a confused look on her face.

"Wait. Didn't you say that you had *two* things to tell me?" she asked me. "And if you say that Ryder asked you to run off to Vegas and elope, I *might* have to jump off the school tower."

"Hey, Arielle," Cade said, appearing out of nowhere and blocking our path. My pulse quickened as I noticed how good he looked. How he managed to make a faded black T-shirt and jeans look insanely hot, I'll never know.

Realizing I was full-on staring at him, I closed my mouth and pulled it into a friendly smile.

"Hey."

"We still on for after school? I'll be over after I pick up the food. I hope you like Indian," he said.

I'd never had Indian food before and honestly couldn't guess what it entailed, but if that's what Cade wanted, I would wolf it down like it was my last meal. And I'd do it with a smile on my face.

"Of course," I fibbed. "Indian sounds great. See you later!"

Cade gave me a little wave and then slipped off down the hallway. McCartney and I turned to watch him go, admiring his laid-back saunter. As soon as he'd disappeared into a classroom, I felt McCartney's eyes attack me like death daggers. Meeting her gaze sheepishly, I held my hands up as I shrugged helplessly.

"*Sooooooooo*, funny story," I said, laughing nervously. "After I got off the phone with Ryder, Cade called and we made plans to meet up after school to brainstorm for the dance. How weird is that?"

"I can't believe Ryder's taking you to Homecoming *and* you've managed to score a date with Cade, too," McCartney said, shaking her head incredulously.

"It's not a date. We're just figuring out decorations and stuff."

"He's bringing food, Arielle," McCartney said. "It's totally a date."

I started to argue with her, but stopped because I knew it was pointless. No matter how much I insisted that things between Cade and me were innocent, McCartney's inner conspiracy theorist would reign supreme.

"I expect a detailed report tomorrow. And if Ryder calls back, I want to hear about that too. No more keeping secrets, capiche?"

"I wasn't keeping secrets, Eve. I was about to tell you about Cade, but then he showed up and beat me to the punch."

McCartney looked down at the ground and then back at me. "I've just been feeling a little left out, lately. I miss being the first to know everything that goes on in your life."

I automatically felt guilty that McCartney was feeling this way. She was my best friend. Of course I wanted her to know everything first. But things had been so crazy lately that I could barely keep up myself. It *was* possible that I'd left McCartney out of the loop without meaning to.

"Got it. Full disclosure from here on out," I promised, making a cross over my heart with my right hand.

"Good," McCartney said.

An awkward silence followed as we both tried to think of what to say next. We'd never really fought before, so this was new territory for us. Were we just supposed to move on, ignore the weirdness until it became normal again? Or was I supposed to give McCartney her space until she came to me and told me everything was fine?

Luckily the bell rang, forcing us to begin walking toward the class we had together. This was when McCartney finally spoke up.

"Since when do you like Indian food?" she asked as we walked through the classroom door.

I looked at her and burst into giggles as we sat down next to each other in the last row. We were back to being us.

I pushed open the front door and ran inside, not even waiting for it to shut behind me before I tore upstairs and into my room. Bree had cornered me in the hallway after the final bell, insisting on talking to me about the dance. I tried to explain to her that I was on my way home to figure it all out, but then she started introducing me to all her friends. Not wanting to appear rude, I stood there for ten minutes answering all their questions. And there were a lot of them.

When I finally snuck away—which was hard to do with everyone focused on me—I practically had to run home in order to get there before Cade. And then I still had to clean my room, since I hadn't done it the night before. I quickly surveyed the damage before picking up the clothes that were littering my floor and bed, and then tossing it all into my closet. Sprinting over to my bed, I pulled my comforter up over my cushy mattress, a half-assed attempt to make it presentable.

With the cleanup done, I pulled off my shirt, which was officially soaked through with sweat after sprinting home, and then stood in front of my closet.

Casual or dressy? Hot or chill? What were you supposed to wear in a situation like this? Not that I really knew what *this* was. Growing frustrated and knowing I was losing time, I put on my softest tee and stepped into a pair of jean shorts.

Then I ran into my bathroom and slicked on more deodorant, blotted my face with a little powder and twisted my hair up into a messy bun on top of my head. I had just enough time to dab on some gloss and spritz myself with perfume before the doorbell rang.

Taking the stairs two at a time, I hustled to the front door and sucked in some much-needed air before pulling it open.

"Hey, Cade. Come on in," I said breathlessly.

"Thanks," he said, before making his way into the entryway. I could smell his cologne as he passed and briefly wondered what kind it was. "As promised, I've got food. Where do you want it?"

I checked out the two big bags that were taking up both of his arms, and looked back toward the kitchen, and then up in the direction of my bedroom. If we ate downstairs and my mom came home, she'd want to chat with us and we'd never get anything done. She'd also likely embarrass me. But if we ate in my room, we'd be alone.

"Um, let's grab some plates and take it upstairs," I said. Realizing what that might have sounded like to Cade, I added, "My radio and computer and stuff are up there."

Cade didn't seem fazed though and followed me upstairs, still carrying our Indian food with him, which I noticed actually smelled pretty good. Whatever it was. I set our dishes on the floor and then plopped down across from him, leaning back against my bed frame. Cade placed the two large bags between us and sat down as well.

"So, what do we have?" I asked, pointing at the bags.

"First off, I have to tell you that this is the best Indian food you will ever eat," he said, his face dead serious. "It might even be the best *food* you've ever eaten."

I laughed. "Really? Where's it from?"

"Sorry, but I can't reveal my source. If word gets out about this place, then everyone will start going and it just won't be the same."

"But what if you're right and this *is* the best Indian food I've ever had? How am I supposed to order it again if I don't know where it's from?" I argued.

"I guess you'll just have to stay on my good side, and maybe I'll order it for us again sometime," he said, with a sly smile.

Was Cade...*flirting*?

With practically perfect timing, my stomach grumbled loudly, and Cade gestured for me to dig in. I didn't want to seem like a pig, but it smelled so good that it was like torture not tearing into the bags. In the end, starvation won over ladylike behavior.

"You drive a hard bargain, Jones," I said, opening up the first container.

Five minutes later, there was a lavish spread in front of us that included a dish of spicy chicken called Tandori, another that looked scarily like baby poop but was actually a mixture of spinach and cheese, and this doughy bread he said was called naan (but pronounced 'non'). I could've kissed Cade for opening my eyes to such amazing food. But of course I didn't. One, because I still wasn't sure if Cade was into me or not. And two, I had the eBay thing to think about. Which I had to admit, hadn't been on my mind much lately.

When we were both disgustingly full, we boxed up what was left and then stood up to find more comfortable spots to brainstorm. I ended up sprawling across my bed while Cade reclined in my desk chair, arms linked behind his head lazily.

"I think I'm falling into a food coma," I moaned, closing my eyes.

Cade just laughed. Finally, I forced myself to pick up my notebook and pen so we could actually get some work done. Flipping to a clean page, I wrote, "Homecoming" across the top and then underlined it.

"Okay. So, decorations," I said.

"Decorations," Cade repeated.

"Opposites Attract," I said. I tapped my pen against the notebook as I tried to think of ways to decorate a gym according to our chosen theme. "How about black and white for colors?"

"Simple, yet effective. They're definitely opposites," Cade said, nodding.

"We could get a bunch of shiny black balloons and some matte white ones, so it's shiny and dull," I continued. "Maybe half the floor could be like that fake plastic grass and the other half can be the gym floor, that way it's rough and smooth."

"And we should make sure the refreshments are salty and sweet, hot and cold, healthy and junk food," Cade said.

"Ugh. Don't even mention food right now," I said, making a face before pushing on. "So now we just have to actually *get* everything."

I walked over to where Cade was sitting and leaned over his shoulder, gently brushing his arm with mine as I reached for my keyboard. "Sorry," I said, though I wasn't really all that sorry.

"No problem," Cade answered.

I could've sworn I saw the corners of his lips turn up into a smile. He swiveled around in the chair as I started to type, not seeming to mind at all that I had to lean over him to get at the computer sitting on my desk.

"Let's see where the closest Party Store is," I muttered to myself as I waited for Google to do its thing.

Within minutes, I was printing out a list of places that sold the decorations we needed for the dance. One was even within walking distance of our school.

"You wanna hit this place after school on Monday?" Cade asked, pointing to the screen and practically reading my mind.

"Sounds like a plan," I answered. "And oh, look! They have puppy dog costumes! Your date could go as a cat...."

"Cats and dogs. Very clever," Cade said sarcastically. "And you and your date could go as Einstein and President Bush."

I acted shocked and knocked him with my hip. He pushed me back gently. "I'm not sure my date would agree to dressing up like Bush," I said, thinking of Ryder. "He may be an actor, but he's not that good at BS-ing." I moved to bump Cade again, but he moved at the last minute and I lost my balance.

And then fell right into his lap.

"Whoa, sorry about that," I said, both embarrassed and slightly exhilarated by where I'd landed.

Cade reached over and brushed a piece of hair that had come loose from my bun behind my ear. I shivered at his touch, but tried to hide it by laughing nervously.

"You already have a date for the dance?" he asked, sounding surprised.

Feeling the moment getting awkward, I pulled myself up off of Cade's lap and moved back over to my bed. I crossed my legs and tried to appear calm, even though my heart was now racing

"Um, yeah. Sort of," I said shyly. "This guy, Ryder, asked me the other day."

Cade's face didn't change, but I could tell that his mood had.

"That guy from the vampire show?"

"It's more of a teen drama..." I started, but gave up when I saw his face. "But, yeah. See, he's sort of a friend of mine now—a new friend, actually—"

"So, he's just a friend?" Cade cut in.

"Uh huh," I answered, because technically it was true. Besides, Cade hadn't asked me if I wanted to be more than friends with Ryder. "He asked me earlier this week. See, he's never been to a school dance before on account of his acting career and all, and he really wants to see what it's like..."

"He asked you earlier this week," Cade repeated slowly.

I nodded. "I'm not even sure if it's going to happen, though. He's in the middle of taping *Night Light* right now, and if they need him to work or something, he'll have to cancel. But if that doesn't happen, then yeah, we'll go together. It's kind of weird to say it out loud, you know? Me. Going to a small-town school dance with a TV star."

"Yeah, *crazy,*" Cade said, running his hand through his hair.

We sat there for a moment in silence, me on my bed, and my now brooding buddy sitting in my desk chair. I faintly heard the front door open and close downstairs, but I didn't bother getting up to see who it was. There was only one person it could be anyway. As mom began to hum to herself as she walked through the house, I turned back to Cade who was now standing up.

"So, who are you taking?" I asked, trying to salvage our conversation.

I watched him put on his jacket. "Huh?"

"Who are *you* taking to Homecoming?" I repeated.

"Oh," he said. "I'm not sure yet. I had a few people in mind, but haven't asked anyone. I'm not even sure I want to go."

"Come on! It's Homecoming. And you're on the *dance committee.* You should at least get to enjoy the fruits of your labor," I said, giving him a goofy smile and then touching him lightly on the arm.

Cade looked at my hand on his arm and then back at my face. We were just inches from each other and I could feel his breath lightly on my face. I wondered if he wanted to kiss me as much as I wanted to...

"Arielle—" my mom said, sounding surprised. I turned to see that she'd appeared in my doorway. Cade took the tiniest step away from me, and then shoved his hands deep into his pockets. My mom looked from me to the boy she'd never met before, and then around my room. It was like she was trying her best to piece together the night's events. And even though we hadn't been caught doing anything, I still felt guilty. And kind of embarrassed.

"Hey, Mom," I said, innocently. "Uh, this is Cade. We're on Homecoming Committee together. We've been coming up with decoration ideas."

"Uh huh," she answered evenly, crossing her arms and examining my study buddy. "It's nice to meet you, Cade. So, what have you guys come up with so far?"

I wasn't sure if she was asking because she was genuinely interested or if she was just grilling us.

"Our theme's 'Opposites Attract'..."

"Arielle actually came up with it, Mrs. Sawyer," Cade added.

"Very clever, Arielle," my mom said.

"Anyway, so we're decorating with black and white balloons, and we thought we'd serve hot and cold food...that sort of thing," I finished, cheerily.

"Sounds like it's going to be a good time," she said. "Do they need any chaperones?"

Cade had somehow made his way toward the door and was standing slightly behind my mom now. So when he smirked at this, I was the only one to see him. I made a mental note to scold him later.

"You know, I think they have enough, but I'll let you know," I said in my best devoted daughter voice.

Cade lifted his bag over his head, the strap hitting just in between his well-toned pecs. He gave me a smooth smile as he stood by the door and I felt my knees almost buckle under his stare. He was the epitome of cool. Bad on the outside and sweet on the inside. Deliciously gorgeous.

Sigh.

"I should get going," Cade said, interrupting my crush session.

I looked around at all the leftovers spread across my floor, and bent down to start gathering the takeout containers.

"Here, let me get some of this for you," I said.

"They're yours. Enjoy," he said. "Who knows when you'll have something that good again."

I could tell he was joking, but it was also just a little bit suggestive. Borderline flirty, even.

"Well, in that case, I think I could have seconds," I countered. Realizing my mom was still in the room and staring at us curiously, I cleared my throat and broke our gaze. "Okay. So, see you at school on Monday then? We'll get the decorations after the last bell?"

Cade nodded and said a polite goodbye, insisting he could let himself out. Once he was gone, my mom walked over to my bed and sat down next to me. When she still hadn't said anything by the time we heard the front door open and close, I started to get fidgety.

"What?" I asked her.

She just smiled and shrugged her shoulders. "Nothing." But I could tell it was *something,* because she had "something face."

"Go ahead. Say whatever you're thinking," I demanded, lying back against my pillows and throwing my arms up and behind my head.

"He's a good-looking kid, that's all," she finally said, her smile growing bigger. "So, you're working on the dance together?"

"Yep."

"Does he have a date, yet?"

"Why? You wanna go with him?" I asked, jokingly. When she gave me the parental warning look, I lowered my level of sarcasm and answered her. "No, *Cade* doesn't have a date for the dance yet. But he's planning on asking someone."

My mom was starting to look like she did after she had a break-through with one of her couples. "You?"

I snorted. "Hardly. We're just on dance committee together. Besides, I already have a date."

"What?" Now she was officially surprised. "Since when?"

"Gee, Mom. Don't seem so shocked," I said slightly hurt by her reaction. "I may not have kissed anyone yet, but it doesn't mean I'm an L7."

"An L7?"

I rolled my eyes. As hip as my mom thought she was, she was always a step behind *cool.*

"L," I said, making the letter with the thumb and pointer finger of my right hand. "Seven," I continued, turning my left palm toward me and showing the number to her. I put the two together, fingertips touching. "It's a square?"

The light turned on in my mom's head and she beamed as if she'd just learned the location of the Holy Grail.

"That's so *crafty,*" she said. "L7. Huh. I've got to remember that."

"Anyway," I said, as she continued to make squares with her fingers, "I'm going to the dance with Ryder."

She stopped what she was doing and blinked at me. "The boy from the TV show? What's it called? *Night Ryder*?"

"*Night Light,*" I corrected. "*Night Ryder* is a show from your day."

"Ah, yes. That Hasseldorf guy who drove the talking car," she said, pulling the name out of her limited celebrity pop culture file. I was always shocked at how little she knew about Hollywood, considering that twenty percent of her clientele were in the entertainment industry. "What's Ryder's show about?"

"It's Hasselhoff," I said. "And *Night Light* is about teen vampires."

"So, you asked him? I didn't know you two were friends," she said, folding her arms across her chest curiously.

"Well, he sort of asked me and I said yes. And I guess we're friends. We swapped numbers that day on the show and we've talked a couple of times on the phone."

I started moving around my room, pulling out all the stuff I'd hidden in the closet before Cade had shown up. I hoped that my mom would see that I was busy and cut our mother/daughter bonding sesh short. Not that I didn't like talking to my mom. For the most part, she was really fun to be around. Definitely cool for an adult. I mean, I don't know any other moms who'd let their daughters sell a kiss on eBay.

It was just that I knew if we kept chatting, she'd ask me if I liked Ryder. And after that, she'd ask if Ryder was into me. And the thing about it was... I didn't know the answer.

I pulled my homework out of my messenger bag and lay it out on the bedspread in front of me. I quickly counted up how many hours of homework I had to do before I could pass out, and the number filled me with stress. I looked up at my mom, who'd grown quiet herself, and saw that she was lost in thought.

"Hey, Mom, you mind if we talk about this later? I've got like, four and a half hours of work here, and then I still have to check on this eBay thing."

Mom's face softened and she smiled at me understandably. "Of course, sweetie. I *do* want to hear all about this, though," she said as she walked toward the door. "You know, I hope you feel like you can come to me to talk about anything. That includes boys and dating. I was a young bachelorette myself at one point, you know."

"I know," I said, forcing my own smile. "Now, you're just a *mature* bachelorette."

"Ugh. The only thing worse than being *mature* is being *old*," Mom exclaimed, throwing her hands up in the air, defeated.

"Well, you're certainly not *old*," I said trying to make her feel better.

"Thanks hon. But I'm old enough to know that you and Cade weren't *just* working on a project."

"But we *were*—"

"It's okay. You don't want to talk to your mom about this stuff and I get it. Just as long as you know I'm here for you if you decide to share."

I knew there was no point in trying to fight her on the subject, so I conceded. "I know, Mom. Thanks."

I watched her walk out of my room and listened as she went back downstairs. A few minutes later, she was puttering around our kitchen. Reluctantly, I turned my attention to my homework. But before I could get completely lost in American History, I found myself drifting back to my conversation with Cade.

Had Mom been right? Was there something more going on there?

Chapter Twenty

I SPOTTED MCCARTNEY almost immediately as we pulled up to the South Kennedy Mall. It was 7:45 on a Saturday morning and I was not at all happy about the fact that I was up so early. I'd always been of the opinion that weekends were meant to be spent sleeping in, then lounging around in your pajamas until at least noon, while you watched your favorite cartoons (which are *not* just for little kids anymore; have you heard some of the jokes on them lately?) and stuffed your belly with sugary treats like donuts, cinnamon rolls or chocolate chip pancakes.

Yet, here I was, pulling up to an empty mall several hours before I should've been waking up. And did I mention this was all totally against my will?

"*There's* McCartney," my mom said a minute after I'd already found her. "So, you guys are shopping for dresses?"

"That's the plan," I grumbled, rubbing at my eyes.

Because of my guilt over my lack of communication with my friends lately, I'd agreed to go dress shopping with McCartney. But when I'd said yes, I hadn't realized she'd want to go before the rooster even got out of bed for the day.

"Okay, well, have fun, hon. Give me a call when you're ready for me to pick you up. I'm just going to be reading for a session I'm having later this week."

"Thanks, Mom."

Once the car rolled to a stop, I pushed open the door and hopped out. McCartney better realize what I was sacrificing for a little girl-on-girl bonding time. I pulled my hoodie up over my head and shoved my hands deep into the soft, fuzzy pockets. Dragging my feet in the direction of the bench McCartney was sitting on, I silently cursed her for choosing such an ungodly hour to get her shop on.

"Great, you're here!" she said, jumping up and walking to meet me halfway. "I was hoping we could strategize before the doors open."

"Mmmggrrrrrrr," I said, doing my best impression of a zombie.

"Oh, here," McCartney said, producing an energy drink from her purse. "I've got a few more stashed in here if that doesn't do the trick. You know I wouldn't make you come here this early and *not* bring you the cure to sleepiness."

I popped open the top and gulped it down, only stopping when the can was empty. McCartney took the drink out of my hands and replaced it with a new one. I could feel the caffeine start to work almost immediately and took my time sipping the second. When I began to feel my annoyance disappear along with my sluggishness, I pulled my hood off and surveyed the few people who'd gathered around us.

"Thanks. I needed that."

"No problemo," she answered, before moving on. "Now back to strategizing. I'm thinking we should start at Forever 21 and then make our way back through the mall. We'll probably need to run to the shop though, because you know that everyone else will be heading there, too. And I want first dibs on all the best dresses. There's no way I'm settling for someone else's castoffs."

"Do you seriously think anyone else from school will get up this early? McCartney, they're *teenagers*. They're probably just going to bed," I said, switching my drink from one hand to the other like a hot potato.

"I love you, Arielle, but have you gone mental? *Everyone* is going to be here today. It's the last weekend before Homecoming and that means it's our last chance to get the perfect dress."

I looked at her. I'd never seen McCartney so worked up over a single event before. In fact, she'd always been kind of anti-school activities. In middle school, I'd even had to trick her into going to our eighth grade graduation ceremony. And now, she was suddenly acting like Mrs. Homecoming Queen.

"You're not fooling me, McCartney Fay Janning. Why are you so worked up about this dance?" I asked. "Come on. Spill."

"What? It's nothing. I just figured that if we were going, we should do it right."

I put my hand on my hip and gave my best "cut the crap" look.

"Okay! Quit looking at me like that. Sheesh, didn't your mom ever warn you that your face could freeze that way?" she said. "So, this only just happened like, yesterday, but I sort of...got a date for the dance."

"And you couldn't have led with that info?" I said, suddenly really excited for my friend. This was practically the news of the century. "Gimme the deets! Who is it? Did he ask you or did you ask him? I bet it's Tommy, isn't it? Oooh, or what about that Italian exchange student? I've seen him checking you out during English class. Why aren't you saying anything?"

"Um, because you won't stop asking me questions," she answered sarcastically. I made a zipping motion across my lips and shut my mouth. When she saw I was serious, she continued. "It's Zack Pinole. He asked me yesterday and it was so cute. He left me a flower in my locker with a note attached asking me to be his date. I made him sweat for a few periods, but of course I finally told him yes. He's cute, right?"

I recalled the guy McCartney was talking about and had to agree with her. The boy *was* cute. Zack was a sophomore *and* a soccer player—which already made him way cooler than anyone she could've gone with from our class. He was tall, and lithe, and walked around as if on air. He was graceful. For a guy at least. His hair was light brown and average length. He was pretty clean cut as far as I knew, a surprising choice for McCartney, considering she usually went after guys who were…complicated.

"So cute! And he scores extra sizzle points for the soccer bod," I said, nodding. "Aw, McCartney, I'm so happy for you!"

And I really was. Now that we both had dates, I knew that I wouldn't have to worry about McCartney having a good time. Or giving me a guilt trip over spending the dance with a TV star.

"So, you can see why I'm going a little mental over this dress thing. Because unlike you, I have nothing stopping me from K-I-S-S-I-N-G at Homecoming," McCartney said, puckering up.

A noise made us turn and we watched as a pimply-faced kid unlocked the mall doors. As he finished, he looked up and noticed the small crowd of teenage girls who'd gathered, waiting for this very moment. I saw a flash of terror in his eyes and wondered if he was recalling the unfortunate accident several years back where a few workers were trampled when they didn't get out of the way of incoming shoppers quickly enough. Of course, this had been on Black Friday, but still.

"Move that scrawny butt of yours, Sawyer!" McCartney shouted, like it was a battle cry. And then she took off at a sprint toward the door, causing everyone behind us to do the same.

Before I became collateral damage myself, I rolled my eyes and began to jog too. The pimply guy fled as quickly as his stubby legs would carry him. A few seconds later, McCartney arrived at the same spot, and pulled on the handle. She held the door open for me, and then turned back and gave me her best "hurry up" stare.

Yeesh. I'd never seen McCartney so serious about something before. In fact, the last time she'd put this much energy into something, her parents had ended up buying her a horse. And the farm that went along with it.

I forced myself to pick up the pace, and was by her side before any of the other shoppers could catch up to me. I felt winded, but McCartney didn't seem to notice. Or maybe she just didn't care. Instead, she grabbed my hand and pulled me along behind her, unwilling to let me fall behind again.

"There it is!" McCartney shouted, like I couldn't see the neon lights of the store with my own eyes.

She let go of my hand then, pulling ahead of me easily, and only stopping once she was right in front of the formal dresses. Then she started grabbing hangers, hugging the gowns close to her body so nobody else could steal them. I don't think she even looked at what she'd chosen. Just took every available dress in her size. The scene was unreal.

At least I know that when the zombie apocalypse comes—and I fully believed it will happen one day—McCartney will be among the survivors. And hopefully, I'll be by her side.

I trudged into the store far less enthused, and still not fully awake. Stopping at the first rack of dresses, I started leafing through the selection. After a few minutes, I'd picked out three dresses that looked like they might be cute on me, and headed toward the back to try them on. I walked up behind McCartney, who'd already made her way back to the dressing rooms too.

"McCartney! How many dresses do you have in there? You know there's a six-item limit, right? And you've got, what," I asked, reaching forward to eyeball count the pile of clothes in her hands, "thirty dresses here."

"It's twenty-two, and I know six is the limit. I'll just leave the rest out here on this rack and exchange six at a time."

I gave her an incredulous look.

"What? I don't want to have to go all the way back out there to get more," she said indignantly. "And what if someone snatched up the one I wanted in the meantime? This way, I have my first pick."

"Okay, okay," I said, shaking my head, and letting it go. For as long as I'd known McCartney, she'd had her own way of doing things. And it didn't matter if that way was completely crazy, because she wouldn't listen to reason once she'd fixed her mind on something.

"You can go into room seven," the store attendant said to McCartney, after taking all but six of her items. Then she loked at me. "And you're in room eight."

"So, do you know where Ryder's taking you before the dance? He is taking you out, right?"

I took off my clothes and stood for a minute in my underwear and bra as I observed myself in the mirror. I grimaced as I saw how the dull lights cast a greyish tint to my skin, and somehow managed to make all my little imperfections stand out like neon signs. If these stores were smart, they'd install lighting that made you look your best. Like funhouse mirrors, except to enhance your *good* qualities.

"Um, I'm not sure yet," I said, sighing and pulling the first dress off its hanger. I fingered the black satin material before pulling it over my head. "We haven't really talked since we decided to go together."

"He *does* know it's only a week away, right? Even if he hasn't been to a dance before, he's gotta know to keep his date informed." Her voice projected over the top of the curtain and probably to the rest of the store.

I could hear her still shuffling around inside as I stepped out of my room and walked over to the full-length mirrors just a few feet away. Seconds later, McCartney exited her room as well, and joined me.

"Woo!" I called out as she sauntered up to me. The dress she had on was purple, with a plunging neckline that tied behind her neck. I looked down to where it extended all the way to the floor.

"Do you think Zack will like it?" she asked, looking nervous.

"Zack will choke on his punch when he sees you in that dress," I said.

"That one's not bad either," she said, motioning to the one I had on.

I made a face and pulled at the bottom of the skirt. "It's too short. *And* too tight."

"It's Homecoming. You can get a little R-O-W-D-Y," McCartney said, making motions with her arms like the cheerleaders.

"I have under-butt cleavage," I said, unhappily. I turned around and showed her how my bottom peeked out from the material.

After a few seconds of surveying my rear end, she nodded. "Too short."

"But I like yours," I said again, as we both walked back into our dressing rooms. "I think you should go with that one."

"You haven't seen any of the others yet," McCartney yelled over the curtain.

"Yeah, but how perfect would it be if you found the right dress on the first try? You'd save yourself so much time," I said, peeling the dress from my body. "And the frustration."

I slipped the second dress over my head, shimmying my way into it and then letting the satiny fabric glide across my body. Without looking in the mirror, I pulled the door open and walked back out to the viewing area.

"Frustration? Are you kidding? Trying on dresses is the *best part*," McCartney answered as she sashayed over to me. "And hello? Now *that's* a dress."

This time I had to agree with her. The pale pink material wasn't too tight, but it managed to show what curves I did have. The top tied at the neck and the material scooped down in the front, gathering beautifully, just above my chest. The gown extended down into a V, with the left side hitting my upper thigh and the right dipping down to my knee. Scattered crystals sparkled all over, shining prisms of light all around. I felt like a princess. You know, like the one in *The Princess Diaries*. Only, without the fortune or kingdom to rule.

"You're *hot*," McCartney said, walking around me to see the dress from every angle. "If this doesn't get you that kiss, then I'm out of ideas."

"This is it. This is the dress," I breathed, running my hands over the soft material. I found the price tag and was happy to see it was well under the limit my mom had given me. I might even be able to snag a pair of shoes with the change. "I'm getting it."

"Good," McCartney said. "Now, back to me. What do you think of this one?"

I looked up to see her striking a pose a few feet away. The new dress she was wearing was also pale purple, only this one was strapless, tight around the bodice but poofy at the waist. Like a prima ballerina.

"I liked the first one better," I said, walking back to the room to change back into my clothes.

I emerged a few minutes later and shuffled my way over to the checkout. Handing the salesgirl the dress followed by my mom's platinum card, I couldn't help but smile over having found the dream dress I never knew I wanted. As I waited for the receipt to print out, I turned around and leaned against the counter. McCartney had already changed into her third dress of the day. This one was electric purple, had one strap on the right side and a bubble bottom.

"How many more dresses are you going to try on before you admit that the first one is *the one*?"

"As many as it takes to make sure that there isn't anything better."

She gave me a goofy grin and turned on her heel. I watched her wiggle her butt as she walked away, aware that she was doing it on purpose. Looked around the store, I spotted a bench right outside the dressing room and made a beeline for it, collapsing onto its cushions gratefully.

If I had to stick around as McCartney tried on multiple outfits, I was at least going to be comfortable doing it.

As I got settled, I felt my phone buzz inside my pocket. I pulled it out and swiped the screen.

> **RYDER:** HEY, SO THERE'S A LITTLE CHANGE IN PLANS FOR SATURDAY...

My heart sank. This was the text I'd been dreading but waiting for, ever since I'd accepted Ryder's invitation to take him to Homecoming. And yet, after all my emotional preparation, I was still disappointed by the news.

Maybe I could still return the dress.

> **ME:** DON'T WORRY, IT'S COOL...I KNOW YOU'RE REALLY BUSY. THE DANCE IS PROBABLY GONNA SUCK ANYWAY.

After all the planning that the Dance Committee had been doing, I didn't actually think this. But what was I supposed to say? "I hate you, cute TV star! You just ruined my first high school dance!" Yeah, right. You played it off like it wasn't that big of a deal to begin with.

RYDER: HAHAHA. YOU'RE NOT GETTING RID OF ME THAT EASILY! WE'RE STILL ON FOR SATURDAY. IT'S JUST THAT MTV WANTS TO TAPE THE WHOLE THING...IT'S STUPID, I KNOW. AND IF IT BUGS YOU, I CAN TELL THEM TO BITE ME.

My stomach rode the roller coaster of nerves back up to the top of the hill as excitement replaced my disappointment. I glanced up and caught my reflection in the mirror. I was grinning so wide that I looked like a Jack-o-Lantern.

He still wanted to go with me to the dance. Ryder Diggs wanted to take me to Homecoming *and* now he wanted to tape it! There would be actual proof that he'd been my date.

ME: OHHHHH! NAH, IT DOESN'T BUG ME... BESIDES, YOU CAN'T TELL MTV NO! I'LL JUST HAVE TO SURVIVE ALL THE CAMERAS. LOL.

And if they decided to give me my own reality show and I become besties with Lauren Conrad, that's a sacrifice I was willing to take. McCartney was going to flip when she heard about this.

RYDER: COOL! I'LL PICK YOU UP AT YOUR PLACE ROUND 4, & WE'LL GO GET DINNER, & DO SOME PRE-DANCE TAPING. THE PRODUCERS ALSO WANT TO MAKE SURE YOU DON'T TELL ANYONE ABOUT THIS. WE DON'T WANT THE PAPS SHOWING UP AT YOUR SCHOOL. TRUST ME, IT'D BE BAD NEWS FOR EVERYONE.

Only, it would be worse news for me if I kept this from McCartney, considering how she'd flipped out the other day. And this was so much bigger than Cade coming over to my house. Not letting her in on the fact that MTV would be taping us *and* breaking our plans to go to the dance in a limo together would leave McCartney furious. I wasn't really sure our friendship could take it.

But I didn't want to betray Ryder, either.

ME: SOUNDS LIKE FUN! I'M LOOKING FORWARD TO IT.

I sent the text and then put my phone away as I heard McCartney come out of the dressing room. There had to be a way to handle this so no one got hurt. I mean, it wasn't like the paparazzi would find out, if I made McCartney promise not to tell.

"What about this one?" McCartney asked.

I didn't even look at the dress before answering. "Buy the first one."

She threw her hands up in the air, clearly annoyed at my refusal to play along with her game of dress up. "You're such a brat," she said. "Change that 'tude or I'll make you sit in the front of the limo with the driver, while I chillax in the back with Zack *and* Ryder."

Crap. I *so* didn't want to have this conversation. But I'd have to fess up to the change of plans sometime. Why not when she's already in a good mood? I said a little prayer that the news wouldn't ruin the rest of our day.

"Actually, I need to talk to you about that," I said gently. "Ryder and I can't share the limo with you guys anymore. Something sort of...came up, that we can't get out of."

McCartney stopped looking at herself in the mirror and turned around to face me. I flinched at the sudden movement and couldn't help but imagine her taking me out once she'd heard what I had to say.

"You're kidding, right?" she asked, the anger seeping into her voice. "We've had this planned for weeks. It's supposed to be you, me, and Phin. And our dates. But it's really about the three of us, and it can't be the three of us if you're not there, too. What's so important that you have to ditch us? Is Ryder too good for us commoners?"

I opened my mouth to tell her about the secret MTV gig, but my phone buzzed just as I was about to spill. I glanced down at my phone nervously, trying not to be too obvious about reading the text. McCartney was already pissed off and I didn't want to send her over the edge.

RYDER: GREAT! I'LL E-MAIL YOU THE NON-DISCLOSURE AGREEMENT. YOU'LL NEED TO SIGN & FAX IT BACK TO MY AGENT. SHE'LL FORWARD

IT ON TO MTV. IT JUST SAYS THAT YOU WON'T SAY ANYTHING TO ANYONE REGARDING THE SHOW UNTIL IT'S ANNOUNCED. PRETTY STANDARD STUFF.

A non-disclosure agreement? If I had to legally promise not to tell anyone about the MTV thing, then that pretty much ruled out any plan I had of involving McCartney. And that made me unbelievably uncomfortable. I could count on one hand the number of times I'd lied to my best friend, and more than half of those incidents had transpired in the last month.

How was I supposed to do it to her *again*?

RYDER: THANKS FOR BEING SO COOL ABOUT ALL OF THIS, BTW. YOU'RE AN AWESOME GIRL. I CAN'T WAIT TO GO TO THE DANCE WITH YOU. TALK SOON.

"Hello? I'm waiting for an answer that's good enough to warrant you backing out of these plans," McCartney said, beyond annoyed.

I read back over Ryder's text, before putting my phone away. As it disappeared, I made a decision.

"McCartney, you know there's nothing I'd rather do than take the limo with you guys, but Ryder just told me he has this whole thing planned out, and we won't be finished with whatever it is until after you guys leave for the dance," I answered, feeling guilty as the words passed my lips. It wasn't totally a lie, but it wasn't totally the truth either.

McCartney just looked at me skeptically, excitement and disdain on her face. The silence between us grew as I waited for her to let me know where we stood. Finally, she turned back to survey her image huffily and I knew this wasn't going to blow over quickly.

"Whatever," she said finally, before stomping back to her room to change. "It was going to be crowded in the limo anyway."

Chapter Twenty-One

THE NEXT WEEK passed by in a blur of dance frenzy. Every conversation had to do with Homecoming. It was all about what people were wearing to the dance, who they were going to the dance with and whether or not they planned to give it up to their dates afterward (and I don't think they were talking about kisses). And if the person wasn't going to Homecoming, they were complaining about how stupid the dance was, what they were doing instead, who *didn't* ask them, or making fun of the rest of us who were excited about it.

It was dance mania.

During this time I tried to keep my focus on my classes, which I'd been neglecting since we'd started project G.A.A.K. But not because I wasn't excited about the dance—actually, it was quite the opposite. I was *so* psyched about going to my first high school dance with someone as cool as Ryder, I was afraid that if I talked to anyone, I might spill the beans. And then, I was pretty sure MTV would sue my mom. Meaning, this would be my first—and last—high school dance.

So, I spent all my free time actually doing the reading assignments, completing my homework and studying for tests that weren't happening for weeks. I ate my lunches in the library and headed straight home after the last bell (except for those days I had Dance Committee meetings).

You know how people say that time flies when you're having fun? Well, it goes painfully slow when you're looking forward to something. Trust me, I learned this the hard way.

By the time the dance finally rolled around, I was officially ready for all the hoopla to be over. But before that could happen, I had to help decorate the gym.

Then, I could hang up my committee shoes and never agree to get involved in a school function again.

"How have we been here for three hours already and only have half the place decorated?" I asked, huffily.

Down on my hands and knees in the gymnasium, I rolled out strips of plastic turf over half of the smooth floor. As I held it down, Cade secured each piece with electrical tape. I wrinkled my nose as the smell of the recently spray-painted fake grass permeated my nostrils.

"Couldn't we have spray-painted this *after* we put it in the gym?" I complained, starting to feel a headache coming on.

"Sure. If you don't mind people getting high off the fumes," Cade said with a smirk. "Actually, that might've made the whole thing a lot more interesting. You should've said something earlier."

I couldn't help but smile at his sarcasm. Cade had been the one bright spot during this non-stop week of stress. It was like he understood how silly the whole thing was, and had made it his mission to get everyone else to lighten up. We'd even started a little contest between the two of us to see who could get Bree to scowl the most. Cade was killing me on this one, as no matter what I said or did, she just wouldn't get mad at me. I could tell I was wearing her down, though.

"Why did we make everything so complicated, again?" I whined, stopping to look around us.

A handful of students were tying dozens of black and white balloons to every table set up throughout the gym. Paper lanterns had been hung from the ceiling, with half the room drenched in red lights and the other lit up in blue. Cade had thought of this as having a sort of heaven and hell vibe.

The rest of the committee members were setting up life-sized cardboard cut-outs of famous couples around the room. Jake's uncle was the manager at Kinko's and had scored us a dozen of them for wicked cheap. My favorite couple was Brad and Angelina. Nobody knew it yet, but I fully intended to take Mr. Jolie home with me after the dance.

I focused myself on what Cade and I were doing, and lay out the remainder of the turf. When we were finished, I stood up and rubbed at my prickly knees until the feeling began to come back to my legs. I felt a little light-headed as I straightened, and closed my eyes to steady myself.

"You okay?"

"Um, yeah," I answered, rubbing at the pain behind my eyes. "I think the paint's just getting to me."

"Have you had anything to drink since we started?" Cade asked.

I gave him a surprised look. "I don't do that kind of stuff."

Cade looked at me confused. Then, he broke into a smile before taking a small step toward me. "I meant...have you been *hydrating*."

"Oh," I said, embarrassed. He hadn't meant alcohol. "No, I guess I haven't had any of that either."

He reached over and grabbed hold of my elbow lightly and began to pull me away from the middle of the gymnasium. "Well then, let's take a break. Grab some water and a little air."

I nodded and allowed myself to be guided away from the noise of everyone setting up behind us. The fact that Cade's hand was touching my arm was something I was well aware of. It was a nice feeling and I wondered how I could get him to do it more often.

As soon as we'd made it through the double doors at the back of the gym, Cade instructed me sit down on the school stairs as he jogged over to the vending machines to get us something to drink. He propped open an emergency exit door allowing the evening air to flow through the hall. I closed my eyes and let the cold hit my cheeks, and blow my hair back over my shoulders.

"Water okay?" Cade asked as I calmed under the drop in temperature.

"Is there seltzer?" I asked.

Cade didn't respond, but I listened as two drinks dropped into the bin below. A few seconds later, he sat down beside me, our bodies connected at the knees. I jumped a little as he pressed the cold can to the back of my neck.

"Oh!"

"You cooling down yet?" Cade asked me quietly. Without opening my eyes, I could tell his face was only inches away from mine. Even with the air moving around us, I swear I could feel his warm breath on my skin.

"Yeah, thanks," I said, feeling flustered by our proximity to one another. I accepted the drink he was holding and popped the top, taking generous gulps of the bubbly water.

"You actually like that stuff?" Cade asked.

I nodded. "It's like water, only fancier."

He shook his head as he watched me down it. My headache started to subside from the fresh air and liquid. I nudged him lightly. "Hey, thanks. I needed that."

"No problem," he shrugged. Then he nodded over toward the gym. "Can you believe how crazy people have been acting over this thing? It's like invasion of the body snatchers or something. Come on people, it's just a stupid dance."

"I know what you mean. After a while I had to tune it all out. I was afraid my brain would turn to mush and ooze out my ears," I said, chuckling.

Cade raised his eyebrows at me, questioningly. "You mean, you haven't been dreaming of this night *all* your life? Won't they revoke your girl card for not obsessing over every little detail?"

"Ha, ha," I said, rolling my eyes at him. "I *am* excited. I just have other things going on, too. Like, the fact that my friend, McCartney, is pissed I had to cancel our plans to share a limo to the dance. And when she finds out why I really had to skip out, she's gonna go all Hulk on me."

"Ah, well, she's your best friend. I'm sure she'll get over it," he said.

I burst out laughing. "You don't know McCartney."

"Are you still going with that vampire guy?"

"Yes. And his name's *Ryder.*"

"Of course it is," Cade said under his breath.

"Huh?"

"Nothing. So, why *aren't* you guys sharing a limo? Is your date too cool to go to the dance with regular people?"

I didn't understand why everyone assumed that just because Ryder was a big-time celeb, he had to be stuck-up. In all the time I'd known him (and yes, I realized that had been less than a month), he'd never pulled a diva move or acted like he was better than anyone else.

"It's not like that," I answered, frowning.

"So then, what's the deal?" Cade asked.

I paused. "I can't really tell *you.*"

"Seriously?"

"Seriously."

Cade blinked at me in surprise. "Okay. Well, I was just making conversation anyway." And with that he got up and began to walk back toward the gymnasium.

Was I hallucinating or did he seem a little...upset?

"It's not like I don't *want* to tell you. In fact, I'm dying to tell someone. Anyone, really," I said, standing up and following him.

"Then tell me," he said, like it was that simple.

Only it wasn't.

"I signed a contract swearing I wouldn't say anything. So, no matter how much it's killing me—" I mimicked hanging myself, "—I'm *legally* not allowed to talk about it. And if you were a teenage girl, you'd realize it's practically impossible for us to keep our mouths shut when it comes to things like this. So, yes, if I could tell you, I would. Happily."

Cade studied me as I finished my speech and then scratched his head as if I'd just tried to explain rocket science. He shook his head and turned away from me again.

"This dance is making everyone freaking nuts," he muttered.

I watched helplessly as Cade disappeared into the gym, and fought the urge to run after him and apologize. But what good would that do, if I still couldn't explain everything to him?

A week ago, I'd been bordering on euphoric over being asked to go to Homecoming by my biggest crush. I never thought that saying yes would cause this much drama. Now, my best friend was giving me the silent treatment, the only person on the dance committee that I could stand, thought I was headed for the loony bin, and I couldn't talk to anyone about any of it for fear that I'd get sued.

To top it all off, even if Ryder and I ended up having an amazing night, and realized that we were totally into each other...we couldn't even *do* anything about it. Because the last official day that people could bid on my first kiss was the day *after* the dance.

Which brought me to the other thing that had me freaked out: In two days I was going to be kissing someone. *My* lips would be touching someone else's. A boy's.

Holy Sundays at church. How did I get myself into all of this?

Groaning, I trudged back to finish setting up for the dance, wondering if I should be going at all.

Chapter Twenty-Two

I SLEPT UNTIL 11:30 the next day, feeling zero guilt over losing my whole morning to extra rest and non-complicated dreams. I couldn't even convince myself to get dressed, opting to stay in my pajamas as I padded around the house looking for something to calm my noisy stomach. Popping two frozen chocolate chip waffles into our toaster, I leaned against the counter and thought about the night before.

I hadn't gotten home from decorating the gym until well after one o'clock. And while there, I'd been doing some serious manual labor, so it wasn't surprising that I was still exhausted this morning. Between lifting props, hanging lights and streamers, assembling tables and carrying supplies in from Bree's mom's van, my body had gotten a serious workout. In fact, I felt a little like I'd been hit by a truck.

And that wasn't even the painful part. After Cade and I had our little talk out in the hallway, things hadn't been the same between us. By the time I'd made my way back into the gym, he'd wandered over to a girl I didn't recognize, and had immediately started chatting her up.

I was still feeling so guilty over the fact that I couldn't tell him about my plans before the dance that I didn't bother asking him to help me finish setting up the floor. So, I did it myself, taking two hours to do what should've only taken one. The few times I'd managed to steal glances at Cade, showed that he was enjoying himself with the cute brunette that wasn't me. I don't know why it bothered me, but it had.

When my waffles popped up, I threw them onto a plate and drenched them in a sea of syrup. It was exactly what I needed. Sugar always made me feel better.

And according to my mom, nearly all of life's ailments could be cured with a little chocolate. So, I figured I was killing two birds with one stone.

Or soothing my sores with sweets.

As I sat down in front of our big screen TV and burrowed myself into a comfy spot on our couch, I entertained the idea of staying there all day. Until it was time to get ready for the dance, of course.

And why shouldn't I? It wasn't like McCartney and Phin were coming over to get ready with me. They were both still giving me the cold shoulder over the whole limo thing, although I was pretty sure that Phin didn't even know why he was supposed to be mad at me. No doubt McCartney had informed him of the ban and he'd just gone along with it.

I laughed garishly as a cartoon character fought with sea creature on the screen in front of me. I had no idea what I was watching, but it was the perfect kind of brainless fluff I needed right then. Something that would keep my mind occupied, but not make it work too hard. I was pretty sure that it was going to hit me soon, that I was about to go to my first high school dance with someone I really liked—and who just happened to be a mega star. And when it did, I'd no doubt experience my second panic attack that month.

Yes. I'd say a distraction was definitely needed.

I pulled the blanket up to my chin and officially set my claim to the living room area. Flipping through the channels, I landed on one of my favorite movies, *Stick It*, and let myself get lost in the world of competitive gymnastics.

Why hadn't Mom ever put me in gymnastics? Then I'd be super-muscular and able to do flips while wearing a formal dress inside a mall. And even though the girls were always busy with training, they were the most hardcore athletes in the world *and* they ended up with guys in the end. Even the bitchy one.

A little after two, I finally dragged myself off of the couch and headed back upstairs to start getting ready. Reluctantly, I shed my comfy PJ's and plodded into my bathroom to take a shower. I turned on the faucet and then headed back into my room to hit play on my laptop. Paramore blared from my speakers as I danced my way back to the now steamy bathroom.

Once I was under the warm spray, I finally began to let myself think about what would be happening in less than a few hours. My stomach buzzed with nervous excitement. I had no idea what I was even supposed to do at a dance. Well, besides dance. And even though it was Ryder's first high school dance, and he wouldn't know the difference, I still felt like I had to do it *right*. Whatever that meant.

I had so many questions and no one to ask them to. Would Ryder think it was weird if my mom took pictures of us before we left? Was he supposed to pay for dinner because he was the guy? Or was I expected to pay for everything, since technically I'd invited him? If Ryder was my "date," did that mean that I wasn't allowed to dance with anyone else? Not that there was anyone else I wanted to dance with. Well, okay, if Cade asked me to dance, I wouldn't be opposed to it—but was that a dance no-no? And how should I greet Ryder when he arrived? Do I hug him? Shake his hand? Kiss him on the cheek like they did on TV? And I didn't even want to think about the end-of-the-night dilemma.

Before I could slip into full-on panic attack mode, I pushed my face under the steady stream and let the sound of the water drown out the noise in my head.

"Whoa, I never meant to break, but I got him where I want him now!" I sang, doing my best impression of an angry rocker chick.

Coming out of the bathroom, I let loose all the stress of the last few days and danced around my room, throwing my body around in a way that was neither cool nor rhythmic, and punching my fists in the air to the music. A few minutes later, I collapsed onto my bed, completely out of breath and a whole lot calmer. I turned down the music and set to work on transforming myself into a princess worthy of a royal ball.

At five after four, I heard the door ring downstairs and even though I'd been ready to go for a half hour, I waited impatiently on my bed as my mom answered it. In every teen movie I'd watched over the years, the girl made her date wait for a few minutes before making her grand entrance. And since my date was an actual movie star, I figured it was appropriate. When in Rome and all that.

"Arielle!" Mom yelled up the stairs to me. "Ryder's here! Come down and let me take some pictures before you guys leave!"

I prayed that she wouldn't say anything to embarrass me as I retrieved the tiny clutch off my dresser and took one last look at myself in the mirror. Every hair was in place, my makeup was impeccable and the dress looked even better on me than it had at the mall. But it still wasn't enough to calm my nerves.

I took my time walking down the stairs, partly for dramatic affect—I was hoping that Ryder would do that mouth-hanging-open, forget-to-breathe thing people sometimes did on TV—but also because I was secretly afraid of tripping over my three inch heels and tumbling all the way down to the bottom of the stairs, effectively breaking my neck before the date even started. So, I put one foot in front of the other and kept my focus on where I was stepping until I'd reached the bottom.

Only then did I dare look up at my date.

I was happy to see that I'd elicited the desired reaction from Ryder and flashed him a shy, but broad, smile. I almost swooned as I took in the sight of him standing just inside my living room, looking more like he belonged on the red carpet than at a small-town high school dance. His tux was a classic black style and fit him like a glove. In a glance, you could tell that it was made for him and not one that he rented from a local formal clothing shop like the other guys in my school would be doing. He looked sharp in a black skinny tie, which hung loosely around his neck in a slightly disheveled way.

But what made the outfit was his dress shirt, which was a bold, dark pink.

He caught me staring at his shirt and began to smooth out the material nervously. "I remembered that you said you were wearing pink," he explained. "Isn't this what people do for dances? They compliment the girl's dress? Or is that lame and I'm going to make us the laughing stock of your school?"

I put my hand over my mouth to keep from laughing. What he'd done was so sweet—and brave, because when the guys at school saw Ryder in a pink shirt, they were going to tease him mercilessly—that I actually wasn't sure what to say. Up until a few months ago, guys hadn't even realized I existed, so the fact that someone was taking my feelings into account for a change officially threw me off balance.

And to my surprise, I liked it.

"You look great," I said sincerely, my cheeks turning a shade that probably resembled my dress.

Ryder seemed relieved by this and immediately regained the confidence I was used to seeing him wear. Stepping forward, he handed me a purple box a little bit bigger than my fist, and urged me to open it.

Oooh, presents!

I opened the package and sucked in my breath at what was inside. Lying on a delicate satin pillow was the most elegant flower I'd ever seen. It was simple, white and had petals that were smooth and perfect. Its fragrance hit my senses like a sweet memory and I sighed with happiness.

"It's a Gardenia," Ryder said proudly. He leaned forward and plucked the corsage from its box and placed it on my wrist. "My sister once told me that Gardenias smelled like 'heaven on earth.' She used to go crazy over them when she was in high school."

"I can see why," I answered, bringing my wrist up to smell it again. "It's better than perfume."

When I looked up from my flower arrangement, I saw that Ryder was standing there, staring at me. Oh, God. Was I supposed to have gotten him something, too? Nobody had told me about this whole present exchange thing and now I was starting to look like the worst date ever. This was why you were supposed to get ready for dances with your friends...so they could make sure that you were prepared for *everything.*

I looked around frantically searching for something in the nearby vicinity that I could pass off as a present suitable for my Homecoming date. I was about to hand over either my mom's iPod which was laying next to her purse or the framed picture of me at my eighth grade graduation party, when Mom cleared their throat behind me.

"Arielle, here's the boutonniere *you asked* me to get for Ryder," she said, walking toward me with a small bag in her hand.

I had no idea what a *boutonniere* was, but I was so grateful to have something to give to Ryder that I didn't care if it turned out to be a fancy fanny pack. I took the bag from her and gingerly peeked inside.

"I know you wanted a lily, but they were all out. I had to go with a classic," she explained.

I smiled as I reached inside and grabbed the fragrant pink rose and displayed it to the room. It was small, and barely had a stem, but it was pretty.

Boys weren't supposed to be into flowers anyway, so maybe Ryder wouldn't care that he got a defected flower.

Keeping the smile on my face, I held out the flower to him, unsure of how this sort of thing usually went.

"Sweetie, it'll be easier if you put it *on* him," my mom interrupted. "Just make sure not to poke him with the pin as you secure it to his jacket."

I could tell Mom was saving me some serious embarrassment by discreetly explaining what I was supposed to do with the boutonniere.

She is so *getting cool mom points for this.*

I pulled the pin out of the stem of the flower, which I hadn't noticed was even there until my mom had mentioned it, and walked slowly toward my date.

"Be careful now," Ryder warned softly. "It's always been a big fear of mine to die at the hands of a needle-wielding crazy girl."

I tried to concentrate on pinning the flower to his lapel *without* drawing blood. It's never a good idea to make a guy bleed on your first date.

"Lucky for you, I'm not crazy, huh?"

"I don't know about that..."

I stopped what I was doing to look up at him challengingly. "Do you *really* think that's a wise thing to say right now? I mean, hello? Girl with sharp object here. I hardly think you're in a position to question *anyone's* sanity."

Ryder abruptly zipped his lip and watched with amused curiosity as I finally secured the flower—without stabbing him, I might add. When I was finished, I took a step back and admired my work. And the guy who wore it.

"Picture time!" my mom chimed in, reminding me that she was still in the room, witnessing our special moment.

Embarrassment spread across my face and I looked over at her with questioning eyes.

So much for the cool mom points.

"We were just going to get pictures at the dance," I said, attempting to keep my voice even. "Besides, I don't think we have enough time. We're supposed to be doing some stuff for the show before we go to the dance."

My mom's face dropped.

"Actually, Ms. Sawyer, we'd love to take a few pictures if you don't mind," Ryder piped up, looking at me and then back at my mom.

He must've seen the confused look on my face, because he moved toward me and lowered his voice. "I think the station wants to tape the whole process. The entrance, the corsage, the pictures...they're gonna want the whole deal. I told them I wanted to go in first. Alone. You know, so we could do this sans camera for a little privacy. But I think we'll have to go back and do it again, for them, if that's okay with you."

He looked at me hopefully and seemed to be slightly embarrassed at what he was asking me. I was guessing that for Ryder, the MTV crew was sort of like having parental units witnessing his first real high school experience. And no one *really* wanted their folks around for that.

"Yeah, sure. No problem!" I said enthusiastically to show him that he had no reason to feel self-conscious. As far as I was concerned, there was a huge difference between posing for your mom's digital camera and smiling for a reality show taping.

"You're the best," he answered, looking relieved.

I watched as Ryder walked across the room, pressing buttons on his phone as he went. Assuming he was letting the crew know they were good to go, I turned and walked over to my mom.

"Thanks for getting the booty-thing," I said appreciatively. "How'd you know I'd need one?"

"It's that Jedi-mom-mind. I know all sorts of things. That's what moms are for, you know."

I raised a skeptical brow.

"Also, I was a teenager once, too. Which means I went to dances with hunky guys and gave away my fair share of boutonnieres."

"Is that what they called it back in the olden days?" I joked.

She looked confused for a minute. When she finally realized what I was alluding to, her eyes grew wide and she shoved me lightly.

"Arielle Anne Sawyer!"

I held up my hands in defeat. "Kidding."

I was still laughing as the crew walked through our front door and began setting up lights and equipment around our living room. Nothing could've prepared me for the sight of so much clutter in our house. I looked over at Mom, expecting to see the panic in her face because of all the people traipsing around. Instead, she was smiling warmly at the crew and asking if she could get anyone a drink.

Shocked by her reaction, I made my way over to Ryder who was still texting on his phone. Once I reched him, he flipped his phone shut and turned his attention to me.

"You sure you're okay with this?"

Was I ready to have my first Homecoming dance exploited by some crazy reality show?

"Let's get this show on the road," I answered.

"Okay people, let's take it from the top of the stairs," a crew member yelled out across the living room.

Chapter Twenty-Three

"I'M SO SORRY about all of that," Ryder apologized once we were inside the stretch limo that MTV had rented for us.

After we'd finished filming at my house, and the crew had gotten the shots they needed for the show, Ryder and I had jumped into the car that was waiting outside, and headed to a restaurant two towns over for dinner before the dance. It was a good thing they'd gotten us a limo, because the cameras followed us inside and taped us as we made small talk and joked around.

It was interesting being on this side of a reality show. I'd always been a fan of the programs in the past, mostly because I was dying to see what it was like to live a celebrity's life. And I know everyone says it's scripted or that reality TV isn't really reality at all, but I didn't buy it. What I was beginning to see is that it's real—to a certain extent.

Like, they'd have us start talking and if one of us said something that was funny, one of the producers would ask us to say it again to make sure they had it. Or if they felt like our conversation was getting a little stale, they'd "suggest" topics for us to talk about. Some of these included celebrity breakdowns and comebacks, what we thought really went on at high school dances and whether the vampire thing was totally dead in its coffin.

Now that we were finally in the car alone and on our way over to the school, we found ourselves falling into a comfortable banter. One that didn't include any of the previously mentioned topics. Instead, our conversation turned to Ryder, his work and the many rumors that were flying around about him.

"Did you really kiss your male co-star when you auditioned for *A New Dawn*?" I asked, unable to hide my desire for a little dirt. "I was looking for it on YouTube, but couldn't find it. Perez Hilton swears he's seen it, though. So, what's the real deal?"

"You went all You-Tubular on me?" Ryder teased. "If you *must* know, there *was* a lip-lock and it *was* between me and a co-star. But it *wasn't* who you think it was."

"Who was it?" I practically shrieked with delight. "Come on, tell me. I promise I won't say anything. I already kept this whole night a secret, which made my friends all pissed at me, by the way. I think I deserve something for keeping my lips zipped."

I crossed my arms and pouted jokingly, while giving him my best version of puppy dog eyes.

"Aw, don't look at me like that," Ryder said, looking pained. "Fine. But it's not in my nature to kiss and tell. Even if it was an acting thing."

"Yeah, yeah, yeah. Spill!"

Ryder laughed and then looked around the empty limo dramatically before leaning over and whispering the name in my ear.

"No *freaking* way!" I screeched, causing Ryder to throw his hands over his ears. My mouth dropped open as I tried to picture the scenario that was now in my head. "Was that...."

"Awkward?" he finished for me. "A little, but that's how it is when you're doing kissing scenes. It's just a job. And not nearly as romantic as it seems."

I shot him a disbelieving look. No way him and his co-star had stopped canoodling when the cameras had been put away. The scene was practically famous among people my age and even earned "Best Kiss" at the MTV Movie Awards. Even *I* wasn't stupid enough to think you could put on a performance like that and *not* enjoy it just a little bit.

I totally loved Ryder, but even *he* wasn't that good of an actor.

"Seriously," he insisted. "When you're shooting stuff like that, it's really clinical. You're given directions on where to put your head, how soft or hard to kiss, and when to hit your marks. You're concentrating so much on everything you have to do, that you forget you're even kissing someone in the first place. It's not as fun as people think it is."

"And what about you? What happens if someone buys your first kiss, and you think he's kind of cool and cute—but you aren't really sure if you like him? If you go through with the kiss, wouldn't you question whether you only did it because he *paid* for it? Or what it would've been like if it had happened organically? Do you really want your first kiss to be like a business transition?"

Huh. When Ryder put it in those terms, he sort of had a point. Did I really want my first kiss to be with someone who happened to have saved up enough of his allowance to buy my affections, instead of because he liked me?

But the alternative was that I might never be kissed if I didn't go through with it. And if I had to go through the rest of the year watching everyone couple up but me, I might have to claw my eyes out or bite the bullet and join a convent already.

To be honest, I wasn't sure which would be more painful.

"Saved by the bell, I guess," he said, interrupting my thoughts. Ryder was pointing outside the car, and I turned to see that we'd arrived at the school. The limo slowed to a stop about 100 feet from the gymnasium and I watched as my peers passed by in their dressiest duds. A group of kids chatted excitedly, making jokes and fooling around as they walked toward the front doors. I felt a pang of sadness and guilt as they stopped to take a group picture, capturing the moment with their phones.

I suddenly realized how much I wished McCartney and Phin were there. If we'd shared a limo like we'd planned, we could've taken silly photos and giggled as we whispered secrets about how cute our dates were. But instead, they'd gone on without me, and my night hadn't been the same without them.

No wonder I haven't been kissed yet. I'm sitting here in this ginormous car with a date who's more famous than Kim Kardashian's booty, and all I can think about is how I wished I *wasn't alone with him.*

"You okay?" Ryder asked, picking up on my silence.

I forced a smile. "Yeah, I'm fine. Just wondering if my friends are inside."

Ryder looked through the back window at the MTV van that had parked behind us. "All we've got left to do, is tape our pre-dance thoughts, and then we can find your friends and get our groove on," he said, flashing me a dazzling smile.

"Pre-dance thoughts?" I asked, confused.

"Like a confessional. It's where we talk to the camera about our expectations, what we're feeling, that sort of thing. Then, we'll do a wrap-up session after the dance and that'll be it," he said. "Don't worry, the producers will prompt you with questions and you won't have to answer anything you don't want to."

"Okay," I agreed uneasily. "Where do we do this?"

"You stay here and I'll do mine in the van," he said. He hesitated before reaching out and placing his hand on mine softly. "You've been really great through this whole thing. I know how hard it can be the first time you have cameras in your face 24/7. I'm impressed. You're handling it like a pro."

"Good to know all those episodes of the Kardashians are coming in handy," I answered jokingly. Even as I laughed, I was very much aware of the fact that Ryder was still holding my hand. And I would've done just about anything he asked as long as it meant I got to hold onto him longer. "Now I know how the celebs feel."

"You have no idea."

Ryder squeezed my hand and exited the limo with a lingering backward glance, leaving me with a tingly feeling inside. But before I could enjoy the feeling, a producer appeared at the door and motioned for a camera to be set up inside. Once again, the bright lights were directed at me and I put on my game face.

"Okay, Arielle, why don't you start by telling us how the night has been so far," the guy behind the camera said.

"Um, well, everything's been great. Dinner was really nice and it's been so much fun getting to know Ryder better. He's a really nice guy and easy to talk to. And this limo is...well, it's bigger than my room!"

"That's great. Now, why don't you talk a little about what you're looking forward to tonight."

"Let's see. I guess, just hanging out with my friends. You haven't met them yet, but they're really great. McCartney and Phin, those are their names. McCartney's going with this guy, Zack? He's a soccer player and I think she really likes him, even though she plays it off like it's no big deal. And Phin's going with," I paused as I searched my brain for the info. "Actually, I'm not sure who he decided to go with. But it doesn't even matter who he takes, he'll be so goofy that he'll be our comic relief for the night."

I couldn't seem to stop my rambling, so I just continued, unloading everything I'd wanted to talk to my friends about all week. Before long, I'd even forgotten that everything was being caught on film.

"You know, originally I was supposed to share one of these," I motioned around the cabin. "We had it all planned out and everything, but then I had to back out because...well, because you guys were going to be taping everything, and I had to sign that paper saying I wouldn't tell anyone, and you made it clear that I couldn't even tell my two best friends. To be honest, they're kind of a little ticked at me right now, on account of the broken plans and all. So, I guess I'm just hoping they'll overlook everything and that we can all still have fun tonight. I want our threesome back. They're the best friends I've ever had and nothing's worth losing them."

When I finished, I took a deep breath, feeling like I'd just purged myself of all of my worries. Confessionals had nothing on these camera sessions.

The producer stared at me, his jaw slightly ajar in what I assumed was part awe and part shock. I felt my cheeks start to heat up. I was beginning to think that maybe there was such a thing as too much information.

I cleared my throat. "I mean…I'm looking forward to hanging out with Ryder and dancing with my friends!" I started over, this time in my most perky, I'm-a-teenager-with-no-problems voice.

"Thanks," the producer answered, slowly. "I think we got it."

And then they were out of there so fast, you'd think the car was on fire or something. I felt bad about going all Oprah on them and spilling my guts like that, so I slid across the seat and followed them out into the parking lot to apologize. The last thing I wanted was to be portrayed as a psycho on national TV.

Only, Phin and McCartney were suddenly right there in front of me. I almost tackled them right then and there, I was so happy to see them. Then I remembered that they were still upset with me and looked away guiltily. My gaze fell on the camera crew that was still walking away, confirming that I had the worst timing *ever.* I turned back to my friends and could see that this was going to be so much worse than the limo thing.

"Hey guys," I said weakly. "You just get here?"

Even if McCartney hadn't been wearing smoky eye makeup that left her looking dark and edgy, I would've still been intimidated by the harsh glare she was sending my way. And one glance at Phin showed me that he wasn't far behind McCartney in the anger department.

"I'm so glad you're finally here!" I said, taking a step toward them. Phin and McCartney's dates stepped around them, and then stopped when they saw the three of us in a standoff. "If you want to wait a minute, Ryder will be finished and we can all go in together."

I was praying they'd say, "Of course! Let's go get our party on!" but I had a feeling that was just wishful thinking on my part. Instead, my friends gave me the stink eye, and promptly turned on their heels and walked away without a word.

"So, I guess that's a no then?" I muttered, my excitement fading. Then, I took off after them to try and apologize. "Come on you guys, don't go! If you let me explain..."

But they were already too far away and I couldn't exactly ditch my date before we'd even gotten to the dance. So, with a final look at my friends, I headed back toward the limo and my date.

Ryder was leaning up against the MTV van watching the whole thing. If I hadn't been so completely horrified that he'd seen my friends reject me, then I would've noticed how incredibly hot he looked standing there like that. When I got close enough, I could see the concern on his face.

"Everything alright?"

I shook my head no, but said weakly, "Yeah. I guess. It wouldn't be a dance without a little drama, right?"

"Sounds about right," he said. "Wanna talk about it? I'm not sure you know this, but I'm pretty good at the drama. *I'll kick your butt for kissing my girlfriend! You never should've been named Homecoming King! How was I supposed to know she was really my cousin?* See?"

I raised my eyebrows at his impromptu performance.

"Hey, I've been a brooding teenager in two different TV shows and three movies. I can *do* drama," he said with a wink. Then he handed me my purse, which I'd left in the car when I'd scrambled out of there to run after the producers. I smiled at Ryder as I placed the strap onto my shoulder and then took his outstretched arm. "Why don't we head on over and you can tell me all about it on the way?"

I nodded in agreement and launched into the story as the camera crew followed behind us, capturing the whole moment on film.

Chapter Twenty-Four

"**YOU DID ALL** of this?" Ryder asked in awe.

We were standing just inside the gymnasium after handing our tickets to a few freshman Bree had suckered into working the door. Ryder looked around the room, taking in the different decorations and pointing out all the things he saw that fit our theme. He seemed impressed and excited and happy all at once. It was really cute.

"I didn't do it all myself," I said. "But yeah, I helped put it together. You don't think it's too cheesy?"

"Are you kidding? This is more elaborate than P Diddy's after-party."

I was grateful for the dim lighting, because I was blushing so hard from his compliment that I could have doubled as one of the Chinese lanterns we'd hung from the ceiling.

"Well, I hope everyone else feels the same way," I said.

And for the most part, everyone *did* seem to be having a good time. Music was blaring from speakers that had been set up around the room. On top of that, a lively chatter served as background noise to the party atmosphere. A hundred people were already inside, gyrating on the dance floor, lounging around tables and snacking on food, and at least fifty more were lined up outside waiting to get in. Based on the smiles on everyone's faces, I'd say we'd planned a pretty great party.

"I don't think you need to worry about that," Ryder agreed.

We watched as a group of kids standing nearby, exploded into laughter, and then posed for a few selfies. Two of the girls pressed their cheeks together and made kissy faces at the camera. I started to smile but felt it fade as I was reminded that *my* friends and I weren't doing the same. The sadness came flooding back.

"Do you want to find them?" Ryder asked, reading my mind. "Your friends? Maybe they're waiting for you somewhere in here."

"I doubt it," I said, frowning. Then, I forced a smile. After all, I *was* here with my dream guy. "I'll let 'em cool down for a while. You want to go find a seat?"

"Sure," Ryder said.

We walked toward the far right corner of the dance floor and snagged an empty table. I placed my purse on the tabletop and sat down, overly conscious of how short my dress was when I did so. Crossing my legs tightly together, I sat up straighter as Ryder filled the chair beside me. Then he scooted his seat closer to mine and leaned in so we could talk.

Or did he want to be closer to me?

"So, what are you supposed to do at these things? Do we sit on the sidelines and make fun of all the people dancing, because we're too cool for it all? Or do we get out there and break out a choreographed dance like they do in the movies?" he asked, mischievously.

He was so close to me that I could smell the clean scent of his shampoo. I had a strong desire to lay my head on his shoulder and stay there for the rest of the night. Who cares if other people thought we were lame? Of course, that wouldn't have really been fair to Ryder. He'd come because he wanted the classic school dance experience. And he wouldn't get that sitting in the corner with me. Still, I wasn't exactly ready for *Dancing with the Stars* just yet, so any fancy footwork was out of the question.

"Well, since we didn't practice any eight counts before we came, I think that doing an elaborate dance number is out," I answered, with a laugh. "And as for making fun of people... I think that'll be kind of hard to do when everyone's staring at us."

I'd noticed it when we'd first made our entrance. Ryder had to have seen it, too. You'd have to be blind not to. All eyes had turned to us as we'd walked through the door and had followed our every move since. People were whispering and pointing, a few were even brazen enough to take out their cameras and snap a few shots in our direction. I couldn't exactly blame them, though. Even if they didn't recognize Ryder—which, let's face it, was a pretty big "if"—the fact that there was a camera and lighting crew following us around would've clued them in.

The whole thing was totally weird, and I began to feel supremely awkward having all those eyes focused on me. I wanted to tell them to mind their own business but had a feeling it wouldn't go over too well. Besides, it was too loud in there for people to hear me anyway. Instead, I turned away from our audience and focused on Ryder.

"How do you deal with this every day?" I asked. "Doesn't it freak you out, having all these strangers staring at you?"

Ryder glanced over at a group of people who'd been dancing together just a few minutes before, but were now fully focused on us. He turned back to me and shrugged. "You know, I don't really notice it anymore."

"How could you *not* notice that," I exclaimed, pointing at a few sophomore girls who were giggling and making a scene not six feet away from us. "There's no way you could avoid the elephant in this room."

"I'll admit, it takes some getting used to. When people first started to recognize me, and they'd stop me on the street for a picture or an autograph, it was surreal. I mean, I'm just *me*. Some kid from Oregon who happened to get lucky and land a few roles," he said. "And suddenly I can't go to the mall without being bombarded by girls who swear they love me, and guys who call me gay or whatever. Even parents would stop me in the middle of eating at a restaurant to ask me for autographs for their kids."

"It got to the point where I was having a really hard time dealing with it all. I started to get anxious about going out in public, and began to hole up in my house, only coming out when I had to do a gig or my family forced me to. Then, I talked to one of my co-stars about it, and he told me just to imagine that I was somewhere I felt safe and happy, and then continue on with my life. So, I tried it and things started to get easier."

It was solid advice, and I could see how it might help, but I wasn't convinced I could pull it off. Right now I just couldn't deal.

"You want some punch?" I asked him. I *was* a little thirsty, but I was mostly looking for an excuse to get away from the spotlight for a few minutes to collect myself and catch my breath. I sort of felt bad about leaving Ryder on his own, but like he'd said, he barely noticed it any more.

Getting up from my seat, I click-clacked my way over to where the refreshments were set up. Checking out the spread in front of me, I had to admit that it was all pretty impressive. There were salty treats like chips and pretzels, teamed up with sweets like M&Ms, brownies and fudge. Fruit and veggies balanced out the junk food and there was an assortment of dark and clear sodas to choose from. I grabbed a plate and began to pile it up. Then I filled two cups with soda and turned to leave.

And ran right into Bree.

"Hey, A! I'm so glad you're finally here! You look amazing! Is your dress Marc Jacobs?" she bombarded me with her questions like a trigger-happy firing squad.

"Hi, Bree," I said, trying to balance everything in my hands without dropping it. "Um, thanks. You look great, too. Are you having fun?"

"OMFG! People are saying that this is the best dance the school's ever had. Even better than when Susie Ferguson was in charge," she gloated excitedly. "But enough about that. Why didn't you tell me that you were bringing *Ryder Diggs* to the dance! If I'd known, we could've gotten at least two hundred more people here, easy. We probably could've even gotten the local news to come. How cool would that have been?"

I stared at her dumbly, as I saw the wheels turning in her head. Did she seriously not recognize that alerting the paparazzi was exactly the *last* thing we needed? Ryder and I had enough people following us around, I couldn't imagine adding flashing cameras and yelling strangers to the mix.

"It's not that big of a deal, Bree," I answered. I knew this wasn't totally true. That having a well-known actor crash our dance was probably the biggest thing to happen in our boring town. But I wanted her and everyone else to leave us alone. Was that too much to ask?

Apparently it was.

"Are you crazy? This is *huge*! Like, Justin Bieber huge," Bree said, her eyes widening. "Do you think he'd perform something from *Night Light*?"

"I don't think he was planning to perform tonight—"

"Can you ask him anyway? I'm sure he won't mind."

"I wouldn't really feel comfortable—" I said, and glanced back in Ryder's direction helplessly.

But Ryder was no longer alone. My eyes narrowed as I saw a tiny blond standing in front of him, hands on her hips suggestively. My heart dropped as she threw back her head to laugh and I realized that it was Kristi. And from the look on his face, Ryder wasn't recoiling in disgust like I would've hoped. In fact, he seemed to be enjoying the company.

Of all the girls he could be talking to, it had to be her. Seriously, why did God hate me?

Leaving Bree to stare after me, I marched over to them, no longer paying attention to the drinks that were sloshing all over me. As I approached, I could hear Kristi's scratchy voice as she fawned all over my date.

"No, *really*. You were my first crush! I saw *The Secrets We Keep* a hundred times in the theater," she cooed. "I thought you were *brilliant* in it."

I resisted the urge to gag. Stepping in between them, I carefully set down the plate of treats and handed Ryder his drink. Then, I turned around and blinked at Kristi, like I was noticing her for the first time.

"Oh. Hey, Kristi," I said flatly. "This is Ryder. *My* date."

"We met," she answered, fluttering her eyelashes at him.

"Great," I said between clenched teeth. "So, who are you here with? Please don't tell me you're here *alone*?"

Please tell me you're here alone, please tell me you're here alone, please tell me...

"Of course I'm not here by myself!" she said as if I'd just suggested she shave her head and start dating a math nerd. Kristi glanced around the room halfheartedly. "My date's around here somewhere."

"Really?" I asked, desperately wanting her to leave. "Maybe you should go find him."

"There he is!" she said, waving in the direction of the stage. The guy, who'd just been lounging up against the wall, saw Kristi motioning to him, and he began to saunter over. Lights were shooting around the dance floor like we were in a club, making it impossible to see who it was. But the guy's walk was slow and cool, like he wasn't in any hurry to get to us. He seemed to almost glide across the floor.

Wait. I *know* that walk.

My eyes widened as the figure got closer. After a few agonizing seconds, Cade came into focus in front of us. His hands were characteristically shoved in his pockets, but that's where the similarities ended. The tux he wore fit him perfectly, hugging all the right places. He looked sharp. Like James Bond or Brad Pitt. You could tell that his hair had just been trimmed and he'd shaved earlier that day. He looked softer somehow. I wouldn't have even recognized him if it hadn't been for that requisite broody look on his face.

Cade stared at me, and then over at Ryder, and then back at me. Though probably no one else had noticed, I could see the flash of intensity in his eyes as he recognized Ryder.

"Arielle," he said way too seriously.

"Hey, Cade," I answered.

I was suddenly furious at both of them for daring to come to the dance together. No doubt, Kristi's motivation had been revenge and all-around torture. Somehow she'd found out that Cade and I'd been hanging out together lately, and figured that by inserting herself between us, she'd succeed in making my life even more miserable than it already was.

And Cade? He was just mad that I refused to tell him about the MTV thing, and was trying to get back at me for it. Why he even cared, I couldn't figure out. No matter who was responsible for the betrayal, my night was slowly heading downhill.

"Kristi was just telling me a funny story about you," Ryder said.

"Oh, really?" I answered as sweetly as I could muster considering how mad I was. "And what story was that?"

"You know, about the guy you tipped over in the cafeteria," he answered, chuckling as he pictured it. "She said he deserved it and that the whole thing was hilarious."

That was enough to knock me off my pedestal. "Really?" I asked, turning to her incredulously.

"Sure," she said, the faintest hint of annoyance in her voice. "It's not *your* fault no one wants to kiss you. And Dan certainly shouldn't try to take advantage of your newfound social status."

What she said wasn't totally mean, but it wasn't exactly nice, either. So I just nodded my head slightly.

"Not that I can blame Dan for noticing the change in you. You *were* always hanging out with those two losers before—he's a big step up for you, by the way," she said, nodding at Ryder, who was now busy having what appeared to be a staring contest with Cade. "Speaking of the socially-challenged, where *are* your friends?"

"Why don't you go find someone else to harass, Kristi?" I asked, growing tired of her. "I'm sure your minions are waiting for you to return to your lair."

A devilish smile spread across her lips. It was the eeriest sight and filled me with icy fear. "Aw, are you and the rest of the Musketeers fighting? What? Did *McCartwheel* borrow your clothes without asking or something?"

"I'm serious, Kristi. Why don't you just leave," I hissed, my blood beginning to boil.

"It must suck to be rejected—again," she sneered.

"Let's dance?" Ryder swooped in, just as I was weighing the pros and cons of going all WWE on my nemesis.

I felt Ryder take my hand, and then he was leading me out to the floor where a slow song had begun to play. When we were safely on the opposite side of the gym, Ryder pulled me toward him and linked his arms behind my back loosely. After a few minutes of swaying to the music, I felt my shoulders start to relax and my anger subside.

I rested my head against Ryder's chest and exhaled deeply, letting go of the last five minutes.

"So...*that* was intense," Ryder interrupted, when I'd had a chance to calm down. What's up with those two? She's straight out of *Mean Girls* and he's—did you two date or something?"

"Me and Cade? No way. We're just on Homecoming Committee together. Why?"

"Hmmm? Nothing," Ryder mumbled into my hair. "Just a vibe I got."

I closed my eyes and let myself get lost in the music. In the moment. I imagined all the drama of the weeks before melting away and tried to focus on the fact that I was experiencing one of the coolest nights of my life. A grin grew across my face without me even realizing it.

Then, I opened my eyes and saw that Cade was twenty feet away, staring at me while he danced with Kristi.

Chapter Twenty-Five

"MIND IF WE sit this next one out? Between drinking all that soda and dancing around, I feel like I'm gonna pop," Ryder yelled over the music.

"Sure. I have to go to the bathroom, anyway," I answered. Realizing how unromantic it was to announce to your very cute date that you needed to pee, I quickly backtracked. "I mean, I think I need to check my makeup."

Ryder just cocked his head at me and smiled. "Okay. You go...check your makeup. And I'll meet you back here in ten?"

"Sounds good. But remember, you promised to show me the dance you did in *Tiki Torch*. All of it. Even the ending 360 to a split."

Ryder's face grew serious as he started to back away. "I don't know what you're talking about," he shouted, innocently.

"You're such a liar!"

I laughed as he motioned that he couldn't hear me over the music. When he disappeared into the men's room, I headed in the opposite direction. I was still riding my Ryder-high when I pushed open the heavy door and slipped into the brightly lit girl's bathroom. As it closed behind me, the music lowered to a dull thumping, and was replaced with a high-pitched ringing in my ears.

Appreciating the relative quiet of the room, I walked over to one of the porcelain sinks and rested my hands on the basin. As much fun as I was having with Ryder, being "on" in front of all these people was exhausting. I mean, I knew that most likely everyone was watching Ryder. But even if they weren't watching *my* every move, they sort of were, since I was with Ryder as he took his every move.

Except for right now, while he was in the bathroom, and I was lucky enough to be in here, alone.

I jumped as I heard the toilet flush in the last stall and turned to see who was there. The door opened and my stomach sunk as I saw who it was. I had to look down at my hands on the sink to steady myself.

"Hey, McCartney," I said, hoping she'd had a change of heart.

No response. Unless you counted the glare she shot me in the reflection of the mirror. Guess she was still mad after all.

"Come on, Cart. Can we *please* call off the Cold War, already?" I asked, facing her as she washed her hands.

Nothing.

"Fine. You don't have to talk to me, but you *do* have to listen. Look, *I'm sorry* that I couldn't go with you guys in the limo. You have no idea how much I wanted to be there with you. But the truth is, MTV is taping our date for a segment they're producing, and they told me that I couldn't tell anyone about it. I think they were worried that the paparazzi would find out and ruin the night…I even had to sign a contract promising I wouldn't tell you or anyone else about it."

"Oh, well, if you signed a contract…" McCartney said, sarcastically.

"How many times do I have to say I'm sorry for you to believe me? All I've wanted to do tonight is hang out with you and Phin," I pleaded. "It hasn't been the same without you."

"If that were true then you should've been honest with us from the beginning. Contract or no contract," McCartney shot back as she stalked over to the door to leave. "Face it, Arielle. You've changed. And *not* in a good way."

Her comment hit me like a punch to the gut. We hadn't fought like this since the great Santa debate of 2008: "Is he real or is he really our parents?" That one had lasted five days. At the time, I was sure we'd never talk again. But we had. This time, however, was a different story.

Because I was currently *furious*.

Practically on her heels, I stomped after McCartney huffily, rejoining the thumpa-thumpa sounds of the dance floor.

"Have you gone mental?" I screeched at her, thankful the music was playing loudly enough to drown out most of the scene I was about to make. "You're just *jealous* because for the first time in the history of our friendship, people are paying more attention to *me* than they are to *you*!"

As soon as I said it, I regretted it. McCartney grew quiet with shock.

When she recovered a few moments later, her eyes narrowed, looking angrier than I'd ever seen her before. It was then that I noticed the camera crew posted just a few feet away from us. And they were capturing our entire confrontation. I looked over at the round lens nervously and then back at McCartney.

I need to get us away from these cameras before we say anything we regret...

Too late.

"Do you *really* think I want to be like you? You're famous for your *inexperience*. And the only reason anyone is paying attention to you tonight is because you're here with *Ryder*."

Her words were harsh and powerful. I'd never thought McCartney was capable of hurting me like this. I knew the tears were coming even before they started to fall. Fighting the pain that was building in the back of my throat, I fled from McCartney and the cameras.

By the time I got back to our table, I was out of breath and out of time. Tears were streaming down my face, taking my makeup along with them. I snatched up my purse, telling Ryder that I had to leave, and then took off toward the door without looking back to see if he was following me. The throngs of people around me were a blur as I passed them on my way to safety. Someone called out my name, but I was so focused on escaping that I didn't turn to see who it was.

The cool night air hit my wet cheeks, making me instantly frozen. But I didn't care. As I tore through the parking lot in search of where we'd parked, I knew that things would never be the same. Not just because McCartney was mad at me, but because I knew that in a way she was right. I *had* changed. Still, I couldn't imagine my life without her and Phin as my best friends.

I replayed everything McCartney had said that night. If I was such a horrible person, then why had they been my friend in the first place? And hello? The whole kiss-selling project was their idea! It's not like I would've come up with it on my own. It wasn't my style. My friends had created this situation, so how could they be upset with the outcome?

"Arielle!" Ryder called out from behind me.

I slowed down, but didn't stop. My chest and head were throbbing, and my body shaking, but all I could think about was getting home—as far away from McCartney, Phin, Crazy Kristi and Cade, that I could get.

"Arielle, slow down," Ryder pleaded, grabbing my hand to force me to meet his pace. "What happened back there? Are you all right? Why are you crying?"

I sniffled, not quite able to take a full breath on account of my extreme sobbing. If my brain hadn't been so messy, I might've been embarrassed that I was having a mini-breakdown in front of a movie star. But acting wasn't my strong suit.

"Thanks, Ryder, but I don't really want to talk about it right now. Do you mind if we go home?" I managed to get out as we reached the limo.

"Of course," he answered, looking concerned. He held the door open for me, taking my hand as I stepped inside and collapsed onto the nearest seat. Speaking quietly with the driver, and then exchanging a few words with the camera crew and producers, he somehow got them all to leave us alone. Sliding into the car behind me, Ryder gently put his arm around me and pulled me into him protectively.

"It's gonna be okay," he said soothingly. "I promise. Everything will look better in the morning."

I wanted to believe him, but I had the sneaking suspicion that things might look even worse in the light of day.

For about twenty seconds after waking up the next morning, I was happy. My lips formed into a smile and I lingered on the memory of the dream I'd been having before I'd woken up.

Then, I was drop-kicked back to reality as I recalled the events of the night before. My grin quickly disappeared. I contemplated forcing myself back to sleep so I wouldn't have to deal with everything. But it was Sunday, and that meant Mom was making her signature double-stuffed French toast; the kind she insisted weren't considered junk food if we ate them together. I usually ignored the lack of logic and happily scarfed down the desert-as-breakfast meal, but as my nerves started to pick up, so did my nausea.

As I pulled myself up into a sitting position and glanced around my room, it was hard to ignore the collateral damage of my emotional breakdown the night before. My dress lay in a heap on the floor beside my bed, collecting wrinkles on the already wrinkled material. It was too late to save it now, so I left it there, and surveyed the rest of the mess. I located my heels over by the door, scuffed up from where I'd thrown them against the wall after prying them off my throbbing feet. My purse somehow made it onto my desk, but the contents had all spilled out.

The familiar ping that alerted me to new e-mails came from my computer. With a grumble, I threw my covers off and trudged over to my desk. Sitting down, I pulled my knees to my chest before clicking on my screen and looking at my inbox. As I scanned the list, I began to feel sick to my stomach for the second time that morning. There were e-mails from McCartney, eBay, and one from Cade.

Without even bothering to look at them, I closed out of my e-mail and turned my back on it all. Why would I give McCartney the chance to tell me off again? Or force myself to deal with Cade's brooding, even though he had no good reason to be upset? And eBay? That stupid site had brought me nothing but frustration. Just *thinking* about kissing someone after all of this made me want to forget the whole thing. Let's put it this way: Becoming a nun was starting to look like a viable option.

If kissing was going to cause this many problems, then maybe I was better off without it.

I forced myself to go through the motions of getting up, heading to the bathroom to brush my teeth and wash my face. As I stared at my reflection in the mirror, I noticed with horror that I had huge bags under my eyes. Probably a result of all the crying I'd done. In short, I looked scary.

Pulling on an old sweatshirt and slipping my feet into my softest pair of slippers, I followed the familiar noises of my mom bustling around the kitchen. She didn't see me right away, but eventually turned around when she heard me pull out a chair and sit down.

"Hi sweetie! I hope you're hungry. I'm making Triple-Stuffed French Toast this morning. I figured you might need a little extra sugar burst after boogying down last night," she said, grinning at me as she threw the dirty mixing bowls into the sink. "I can't wait to hear all about it!"

My response was to place my forehead down on the top of the table. I prayed that she wouldn't push the subject. But either her mom-dar was on the fritz or her parental intuition had screamed for her to interfere, because she wasn't having it.

"Uh, oh. What happened?" I groaned as she asked it.

"Do we really have to do this now? It's still early and I'm really tired," I answered, hoping she'd take pity on me and just leave me alone.

"Well, we can either talk about this now while we eat this amazing breakfast I just slaved over, and try to figure out how to fix whatever is bothering you. Or you can choose *not* to tell me, which will result in me repeatedly asking you about it all day long, until you give in," she said as she walked over to the fridge and pulled something off the shelf. Returning to the table, she placed a cold can of Red Bull in front of me, but kept her hand on it for leverage.

I couldn't believe that she was blackmailing me into telling her what happened! My own mother. I was shocked. I was outraged. And to be honest, I was a little impressed that she'd gone with a more direct strategy than her usual reverse psychology bit.

I wanted to refuse, but between the smells that were coming from the frying pan (the tri-fecta of chocolate, bananas and peanut butter) and my extreme need for caffeine, I reluctantly gave in.

"Fine," I said, without energy. I snatched the Red Bull from her hand and popped the top. "The dance was a disaster."

"How so?" Mom asked as she walked over to the stove to flip our breakfast.

"Well, everything was fine until we got to the dance. Ryder was the perfect date. We went to this really nice restaurant for dinner..."

"What'd you get?"

"Ravioli."

My mom nodded her approval and then motioned for me to go on.

"And I even started to get used to the cameras following us around the whole time. But then when we got to the dance, I ran into McCartney and Phin, who are officially pissed at me."

"Why?"

"Because I didn't ride in the limo with them to the dance," I said, shrugging. "I guess they felt like I ditched them or something. And then when I showed up with an entire TV crew—that I didn't tell them about—it pushed them over the edge."

"Did you explain that you *couldn't* tell them?"

I rolled my eyes. "I tried to. But then McCartney accused me of *changing* and then said some really mean things about me while the cameras were taping. I was so humiliated that I ran out of there before the dance was even over."

"I'm sorry, baby," she answered, giving me a tight hug.

As she rubbed my back, she grew silent. Which was unusual for her. Mom *always* had an opinion.

"What?" I asked, knowing that I was about to be "shrink-ed."

"Well, I was just thinking that McCartney is...kind of right," she said carefully.

Are you kidding me? What was this, bash Arielle weekend? I looked at my mom incredulously.

"Hear me out," she answered, searching my face. "You *have* changed, Arielle. Over the past month, you've grown more self-assured, confident and adventurous. You've come out of your shell, and for the first time, you've really stepped out from behind McCartney and Phin's shadows and into your own spotlight."

I blinked in surprise. Was it possible Mom was right? Had I changed that much? Sure, I'd been more outgoing in general lately. I mean, going on that talk show and getting back at Dan Stevenson for spreading those rumors about me—the old me would never have done all that. And it *was* sort of true that I hadn't been as dependent on McCartney or Phin lately. Before the last few weeks, I never would've been able to survive a whole night alone with a guy as cute as Ryder, let alone as famous. And agreeing to be on the Dance Committee? Forget about it. Before, I only would've signed up if McCartney and Phin were doing it, too.

So, maybe I had changed...slightly. But I couldn't see how being more self-sufficient and sociable would be a bad thing.

"McCartney sort of said the same thing to me," I confessed. "Only she wasn't as nice about it."

"I bet she was just hurt and scared, and that made her say some things she didn't exactly mean," Mom said.

"Nope, I'm pretty sure she meant it," I said recalling how mad she'd been. "Besides, what could she possibly be scared about?"

My mom turned off the stove and brought over the ginormous plate of French toast, placing it in the middle of the table. I grumpily snagged a few pieces of the stuffed bread and slathered it in syrup. Across the table, my mom did the same.

"Did you ever think that maybe she's scared that you're going to outgrow your friendship and pretty soon you won't need her anymore? Or maybe she's worried that you'll move on without her?" Mom answered, between mouthfuls.

"McCartney knows I'll *always* be her friend," I said. "Well, if it were up to me, at least. How could she even think that I'd ditch her?"

My mom finished chewing what was left in her mouth and then washed it down with a gulp from her "Mommy Dearest" mug.

"Didn't you kind of already do that?" she said, evenly. "I'm not trying to be mean here, Arielle, but didn't you choose to go to the dance with Ryder instead of with your friends?"

I frowned as I stuffed a forkful of food into my mouth.

"Now, I'm not saying that what you did was wrong, and I think that both of your emotions are running a little high right now, but maybe before you write her off, you should try to see things from her perspective."

"But I already tried to talk to her about it and she said all those horrible things..."

"So try *again*," Mom said, taking another sip of her coffee. "Don't you think that seven years of friendship is worth more than one attempt at a reconciliation?"

She had a point. And I didn't exactly like the idea of holding auditions for a new BFF or going through the rest of my high school experience solo. But getting back to where McCartney, Phin and I had been wouldn't be as easy as Mom made it sound. "Fine. But I'm still mad at her for the things she said."

Mom just nodded, knowing that once I'd cooled down I'd do the right thing.

When she was finished, she got up from the table to clear her plate and give me some time to think about everything. Oddly, as I sat there, I felt my anger start to subside and fade into guilt. Deep down I knew that McCartney was just scared of losing our friendship, and I could sort of see why she felt that way. In fact, I was beginning to think that our fight was mostly my fault.

God, I hope it's not too late to make things right between us and save this friendship.

"Thanks for the talk, Mom," I said, bolting out of my chair.

I started to gather my dishes, but she waved me off. "Go talk to McCartney and Phin. I'll clean up."

I gave her a smile I hoped showed how much I appreciated her, and then rushed upstairs into my bedroom. Crashing down in front of my computer, I signed into

IM and to my relief, saw that both McCartney and Phin were online. I opened windows with both of them and started typing.

> **ME:** YOU THERE? LOOK, I'M REALLY SORRY. ABOUT EVERYTHING. CAN WE PLEASE TALK ABOUT IT?

I waited for a response, but it never came. As the minutes ticked by, my heart sank a little lower. I wanted so badly to fix everything that had happened, but their lack of response wasn't looking good. I leaned my head back and closed my eyes. An ache began to form in my throat as I thought about what I might have lost.

"I leave you alone for *one week* and this is what happens?" a voice asked from behind me. "You're sitting in the dark, looking like the unibomber, and I've gotta be honest—you could use a shower."

I turned around and saw McCartney and Phin standing in my doorway. To say my heart soared would've been an understatement. McCartney leaned against the wall, her arms crossed in front of her chest and a wry smile on her face, while Phin stood behind her like a bodyguard.

Though I was happy to see them, I was also totally confused. The last time we'd been in the same room together, we'd been at each other's throats. Now, they were standing in my room, smiles on their faces. I decided I didn't care why they were there or what had changed since the night before.

Without thinking, I jumped up and ran over to them, throwing my arms around their necks and squeezing tightly. When I'd gotten my fill, I let go and took a step back.

"I'm sorry!" I blurted out, at the same time McCartney said, "We're sorry!"

We all looked at each other in disbelief and then burst out laughing.

"Why are you sorry? I'm the one who totally left you guys hanging with the whole limo and dance thing."

"But *we're* the ones who pressured you into doing this whole eBay thing in the first place. And then we got weird when the whole plan actually worked..."

"I let my worry over a stupid kiss get in the way of our friendship and that wasn't fair, either," I admitted, looking down at the ground.

"And I was scared that we were growing apart. That eventually you wouldn't need us anymore," McCartney said, her lip trembling slightly. "You have to know that *nothing* I said last night was true. People don't really think you're lame because you haven't kissed anyone. I was just pissed."

I nodded, noting that Mom had been right all along. I hated when that happened.

"Yeah, but contract or no contract, I should've told you about the MTV thing. I *know* I can trust you guys with anything."

"I feel the same way!"

"Can this fight be over now?" I asked

"Yes, please!" McCartney exclaimed.

Then we practically lunged at each other. As we hugged again, I felt a third pair of arms reach around the both of us, completing the threesome.

"You guys are such *girls*!" Phin said, sarcastically but clearly happy about our reunion.

"You're one to talk, *Phinelope*," McCartney answered, between sniffles.

"I've missed you two so much, you have no idea!" I said as I listened to them bicker like usual.

After a few minutes, we turned down the dial on the dramatics, and looked at each other expectantly.

"You guys wanna do something today? Watch a movie, go to the mall? I'll even let you guys pick," I said, hoping they didn't already have plans.

"Actually, we sort of had something *else* in mind," McCartney said, looking over at Phin conspiratorially.

"Oh no. Should I be worried?"

The two walked further into my room, until they were standing right in front of my computer. McCartney leaned down and read the messagess I'd sent them before they'd shown up. Then she looked back at me, with a smile. "We were already on our way."

They *hadn't* been ignoring me after all.

"Not that I'm unhappy about it or anything, but what made you come over here? You guys were so mad at me last night and you wouldn't even let me explain..."

"Yeah, sorry about that," Phin cut in. "We were too invested in our pity party to stop and listen."

"After you left, Ryder came back to the dance," McCartney said.

"He did?" I asked surprised. "Why?"

"He said there was something we had to see. And then he showed us the tape," she said. I looked at them, confused. "We saw the interview you did in the limo."

The confessional. What had I said again? "Oh."

"We had no idea you were such a *cheeseball*."

I'd always loved McCartney's ability to underplay a sentimental moment. Even so, we all knew what that video had meant to our friendship. Before things could get all mushy again, she seemed to snap out of it, and turned back to my computer, letting her fingers flutter over the keys at a pace much faster than my own.

"You know what today is, don't you?" she asked, changing the subject.

"Sunday?" I answered.

"Yes, *smartass*," Phin said, rolling his eyes. "But it's *also* the day we find out who will become your first kiss."

I looked at them blankly.

"The bidding on your kiss ended this morning," McCartney explained, still focused on my computer.

Nerves suddenly filled my system and I felt the need to sit down.

"Wow. Okay," I said in a daze. "So, what do we do now?"

"We take a look at who put in the final bid," she answered, softly. "Are you ready to do this?"

That was a good question. The idea of coming one step closer to my first kiss made me want to hurl. But after everything that had happened how could I say no?

"Um, sure. Yeah. I mean, that's why we did all of this, right?"

McCartney gave me an encouraging look and turned back around to stare at the screen. "Okay, I'm logging in now. Clicking on the winning bid and waiting for the buyers information," she said. "You want to do the honors?"

I nodded, unable to speak. She got up and we switched spots. I kept my eyes locked on the keyboard to stall. My heart was pounding so hard, I thought it might burst from my chest. Slowly, I looked up at the screen in front of me. Then, I sucked in a sharp breath as my eyes focused on the name of the person with the winning bid.

You've *got* to be kidding me.

Chapter Twenty-Six

"**HEY, ARIELLE! YOU** feeling any better?"

"Hi, Ryder," I said tentatively. "I'm doing a lot better now, thanks for asking."

"That's good," he said over the phone. "I knew things would work out in the end."

"Yeah, I guess they did," I answered. I was growing antsier by the minute and couldn't help myself as I blurted out what was on my mind. "Ryder, did you bid on my kiss? Because according to my account...you won."

He fell silent.

Finally, clearing his throat he answered. "Yeah, I got the confirmation this morning."

As the admission hit me, I started to sweat a little.

"If you bid because you felt bad for me or something, you didn't have to do that," I said, stammering. I was nervous about this next part, but forced myself to keep going. "And if you really *do* want to kiss me, you could've done it for free last night, you know."

When I'd first discovered that it was Ryder who'd won the eBay listing that morning, I'd nearly passed out. It didn't make sense. He was a celeb. He could kiss anyone he wanted to. Why would he choose me? Also, if I was being honest with myself, I'd never really gotten that vibe from him.

Don't get me wrong. Part of me *wished* Ryder felt that way about me. I even daydreamed more than once, about him confessing his undying love. But things between us had never dipped into the romantic end of the pool. With the exception of a few moments of hand-holding and a slow-dance, we'd remained firmly in the friend zone. The surprising thing was that I was almost okay with that.

I held my breath as I waited for his answer.

"Look, Arielle, I didn't do it because I felt bad for you. You're one of the coolest, down-to-earth, funniest people I've ever met. You don't need *my* help in that department. In fact, I think the only reason no one's kissed you yet is because no one worth kissing has come around," he said. "And believe me, if I thought you actually *liked* me like that, I would've made a move on you the first day we met. But we both know that your heart's not totally in it. You feel that too, right?"

And I did. It was hard to explain, but even though I loved Ryder as a person and as a friend, I couldn't picture us working out as a couple. Of course, if he understood this, then what was going on?

"I'm sorry, I'm just a little bit confused. Why did you bid then, Ryder?"

"The more I thought about it, the more I realized that you deserve to have that *magical* first time," he said slowly. "Your first kiss should be with someone you really like. It should be special. Not something you do just to 'get it over with.' So, I bought your first kiss—and I'm asking you to give it to someone who's worthy of being that guy for you. Because you deserve it."

"Oh." It was possibly the sweetest thing anyone had ever said to me. Why wasn't I in love with this guy again?

"Listen, I have to run. We're shooting *Night Light* tonight and I have to get back," he said. As he said it, I could hear people in the background. "But before I go, can I give you some advice?"

"Sure," I said, my head swimming.

"That guy, Cade? The one who was staring me down for just being at the dance with you? I think you should see if there's something there."

"You think?" I asked, surprised to hear him say this.

"Yeah. He seems like a good guy—and he's *crazy*-into you," he said, then chuckled. "For a second there, I thought he was going to fight me."

"Okay," I said, overwhelmed by all this news. What else were you supposed to say to the guy who'd just bought your kiss but didn't want to kiss you?

"Okay—but if I still haven't kissed anyone a year from now, then I'm coming to collect."

He laughed. "It's a deal."

We said our good-byes and hung up. I sat there on my bed for a few minutes, going back over what had just happened. In a way, I could see what he was saying. And I knew that I should feel lucky to have such a great guy looking out for me. But the fact was that I was back where I started.

Kissless and alone.

But what about Cade? How weird was it that Ryder had brought him up? Had he seen something that I didn't?

I mean, Cade *was* good looking. He had that tall, dark and handsome thing going for him, and had perfected his smolder so well that any girl practically melted in his presence. Also, we got along. At least, when he wasn't upset with me because I was keeping things from him or going to Homecoming with another guy. And he had great taste in food...

Wait, where was this going? Did I *like* Cade? More importantly: was Cade into me? I couldn't forget the fact that he'd gone to the dance with Kristi. And in my world, that was a capital offense punishable by public shunning.

Still, I couldn't shake this feeling that was growing in my gut. I got onto my computer and looked over my new messages again. Right in the middle of about a dozen, was Cade's e-mail, sitting where I'd left it, unopened. Taking a breath, I clicked on the subject line and felt a tingling bubble up in my stomach as I began to read.

TO: Arielle Sawyer
FROM: Cade Jones

Hey. I saw you run out of the dance last night. You looked upset. Sorry I was sort of a dick about everything. It was a weird night. Can we meet up? I'd like to explain, if I can.

Cade

P.S. I don't like Kristi. I owed her a favor and she asked me to help her out. I had no idea she was going to say all those things.

I smiled and without thinking, hit reply and started writing back.

TO: Cade Jones
FROM: Arielle Sawyer

Can you be at Chat & Chew at 3pm? I want to talk to you about something, too.

;)

Arielle

P.S. I'm glad you don't like Kristi.

I hit send and started to get dressed while I waited for his response. Jumping into the shower, I attempted to wash away all the bad memories of the night before. The more I thought about this new thing with Cade, the more excited I got to talk to him. After a few minutes, I emerged from the steaming room clean, refreshed and on a mission.

I glanced at my e-mail and saw that Cade had responded.

TO: Arielle Sawyer
FROM: Cade Jones

I'll be there.

Cade

P.S. I'm glad you're glad.

I shut down my computer and finished getting dressed, throwing on a pair of ripped jeans and a striped tee. I brushed through my wet hair and pulled it back into a messy bun, before slicking some color quickly across my lids. Inspecting myself in the mirror, I was satisfied with my low-key look. The truth was, I was sick of worrying so much about what other people thought of me. From here on out, I was staying true to me.

I snatched my purse off my desk and ran downstairs and out the front door.

The window table at Chat & Chew, was the best one in the place, because you could people-watch for hours. I liked to imagine the conversations that passersby might be having, while sitting there. It was also the easiest way to see people coming when you were waiting for a friend—or maybe even a cute guy—to show.

The diner was only 10 minutes away from my house, so it was easy enough to get to. It was my favorite diner in town, mostly because they had this desert sampler plate, where they'd bring you a small slice of all the cakes, pies and cookies they had for the day. I loved tasting a little bit of everything, because I never knew what my craving was going to be until I started eating.

My legs jumped up and down nervously as I waited for Cade. A glance at my cell told me that he was already six minutes late. I didn't want to let myself wonder whether I was being stood up, but of course it's where my thoughts wandered to. Had I completely misread the situation? Suddenly all my confidence and excitement started to fade as doubt crept slowly in.

Then I saw him. He walked down the street toward me, hands hidden in his pockets and his face stuffed inside the collar of his jacket. He looked down at his feet as he walked, and didn't seem to notice me sitting there until he was less than five feet away. When our eyes locked, he gave me a little smile and a half wave, before pulling open the restaurant door.

"Hey," he said, as he sat down across from me.

"Hey," I repeated.

We sat there for a minute just staring at each other and waiting for the other to speak first. I must have won the stare-off, because Cade finally cleared his throat and sat up straighter in his seat.

"Thanks for meeting me," he said finally. "I just wanted to talk to you in person and try to explain why I acted the way I did last night."

"Yeah, what was up with that?" I asked, curiously.

Cade ran a hand through his hair, like he was trying to figure out what to say. "I was just...frustrated, you know? You're such a cool girl and it's been nice hanging out with you the last few weeks. And then you went to the dance with that actor guy and I kind of freaked."

"So, when Kristi asked me to go with her to the dance to pay off a favor she did for me last year, I said yes. I didn't know you guys hated each other. I just wanted you to know that I wasn't there *with* her. Like that. It didn't mean anything."

I nodded as I processed what he was saying.

"And I get that my reaction to your date wasn't cool. I just couldn't stand to see you there with him. Dancing with him. Laughing with him. It made me mad."

"But why?" I asked finally. "He's not a bad guy, you know. I think people just see him as this stuck-up celebrity and that's just not him."

"I know. And I'm sure he's a good guy. I guess I would've been jealous of whoever you went with," Cade admitted, looking around at anything but me.

Whoa. Cade Jones was *jealous* of Ryder? Because he went to the dance with *me*? This was turning out to be the weirdest day.

"And I know that's not fair to you. I just want you to be happy, and if that means being with him, then I'll learn to deal," he said, sounding pained.

"We're not together," I blurted out. "We're just friends. Besides, there's someone else who I'm sort of into right now."

"Oh. Okay," Cade said, suddenly looking even more uncomfortable than before. "Well, like I said, I'm happy if you're happy."

I couldn't believe what I was about to say, but I channeled my inner McCartney and said it anyway. "I think I'll be happiest if I'm with you."

Cade's head shot up in surprise. He searched my eyes for confirmation that I wasn't joking. When he saw I wasn't, relief washed over his face and he smiled.

"You don't have to say anything right now, and I'll understand if you don't want to, but I was wondering if maybe we could hang out some more..." I began tentatively.

Before I could finish my sentence, his mouth was on mine and we were kissing. His lips were soft as we gently pressed them together, getting closer than I'd ever been to a guy before. I could smell the soap he'd used in the shower before he met me and sighed just loud enough for him to hear. Time could've stopped around us and I wouldn't have noticed.

What felt like an eternity, but was probably just a few seconds later, we pulled away and I kept my eyes closed for a moment, reveling in the experience. I committed how I was feeling to memory, since I knew that I'd be recalling the experience for the rest of my life.

"Wow," I said, when I could finally speak again.

"Yeah," he agreed, now fully beaming at me. "Wait, what about your eBay thing? Did I just ruin it?"

"Actually...Ryder had the winning bid," I answered. I watched as Cade's face fell. "But he told me I should wait until it was the perfect time, with the perfect person. And as far as I'm concerned, you're it."

We grinned stupidly at each other again, and then leaned in for what would be my second kiss. And third. And fourth.

Acknowledgments

I CAN'T EVEN begin to thank everyone who has helped to bring this book to life. But I'm going to try anyway.

First, I have to give a huge THANK YOU to everyone who supported me during my fan-funding campaign. Publishing a book takes money and without your generous donations, *Kiss & Sell* wouldn't be available to the world at large today. So hugs and KISSES to (in no particular order): Kate Chapman, Rusty Hendrix, Ajiamarie, Rose Kahn, MadHatter007, Katherine Pocock, PeridotAngel, Ivette Barrera, Bella Donatella, Rhonda Lane, Rebecca Barfield, Alys Arden, Samantha, Pam, Kallie27, Jake Van der Ark, Adam Stewart, Mary Eustace, Anne Langer, Diane Geragotelis, Seema Lakhani, Candice Faktor, Allen Lau.

Everyone at Wattpad: You have been there from the beginning, have always supported me and my books. Thank you from the bottom of my heart for helping make author's dreams come true.

Every author has a dream team and I couldn't exist without mine: Big thanks to Kevan at the Marsal Lyon Agency, Taryn at the Taryn Fagerness Agency, Brandy at Gersh, Deb at Frankfurt Kurnit Klein & Selz, Sam, Sandy and Anna at Media Maison, and everyone at Simon & Schuster.

Thank you to my good friend, Coffee—without you, I wouldn't be able to churn out my books in six weeks. And my stomach thanks Denise at Pips Place

NYC for supplying me with all the sugar I need to remain happy through re-writes and slow writing days. And so much gratitude to the other creative people (writers, actors, singers, directors, producers) who remind me that failure and road blocks are normal, and that rejection and difficulties are just a part of the process. Thank you for inspiring me.

To my friends and family, who keep me sane, centered and happy. I love you all. Every part of my success is because of you. Thank you for believing in me, when I couldn't believe in myself. You know who you are (but I also know you like seeing your names in print): Mom, Dad, Jacey, Amy, Cody, Cash, Andrea, Price, Ryan, Katy, Chelle, Maya, Tammy, Amanda, Kate, Jess, Zach, Courtney, Mary, Colleen, Siena, Schuman, Darcey, Amanda Havard, Calvin Reid, Lady Dawn, Aunt Denise, Auntie Anne, Becky, all my Friday the 13th buds, and Mexican food and movie night attendees, and everyone else who's ever made me laugh or laughed with me.

Lastly, to my husband, Matt: thank you for never letting me give up and for always encouraging me to write the next book. You're the bravest, strongest, most impressive person I know. I looooooooooooove you!

Made in the USA
Lexington, KY
18 July 2015